MW00532316

A Poisonous Palate

Also available by Lucy Burdette

The Key West Food Critic Mysteries

Other Novels

A Poisonous Palate

A KEY WEST FOOD CRITIC MYSTERY

Lucy Burdette

CROOKED
LANE

NEW YORK

Copyright © 2024 by Roberta Isleib

Published in the United States by Crooked Lane Books, an imprint of The Quick Brown Fox & Company LLC.

Crooked Lane Books and its logo are trademarks of The Quick Brown Fox & Company LLC.

Library of Congress Catalog-in-Publication data available upon request.

ISBN (hardcover): 978-1-63910-847-3
ISBN (ebook): 978-1-63910-848-0

Cover design by Griesbach/Martucci

Printed in the United States.

www.crookedlanebooks.com

Crooked Lane Books
34 West 27th St., 10th Floor
New York, NY 10001

First Edition: August 2024

10 9 8 7 6 5 4 3 2 1

For the heroic librarians of the world
who place books in the hands of
readers and stand up for everyone's right
to read whatever they choose.

Chapter One

"At times, I felt like a food writer who was assigned to cover a trendy new restaurant, only to discover that the kitchen staff wanted to talk about nothing but food poisoning."
—Kevin Roose, "Inside the White-Hot Center of A.I. Doomerism," *New York Times*, July 11, 2023

I loved every time of day in my home on Key West's Houseboat Row, but I loved mornings most of all, enjoying the view from my deck with a steaming cup of coffee laced with milk, thinking about the day to come, and watching the rest of the world wake up. From the month of May onward, it got too hot to sit out during the day, so I tried to seize these early morning hours, and later, the evenings. Maybe I had a few tiny quibbles about our neighborhood, like the high season rush hour when the traffic backed up on Palm Avenue, with its plumes of exhaust and incessant honks of annoyance, but all things considered, my houseboat home felt like a jackpot won, a piece of heaven, a slice of paradise.

I sipped on the coffee my husband had delivered on his way off to work (another jackpot!) and scrolled through my stuffed inbox, deleting all the messages that were spam, junk, or stuff that I'd sat on too long to bother answering. I paused over one email that had arrived the night before from a name and address that I did not recognize. As my finger hovered over the Delete key, the alluring subject line made me pause: *Hemingway's toxic love and an old story.* I couldn't imagine what kind of clever angle this spam might hold, so I opened it up to see.

Dear Ms. Snow,

You don't know me, and I apologize for intruding into your inbox. I have read a lot about you, both your restaurant criticism and your crime solving. I would like to talk to you, at your convenience of course.

Below this introduction was a screenshot of a yellowed newspaper clipping.

Monroe County Sheriff's Office Investigates Report of Missing Woman. May 13, 1978. A 22-year-old woman approached the Sheriff's Office reporting that the friend she had traveled with several months ago from Michigan to the Florida Keys has disappeared. Deputies interviewed all available witnesses and investigated the area where the alleged victim was staying with her friend. There was no sign of criminal activity, although the alleged victim had been living in a commune-type encampment, which was subsequently evacuated by the Sheriff's Office. Several people familiar with the situation reported that the missing woman had been restless and eager to leave the Keys.

The email continued: *I was the one who reported Veronica missing, As you can probably read between the lines, the authorities brushed me off, insisting that she'd left the area of her own volition. But she never turned up in Michigan after I went back home, nor have I heard from her since. I even hired a private investigator, Simon Landry. He was supposed to be the best, but his trail ran ice-cold once he hit the Keys. He returned part of my deposit, if you can believe it.*

You've had some experience solving mysteries, and I'm hoping that you might help me look into this one. I will be staying at the Gardens Hotel this week, working on my book about what women can learn about toxic love from Hemingway's wives. I'll spend most of the day tomorrow at the Hemingway Home and would love to chat with you there or meet for dinner, or whatever might suit your schedule. Text me anytime.

Signed Catherine Davitt. Then she'd added her phone number and a crossed fingers emoji.

Again, I thought about deleting the message. My husband, Key West Police Department lieutenant Nathan Bransford, was not a big fan of me getting involved in possibly dangerous situations. Not that this would be dangerous, but it sounded like it ventured into law enforcement territory. On the other hand, how much trouble could I get into if the woman had disappeared forty years ago? Now I was super curious.

A text arrived on my phone from my dear friend down the dock, Connie, directed both to my next-door neighbor, Miss Gloria, and me. *The new baby is up wailing, toddler Claire is hysterical, and I desperately need caffeine. Not to be too needy but I could murder some breakfast.*

An SOS if I'd ever heard one. *Be right there,* I texted back, and Miss Gloria added her thumbs-up. I packed up the breakfast muffins chockablock with crispy bacon and sharp cheddar that I'd baked yesterday, poured coffee into an insulated carafe, and headed for her boat. Evinrude, my gray tiger cat, and Ziggy, Nathan's little dog, trotted along in my wake. Connie had taken me and my cat in several years ago when we had been kicked to the curb by a bad boyfriend choice. She had also been my college roommate. My mom and I had seen her through the dark days after her mother died of cancer. Now she had an infant and a needy toddler—a stressful even if temporary transition of a different kind. When she cried uncle, I came running. And vice versa.

By the time we arrived, everyone had climbed up to Connie's second-floor deck. Toddler Claire was gnawing on a wedge of apple and distributing LEGO bricks over the floor. Miss Gloria had gotten there ahead of me and was rocking the baby gently and crooning baby nothings. The infant's eyes were pinned to our friend's face. I met Connie's gaze and knew she was thinking the same thing I was—how sweet it was to see the juxtaposition of the old and the new. I settled the animals and gave them treats, then poured cups of steaming coffee, added milk, and passed around the muffins on Connie's flowered plates.

"You're a lifesaver," Connie said, nearly inhaling her first muffin and cup of coffee.

We chatted about the baby's sleep pattern (not terrible for three weeks old), Claire's upcoming toddler preschool session at the Key West library, and then my unusual email. I read it to them, including the text of the old newspaper article.

"What do you think?" I asked them.

Miss Gloria said, "Of course you should go. She needs your help."

Connie was not so sure. "Why is she looking for her friend now?" she asked. "She's been gone for over forty years. Plus, why you? Why not go to the authorities like a normal person would?"

These were good points. It was hard to argue with her reasoning.

"Here's what you do," said my octogenarian friend, jostling the baby a bit in her excitement. "You tell her two o'clock but go early so you can lurk in the background and follow the one o'clock tour as if you're one of the tourists. She'll probably be in the crowd, listening for Hemingway tidbits for this project she's writing. Use your honed detective skills to try to pick her out. If she looks suspicious, book it out of there. If she looks normal, take her across the street to the Moondog Café, buy her a cup of coffee, and hear the story. Then tell her to call Nathan because you're going to talk to him if she doesn't."

"Actually, that's brilliant," I said. Even Nathan would have a hard time complaining about that plan. It was well thought out, cautious, yet potentially helpful to a person in trouble. Miss Gloria sat back with a satisfied smirk, shifted the squawking baby to her shoulder, and patted the baby's back.

"I probably should google her first to make sure she isn't a serial killer on parole." I typed Catherine's name into the search bar on my phone, scanned the links that appeared, and finally clicked on the link leading to her website. "She appears to be exactly as described, a self-help maven, specializing in articles and books for women about managing anxiety, fostering self-love, body image, toxic love, the usual. Not a single mention of prison or criminal acts, although she wouldn't post that sort of thing on her own website, would she?" I read a little further and glanced up at Miss Gloria. "Her home is outside your old stomping grounds in Detroit."

"She's practically a neighbor, then. Go for it!" she said.

I grinned at my friend and texted Catherine Davitt's number.

Hayley Snow here. I can meet with you for a few minutes, early afternoon, say 2:00 pm, near the swimming pool.

The swimming pool was positioned outside the Hemingway Home next to the gift shop. The pool was a luxury for a 1930s home, and by all reports, a bone of contention between Hemingway and his second wife, whose marriage was already in trouble. A penny had been glued to the pavement, and every tour ended with a joke about Hemingway telling Pauline she'd spent so much on the showpiece pool, she might as well have his last penny too.

By the time Catherine Davitt reached this point in the Hemingway saga, I hoped I would know enough about her to decide whether or not to show myself.

Chapter Two

"I thought about how, when you get to know someone so well at the same time that you're also just getting to know yourself, your identities can seem almost inextricable, much like the cheese and butter melting into each other in my bowl."

—Joe Yonan, *"Creamy Cacio e Pepe Soup Served Up Comfort When I Needed It," Washington Post*, October 1, 2023

I had visited the Hemingway Home on Whitehead Street many times since moving to Key West. It was one of my favorite places to unwind. The home itself was a beautiful two-story, cream-colored French colonial structure, with lemon lime shutters and a wide front porch. The grounds, expansive and luxurious for tightly packed Key West, were surrounded by a tall vintage brick wall and populated by fifty or so polydactyl cats. The first cats were either the offspring of Hemingway's white cat, Snow White, or they belonged to the neighbors, depending on who was telling the story. These days, they had the run of the house and grounds and garnered a lot of admiration from visitors.

I usually skipped the formal tour of the house, which focused on the years 1931–1939, when Ernest Hemingway lived here with his second wife, Pauline. I'd heard the story often enough that I could almost recite it by heart. Instead, I favored relaxing on one of the benches and hoping a polydactyl cat would saunter by to visit while I worked on a story. Sometimes I climbed the stairs at the back of the house to look at Hemingway's perfect jewel of an office. I liked to imagine the writing I could do there while sitting in the rattan recliner, my feet up on a sage-colored cushion. On other visits, I browsed the stones that marked the lives of cats that had lived here and passed on to their feline rewards. I had also helped my mother cater a wedding on these grounds several years ago on New Year's Eve—a debacle for sure.

Today, I'd planned my visit so I could join the tour that would finish around two. I stayed at the back of the group of tourists, remaining unobtrusive in order to see if I could spot the mysterious Catherine.

The tours began in the living room of the old home. Each guide gave a personalized overview of Hemingway's days in Key West, including the apocryphal story about using the lighthouse across the street to lead him home from late nights when he'd been overserved at his favorite bar. The history that I thought would be most important for the book this woman claimed to be writing began in the room across the hall. Here, the tour leader would talk about Hemingway's four wives, particularly Pauline. I stood in the hallway listening to the guide's opening.

This afternoon, my friend Rusty was warming up a medium-sized crowd of tourists dressed in shorts and ball caps or straw hats, some aglow with painful-looking sunburns. I tried to guess which one of them might be Catherine. Several women stayed near the front of the group and appeared especially attentive to the guide's descriptions of Hemingway's time in Key West. Only one of those women was obviously taking notes. She had chin-length brown hair that was streaked with silver, and a fringe of bangs. Her skin was ivory-colored, suggesting she had not spent time in the sun lately. She was wearing Capri pants and comfortable sneakers and looked to be in her sixties.

"Next stop, the dining room," Rusty said, beckoning the group toward me. I faded back next to the wall. "I will give you a very, very brief biography of Ernest Hemingway," he added, then swept his hand over the collection of photographs of his four wives and himself. "We call this Ernest Hemingway's 'gallery of wives.' He had four of them, if you can believe that." The woman in Capri pants scribbled furiously, while others in the crowd snickered.

As Rusty's tour group trooped toward the back of the house to see the kitchen and then climb upstairs to the second floor, the note-taking woman stayed behind. I watched her study the photos of Hemingway during his happiest times with Pauline, and then take photos of the pictures on the wall. Those happy times were short-lived, as they'd stayed married for only thirteen years, long enough to produce two sons. Just as Pauline had flirted with Hemingway while he was married to Hadley, Martha Gellhorn flirted with him during his marriage to Pauline. In fact, I had read that Hadley and Pauline were best friends before their mutual love for Hemingway destroyed their relationship.

I would be interested to hear how this Catherine Davitt planned to develop her treatise about toxic love. To me, the marriage/love question boiled down to one bare fact: if a man is married when you meet him and shows no concrete sign of heading for divorce, then it's best to stay away from him. You and the other woman are bound to suffer. That realization brought a short pulse of pain to my heart. My own husband had been separated when we first met. We felt a mutual zing of attraction. Luckily, we both realized quickly enough that he needed to sort out his old business before he could explore the possibility of a relationship with me. Hemingway, on the other hand, seemed to always have a new love lined up before he left an old one. Would that thesis provide enough material to fill a book? I was definitely curious. The woman tucked her notebook into her backpack and followed her group and guide upstairs to the second floor. I trailed along behind.

By the end of the half hour with our docent, Rusty, I was convinced that this woman was what she said she was. If she wasn't a writer doing research, she was doing a darn good job of faking it. Outside the gift shop, where the guide wound up his description of the tiled urinal that came from Sloppy Joe's bar and doubled as a cats' water fountain, I saw her hand Rusty a tip and then look around at the people milling about the grounds. She was looking for me, I assumed. I held my hand up and waved.

"Catherine?" I asked.

"Hayley?" she answered, flashing a warm smile. "Thank you so much for coming. I wasn't at all sure you would."

"I wasn't sure either," I said, adding my own smile. "If you're finished here, we could go across the street to the Moondog Café and get a coffee."

Once we were settled at a table for two under a turquoise umbrella on the front porch bordering Whitehead Street, we ordered iced tea and pastries at her insistence. "I read online that they have an excellent pastry chef," she explained. She called the waiter back before he'd disappeared inside. "In fact, please add a grilled vegetable charcuterie, an order of chicken potstickers, and an artichoke chicken pizza too." After the waiter left, she said, "I'm starving. I haven't had lunch yet because I went through the tour twice. Every guide tells the story a little differently, and I didn't want to miss any possible angles. Hopefully you'll be tempted to nibble and prevent me from eating all of it." She flashed a friendly smile.

"If you don't mind, let's start with why you reached out to me," I said. "Even with a cold case, the more useful contact would probably be with the police or the Sheriff's Office."

"So you might think," she said, keeping her cool gray eyes focused on my face.

The waiter arrived to deliver our food, and Catherine gestured for him to leave everything in the middle of the table. "She said she's not hungry," she told him, with a tip of the chin at me, "but she looks like a woman who enjoys her food, doesn't she?" They both laughed, and I grinned back, taking no offense. I *was* pleasingly plump these days, as Nathan put it. Like my mother, I enjoyed eating too much to worry about staying model thin. I mostly beat back the addition of any extra pounds by working out at the gym and running with our dog—though trotting or ambling might describe it better.

Sitting across the table from this woman, watching her cut a piece of the pizza, I noticed the webbing of fine lines radiating from the corners of her eyes. I wondered if she was a bit older than I'd first guessed. In her late sixties, maybe? She added two potstickers to the plate holding the wedge of pizza and pushed it over to me.

"Back to your question about the authorities. They were not helpful back then, and I have no reason to believe it would be different now. Here's my promise: if you can find a thread in the history that the department might reasonably pick up, I guarantee I will get in touch with the Sheriff's Office."

"Hmm," I said, thinking she was a smooth operator. For one, I'd told her I only had a few minutes and suggested we have a quick coffee. Instead, we were zooming head on toward a full, if late, lunch. I also suspected she'd thought through any possible objections and had prepared packaged replies well in advance of this meeting. "I have a lot of questions before I could commit to anything."

"Of course," she said. "I have all afternoon."

"I don't. But I would love to hear about your book project before we get to your missing friend. How do you see this going? Is your research anything more complicated than how many marriages somebody has in their back pocket when you meet them? Perhaps equally, if not more, important, are you looking into how they explain the demise of those relationships?" I nibbled on the chicken potstickers as we talked, dragging each bite through the wasabi-soy-ginger sauce, enjoying the salty tang.

"As you may know," she said, "Hadley Richardson was his first wife. So those rules of thumb would not have helped her. You've probably heard the story about how she lost his manuscripts when she left them unattended in a train compartment. Of course he would be upset. It was his life's work, and he hadn't made any copies. But he never was able to forgive her. I think her error in judgment and his reaction to it paved the way for the demise of their marriage." She sighed and looked away, her gaze landing on the lighthouse behind me.

A Poisonous Palate

She continued. "People make mistakes, even grievous errors. If there isn't room for forgiveness, the relationship is doomed. Don't you think?" She paused until I nodded in agreement. "In a nutshell, I think we can look at each of his marriages and see different problems. For Hadley, Pauline—aka Fife—was in their marriage constantly, like Camilla was for Charles and Diana. For Pauline, there was always a trio including Martha Gellhorn, with lots of drinking and partying involved. Finally, along came Mary Welsh, who described time spent with Hemingway as 'in the beam.' Like a beam of light. Get it?" She gestured across Whitehead Street, where we could see the tip of the lighthouse. "There was something about Hemingway's attention that lit up the woman receiving it. But in each case, there were so many secrets. Everyone has them, of course, but in a good relationship, the secrets are revealed slowly as more trust is developed. My research tells me that he was much more likely to talk to the new lover about problems and feelings than hash them out with the old one."

"Go on," I said. "You've really thought this through."

"I've got a few other angles to investigate as well. A man who insists he can love two women equally at once has a problem. Here's another: a man who says a woman is his other half needs to first do some work on making himself whole. Watch out for what might be underneath a "man's man" facade. This kind of man may be working too hard to prove he's a perfect masculine specimen, especially when he feels weak or damaged inside. Bullfighting, war, prizefighting—Hemingway adored them all. He appeared on the outside to be such a tough guy, but inside was much more complicated, softer and weaker. I shouldn't forget this—Martha Gellhorn said she should have known better than to marry a man who hated his mother."

I was impressed. She had thought this through well and developed more interesting points than I would have imagined possible.

Catherine asked, "Did you know he wrote a collection of short stories called *Men Without Women*?"

I shook my head. "I'm fascinated with the man, but not a big student of his work."

She pointed at me with the tines of her fork. "You aren't alone. If I have space in the manuscript, I'll try to make some connections between his work and his relationships. I suspect my readers will be less interested in the work, like you, than they will be about the lessons that can be applied from his failures to theirs. I believe that's my audience, and that's how I pitched the book idea."

She looked at me steadily, as though she was trying to read my thoughts and my history. *Another beam,* I thought. This time I was in hers. Then she said, "You're married?"

I nodded again. "Still something of a newlywed. How about you?"

"Came close a few times," she replied, with a look of possible regret on her face. Or was it bitterness? Maybe even relief. "My radar for toxic love can be a little stunted, so I had some near misses with terrible choices. Nothing I really mourn, looking back in the mirror. I'm not the kind of person who can't enjoy her own company. I'm afraid Hemingway was one of those."

This was turning into one of the odder interviews I'd ever experienced. I had no way of knowing whether she was lying to herself, lying to me, both, or neither. "Tell me about your missing friend."

She collapsed back into her chair and poked at a piece of limp grilled onion on her plate with her knife. "We were both at Loose Ends—with a capital L and capital E. I was terribly unhappy in my first year of college, and Veronica had a dead-end job and a living situation that was going downhill fast. I fought about this all the time with my mother, who insisted I stay in school and finish what I'd started. On top of all that, it was bitterly cold—there is nothing like a Michigan winter to chill you to the bone. This was January, and we'd already had more snow than we could keep up with. Picture ugly gray hillocks of ice that won't go away because the temperature never rose over about twenty degrees. I met Ronnie in a local student dive, and somehow the idea came up that we could do a road trip. We cobbled together a tent, sleeping bags, a cooler, and a few books to read along the way. There wasn't a whole lot of thought that went into the decision. We were running from what we had, plain and simple.

"We took some crazy chances," she said. "We did things I'd never do today, but everyone was so friendly, and we were so far from our problems at home. It felt magical. Until it didn't."

"I had one of those escape trips," I said, remembering what I thought was the magic of Chad Lutz's proposition that I travel to Key West and move in with him, even though we barely knew each other. The one thing that saved me from total disaster was that my dear friend Connie already lived here. She took me in when things went south. "Some of that—making dumb mistakes—goes along with being young, right?"

"I suppose," she said, letting her cutlery clatter on the china plate. "Initially, we stopped in North Carolina, but they were having a cold snap too. So, we kept driving. Ended up in a bar near Big Pine Key. It was the late seventies, different times. The island was barely developed, but we were out of gas and nearly out of money. Someone told us about a local motel that was cheap and probably had a room."

She squinted and frowned, and her next comment felt like a criticism: "You probably weren't even born by then."

1978

Catherine

You really get to know someone while living with them in a tent. I hadn't completely thought it through when Veronica proposed the road trip. But living with my mother was a nightmare, and my job was a dead end, and so was my boyfriend. Michigan in January is frigid, just as he accused me of being.

For the first couple of weeks, we skated on the surface, singing along with my cassette tapes. David Bowie, Pink Floyd, the Rolling Stones—those were my favorites. She leaned toward Elton John, the Eagles, and the Bee Gees. We both loved Queen. Ronnie had brought a stash of killer weed, and we slept at rest stops when we got tired. She took the front seat and I took the back, being seven inches taller and a good twenty-five pounds heavier. Ronnie had wavy blond hair that I would've killed for, but she said I had the long legs that she'd always wanted.

The solenoid and then the water pump burned out somewhere in North Carolina, so we found a mechanic and spent two nights in a motel while the car was repaired. A waitress at the drugstore counter in the little town nearby noticed we were shivering and wondered why we didn't go to the Florida Keys. She said her friend's sister had spent last winter there and couldn't say enough about how friendly everyone was—and the weather. She leaned her elbows on the counter and rested her chin in her hand. "Oh, the weather. I'd kill to spend the winter down there."

Once we'd picked up the car and spent pretty much all the money we came with on repairs, we figured, why not? We could find some kind of work. If it was warm, we could stay in the tent, and it wouldn't cost a penny. Neither one of us was ready to go back home. Three weeks after we'd crossed the Michigan state line into Ohio, and then on through West Virginia and Virginia into North Carolina, neither one of us had talked about what we were running from.

Chapter Three

"A certain kind of connoisseurship of taste, a mark of how you deal with the world, is the ability to relish the bitter, to crave it even, the way you do the sweet."
—Stephanie Danler, *Sweetbitter*

By the time I finished talking with Catherine, she had plowed through all the dishes she ordered—and I'd nibbled and made notes and taken photos in case I wanted to use this meal in a future article, "Bunches of Lunches," or hopefully something way more clever. I was also leaning toward accompanying her tomorrow to Big Pine Key. She had said that she would love some company while she looked around to see how things had changed. I could try some local food while we were there.

I glanced at my phone—I was close to late for my date at the dog park with my pal Eric and his dogs, Chester and Barclay. I told Catherine I'd text her later and zipped home on my scooter to pick up Ziggy. He was sitting by the houseboat door, looking a bit forlorn.

"I didn't forget you, Ziggeroo," I said. We jogged back down to the parking lot, and I scooped him up and tucked him into the crate fastened to the back of the bike. Then we headed over to the small dog park on White Street. Located at the corner of White and Atlantic, this might have been the only park in the country with a glorious ocean view—not that the dogs cared a bit about the scenery. Eric and his guys were inside the chain-link fence, waiting on one of the concrete picnic tables.

I kissed my friend's cheek, and we watched the dogs sniff each other in greeting and then take a lap around the edge of the fence, barking joyously as they ran. "You'll never guess what I've been up to," I said.

Eric laughed. "With you, I never know."

I pulled up Catherine's email on my phone and showed it to him while I told him about our conversation. "I judged her to be authentic," I said while he skimmed, thinking he might be suspicious of my conclusions and concerned about me getting involved, the default position for most important men in my life. Eric would definitely be more subtle about his worries than Nathan would. "During the tour of the Hemingway Home, she was taking notes exactly like a writer would, and later, she answered all my questions without sounding defensive. And PS, I did google her before we met. She appears to be what she says she is." Then I described how she'd come to the Keys more than forty years ago and spent several glorious months camping in the mangroves.

"She remembers that time as magical. They took crazy chances trusting people they didn't know, but she insisted everyone was so nice and so helpful—until Veronica disappeared. Then people clammed up. Maybe they didn't want to be blamed for what happened, or they knew something they weren't comfortable sharing."

Eric looked thoughtful. "Those were different times. Did she say what she meant by crazy chances? That phrase could have a lot of meanings. You can't assume what she meant."

I scanned my memory of our conversation. "You know, I didn't ask that question exactly. We talked a lot about her book project and about her missing friend. Then I got a little distracted thinking about why I came to Key West." Eric nodded. He knew the whole sordid story. "I'm taking her up to Big Pine Key tomorrow, so I'll find out more."

"I've had a couple of patients who grew up in the Keys back in those days," he said. "Lots of folks were laying low because they were involved in things that weren't strictly legal. I can imagine that some people felt the law didn't apply to them down here in the Keys."

"She mentioned marijuana several times," I said.

"I suspect there were more serious things being shared than pot," Eric said. "People came down to disappear for lots of reasons, some of them complex. When their time here ran out, reentry into mainstream culture after life in a commune could be difficult."

As always with Eric, I wondered how much he knew because of his psychological training, how much he'd heard from his patients, and what might have come from his own life. We'd known each other since I was ten and he was a teenager. He hadn't had an easy time in his late teens and early twenties. I always thought that those experiences laid the groundwork for the empathy that his patients deeply appreciated.

"How long did she stay after her friend disappeared?" he asked.

"She told me that by May it was getting hot, and the air was swarming with some kind of saltwater mosquitos that tortured them. She knew she couldn't stay in a tent all summer. Veronica's disappearance had begun to eat at her and freak her out. She didn't feel safe alone anymore. Some of the other campers that she'd gotten to know well decided to move on and resume or begin their other lives."

"Her friend never warned her that she was leaving? Did she take the car?"

"No warning that she remembers, or that she told me about. The car belonged to her, not Veronica." His questions made me realize that I still didn't know a lot about this time in the girls' lives, such as why they ran away to the Keys, what their relationship was like, and who specifically they bonded with and relied on while camping in the mangroves. I glanced at my phone. It was getting toward dinnertime, and I had a few things to finish before Nathan got home. We collected our dogs and began to walk toward the exit.

As we stood inside the double gates meant to keep errant pets from running out into the road, Eric turned to ask another question. "After listening to her, why do you think she's looking into this now?"

I ticked some things off on my fingers. "She's working on this Hemingway project and needed to do research here on the island, so it's convenient. Maybe this is the first time she's been back to the Keys since the seventies."

"That sounds like a believable reason on the surface, but keep thinking. Go deeper. Did something happen back home recently that's triggering this quest now? We humans are wired to repeat old traumas until we identify the ghosts that haunt us, determine they no longer fit with our current lives, and let them go." His head was tipped sideways, as if to ask whether I understood.

I laughed. "This is a little bit over my head, but I think I get the gist. She's stuck on something, a wound from her past, from her days on the Keys in the seventies, which would explain why she's back."

"Yes, keep asking until you have the answer: *Why now?* Have you thought about the book that she's writing? Could there have been a toxic relationship related to her friend's disappearance?"

"I did wonder about her love life—in fact, we talked about that a bit—but it also seemed like there had been enough in Hemingway's life to explain why she chose this topic." I paused for a minute, watching the dogs wrestle, trying to formulate a thought from the recent *Key Zest* staff meeting that had flitted into my head. "Palamina's been bugging me about how we can reach more people with our e-zine, so I've done some reading about how to increase your promotional platform. One way is to choose a topic that has a built-in platform, like Poe or Hemingway. That way, people will gravitate toward it even if they have no idea who you are.

"No one's had more play than Hemingway, and Catherine chose an interesting angle. It could be as simple as that. But your theory that she chose this because of something in her own life makes a whole lot of sense. I count on you for that." I grinned. "Plus, you'll eat anything I ask you to. We need to grab dinner very soon."

"Anytime," he said. "Make sure you run this by Nathan before you get more involved."

"I will. I'm glad we had the chance to talk before I bring it up with him." I grinned and whistled for Ziggy. "You can picture what he's going to say."

"I can," said Eric as he snapped the leashes onto Chester and then Barclay.

Chapter Four

"When it comes to secret family recipes, people just want to believe."
    —Alex Mayyasi, "The Dirty Secret of 'Secret Family
        Recipes,'" *Gastro Obscura*, February 27, 2018

After sitting down to dinner with Nathan—one of his favorites: an Italian pot roast that I'd loaded in the crockpot this morning, served with a pile of mashed potatoes and some steamed broccoli (not his favorite)—I showed him the email with the old newspaper clipping about Veronica's disappearance. I confessed that I'd already had lunch with Catherine, and I told him I was tentatively planning to see her again tomorrow.

"We're going up to Big Pine Key to have lunch at the No Name Pub. It's nothing to worry about because I'll be the one driving, so she can't whisk me off into the woods, strangle me, and dump my body somewhere. Besides, I did a search on her before I met her, and she's quite legitimate. She's written a number of modestly successful books in the self-help genre, but it looks like she's gotten a big advance from a major publisher for this one. Hemingway, anything Hemingway, sells. People are fascinated with his four marriages, so it's the perfect topic." I was babbling a little bit here, but I was slightly nervous about leaving too much silence for him to comment.

He stared at me for a minute, his expression worried. "What does she think happened to her friend?" Then he held a hand up before I could answer. "Let me be clear about this: I don't really like your plan. Can you agree that the minute anything seems dangerous or fishy in any way, that you call the Sheriff's Office and then call me?"

"Of course," I said. "I have no interest in putting myself in danger. I'm super curious though, and I feel a little bit sorry for this woman. I googled the incident while I was waiting for you. As she pointed out, it made very little splash in the papers. Look." I showed him my phone again with the email from Catherine. "They didn't even mention the missing girl's name. Doesn't it sound like they assumed that she had left the Keys of her own accord?"

Nathan read it over, and then read it a second time. "I agree. There is a value judgment implied by the commune comment. On the other hand, the article says they interviewed witnesses and investigated the surroundings. I would not assume they brushed it off and nor should you." He put down the forkful of mashed potatoes that he'd loaded just before I handed him the phone. "Tomorrow I can call Darcy Rogers at the Sheriff's Office and ask whether they have anyone on staff who was there at the time."

"I would appreciate that," I said, grinning and squeezing his hand. "That would be a perfect compromise between my instinct to poke around and yours to protect me."

A Poisonous Palate

Once we'd cleared away the dishes and Nathan was walking Ziggy, I texted Catherine. *Pick you up around 10:00 tomorrow for lunch at the No Name Pub. Where are you staying?*

Her return text came back instantly. *The Gardens Hotel. Thank you!*

1978

Catherine

We couldn't wait to get out of the first motel we'd found, which smelled of mildew and cigarette smoke and had a black and white TV that received one fuzzy station. A lady at the laundromat had mentioned the only real action in town—the bar at No Name Pub. 'Head out toward No Name Key', she'd said. 'Left on Key Deer Boulevard, then right on Watson. You can't miss it on the left before the bridge.' We'd driven over and parked. The first thing I noticed inside the building were the dollar bills stapled to the ceiling—every square inch was covered. Then the dusky smell of marijuana, and finally the silver hats that the patrons were wearing. A waitress approached us carrying two pieces of foil. 'Make a hat and make yourselves at home', she yelled over the din. 'They will protect you from radiation'. She laughed and laughed. We ordered beers and a pizza and fashioned headpieces with horns and tails.

'Welcome', called a blond man behind the bar, 'to the bar where nobody knows your name.'

Chapter Five

"He was married then, to a woman named Cloris, who was as well intentioned and charmless as a store-bought pie."
—J. Ryan Stradal,
Saturday Night at the Lakeside Supper Club

The trip up the Keys to Big Pine was only thirty miles, but it could take from thirty minutes to two hours, depending on traffic, unfortunate accidents, or construction. This was the hazard of a two-lane road with too many people driving it. The No Name Pub was about a mile off the main road, past the so-called downtown of Big Pine Key. We drove for what seemed like miles, passing a landscape of shrubs and the graying, bare trunks of what might have been pine trees. I began to wonder if we were lost.

"It looks spooky," Catherine said, gesturing at the skeletons of dead trees. "There used to be so many more pines."

"Hurricane damage," I said. "Irma hit this island hard. Look at all this open space. I had no idea the island was this big." I turned off Key Deer Boulevard onto Cypress Drive, wound through a small neighborhood of mostly concrete block homes, and finally spotted the No Name Pub.

"This part hasn't changed," said Catherine as I pulled into the parking lot of the restaurant. "Aged better than the rest of us, including Key West."

I glanced over at her, wondering what she meant. "I would have liked to have seen this place back in the old days."

Most of the seating was outdoors at painted picnic tables shaded with big umbrellas, or under a thatched tiki hut roof. I ducked inside to check out the bar, which was dark and cozy, the ceiling papered with dollar bills.

"Grab a couple of menus and seat yourselves anywhere, I'll be with you shortly," called a waitress in a tie-dyed T-shirt and Birkenstock sandals.

When I returned to the outside tables, a miniature Key deer with enormous ears had approached the table where Catherine sat. It was the size of a big dog, like a Great Dane, maybe. "I'm not sharing, buddy," she told the deer and then winked at me. "It's illegal to feed them."

"This is my first Key deer, believe it or not," I said as I snapped a quick photo. The animal turned away and trotted off. "It's adorable."

For a few minutes, we studied our menus, which focused on tropical bar food, including seafood pizza, burgers, fish sandwiches, and fish dip. The list made my stomach growl in anticipation. I'd explained to Catherine on the way up the Keys that I'd be choosing multiple dishes for a future review, but that she was welcome to eat any or none of it.

When the waitress emerged from the bar to take our orders, I realized that she was older than she'd appeared from across the room in the darkened bar. Her face was lined, maybe from smoking or too much sun, and her lipstick had settled into the cracks and chips of her lips. Those observations faded when she smiled broadly. "Welcome to No Name Pub. My name is Ginny. You look like first timers to me, no? We are famous for our white shrimp pizza, sangria, and fish dip. But folks love the burgers too. Please don't feed the wildlife." She gestured at a trio of tiny deer who had edged closer to our table, almost as if the one deer we'd seen earlier had gone to tell its friends it'd found some tourists. "Are you ready to order, or should I give you more time?"

If there was one thing I'd learned as a food critic, it was to order when you had the chance in a busy place. I listed off the items I wanted to try. "Iced tea to drink for me," I added.

"Sangria, please," said Catherine.

"I can't believe she's still here," she said to me in a low voice once the waitress returned to the restaurant.

"You know her?" I was surprised because the waitress hadn't acted like she recognized Catherine.

"She floated around the fringes of our crowd. She always said she couldn't wait to get off the Keys and start her real life. Yet here she is, stuck at No Name Pub on Big Pine Key." Catherine spread her arms out as if wondering who would possibly make that choice.

Something felt off about this. I paused, then asked, "Did you know she was working here? Is that why we came?"

Catherine leaned over to take a sip of water. "Nope. I'm as surprised as you are."

Was she telling the truth? Anything seemed possible. "I suppose she could have moved away and later realized that she belonged here," I suggested. "From one who started life in New Jersey and moved to Key West, I can say from personal experience that running away from home doesn't always work out. Thank goodness it did work out for me once I straightened out a few almost-fatal kinks in the plan."

The woman approached our table with our drinks and a bowl of fish dip and crackers. "I'll be right back with the rest. We're not known for the timing of our courses," she added. Several minutes later, she returned. "The chef's a little grumpy, so you get what you get when you get it." She smiled again and winked, depositing a fried grouper sandwich in front of me, a Hawaiian burger for Catherine, and the shrimp pizza to share. "Can I get you anything else?" she asked.

Catherine smiled and said, "You might not remember me, but we met back in the late seventies. You used to come to the bonfires in the mangrove camp, didn't you? I'm Catherine Davitt. Some people called me Kit Kat."

That nickname surprised me, as it seemed like something belonging to a bubbly little girl. Maybe someone more like her friend Veronica, the way Catherine had described her.

The woman looked puzzled at first, as if she was clicking through the Rolodex of her mind. Then her eyes got wide. "Kit Kat! Of course I remember you. You don't look a day older than me." She patted her cheek and cackled with laughter. "What brings you back to the wilderness?"

"I'm here on a research trip. I'm writing a book about toxic love and Hemingway's wives."

The waitress said, "There's a lot of material in that man's failed marriages."

Catherine offered a thin smile, pulled the creamy dip closer to her, and spread it carefully on a saltine. "I thought I'd look up folks I used to know while I was here, reminisce a bit and all that. Are there any others from back in the day who are still on the Keys?"

"Most of those people have moved on. Personally, I've not kept in touch with anyone." Her eyebrows lifted as if to ask whether Catherine had done better.

"Me neither," said Catherine. "I never heard a peep from Veronica, remember her? Ronnie?"

"She would have been hard to forget. She looked like a fairy princess and talked like a trucker." Ginny snorted with laughter. "I have to deliver a few more orders, but I'll try to stop by again before you finish lunch." She wiped her hands on the bar towel hanging from her apron and bustled off toward the building that held the bar and the kitchen.

"Either she was really busy"—Catherine glanced around the patio where five or six other couples were seated—"or she didn't want to talk to me."

I cocked my head and shrugged. "I have a smart psychologist friend who always tells me not to assume that people's reactions are all about me. They have entire lives in their heads, about which we have no idea. Was this waitress part of your regular gang?"

Catherine finger-combed her bangs. "She was a local, five or six years younger than we were. Probably still in high school. She looks older than me now, like she's lived a hard life." She took a bite of her burger, chewed, and swallowed. "She'd come to our camp most nights for the bonfires, but she never stayed overnight. I assumed she had to be home at a certain time to check in with her parents. But she was watching all of it, everything we did, taking it in. She was a little mean in the beginning. When we first arrived in the camp, she tried to scare us

30

off by listing all the poisonous insects and animals and plants in Big Pine."

"Are there really poisonous plants on this island?"

"Yes, of course, but I knew she was full of baloney because she told us a crocodile was living in the Blue Hole. That's a freshwater sinkhole, so it would've had to have been an alligator."

This made me think of Eric's question about what Catherine meant exactly when she talked about taking crazy chances. "Did Ginny have a particular boyfriend?" I asked.

"Hard to say. There was a lot of flirting and romantic musical chairs. I suspect that the guys realized she was too young for consent, and no one wanted to bring the law in and close the camp down." She leaned her chin on her fingers that had clenched into a fist. "She was close to Ronnie, I'm almost sure of it. She worshipped her as only a teenage girl can. I can picture them chattering and laughing, a little apart from the rest of us. God, how we've all aged." She patted her fingers on the skin under her eyes.

"Yet she didn't seem too interested in talking about Veronica when you mentioned her name. She didn't say anything about the disappearance. Maybe she wasn't around for that?"

"She would have remembered," Catherine said, her face rigid. "It changed everything. Right after I went to the Sheriff's Office to report her missing, they cleared out the whole camp. The deputies said people were complaining about gypsy trash living in the mangroves." She barked out a laugh. "We thought that was so funny. A few of us stayed to camp for a week or so at Bahia Honda, but it wasn't the same."

Ginny swooped back in as we were finishing lunch. "I thought about your question about whether any of the old

31

gang are still around. That reminded me that Arthur Combs and Ned Newman are still here," she said, picking up the conversation but leaving out Catherine's question about Ronnie. "Tomorrow's ukulele night at the Green Parrot. A bunch of Big Pine musicians always perform, so you can probably catch them there. Buy them a beer, and they'll talk to you for the rest of the night."

"What's Arthur up to?" Catherine asked. I thought I detected a sense of yearning, probably about time passing and old friends disappearing.

"He's a veterinarian," said Ginny. "I don't have animals, but he's apparently quite popular with that set."

"He had a kind way about him, even back in those days," Catherine said. "And Ned?"

"You remember him, right? He was creepy, too old to be hanging around with the rest of us, really. He's still running that dreadful motel. You can tell by the way he dresses and acts that he still thinks he's in the seventies. It's sad, really." Ginny made a face and looked at her watch. "Can I get you anything else?" After we'd shaken our heads, she pulled our check out of an apron pocket and slapped it on the table. Then she loaded our empty plates onto a tray and carried them off. "Nice to see you again," she called back over her shoulder.

At my insistence, Catherine let me pay. "It's work," I said. "I have an expense account. I have to spend it, or my boss will cut me back." I picked up my copy of the bill and we headed back to the car. "Where to next?"

"Do you mind checking in at the motel?" she asked. "Ginny said we could probably chat with him at the Green Parrot tomorrow, but I'd rather catch him one on one, if he's in."

"That's why we came," I said, sliding back into the car, "to talk to your friends."

She wrinkled her nose and slammed her door shut. "I'd hardly call them that. They were marginal friends back then, and certainly not now."

Ned and Nora's motel was located on an inlet off Pine Channel. It didn't look like much from a distance, more shabby old Florida than anything else—a one-story concrete block structure with faded turquoise paint and louvered shutters. I paused along the sandy driveway in front of the building and looked over at Catherine, who had an expression on her face that was a combination of nostalgia and dismay.

"Might as well go in since we came this far, right?" she asked.

I nodded with reassurance. It seemed like she needed it. Then I parked next to a building that looked like it might be the office, although the sign above the door was missing the I and the C and the E. OFF! the sign flashed in faded pink neon. The vegetation around the building was creeping over the roof and shading the windows. Two rusty chairs with torn vinyl seats flanked the door.

"It looks like nothing has changed. Nothing good, anyway. Surely they've had to do some maintenance over the years to keep it open, right?" Catherine asked.

I shrugged, because really, I had no idea. Besides, I got the sense she was talking herself through something, not asking me.

"There was nothing fancy about the place then—in fact, it was a dump—and it doesn't look like they've done any upgrades. We stayed a couple nights here when we first arrived, but then we met some people at a bar and realized we could camp in the mangroves, and it wouldn't cost a penny."

"I assume that the owners were Ned and Nora?"

She nodded. "We never met Nora. There was a rumor that she'd left him not long after we arrived. Maybe his lousy marriage made him sour, I don't know. But when we complained about roaches, he insisted that we were the ones who'd brought them in. Seriously, there was a carpet of bugs any time you turned the light on at night. Hundreds of them would scuttle away to cracks in the baseboard." She shivered, glanced over at me, and shook her head. "Besides, we don't have roaches in Michigan, the winters are much too cold. At one of our big bonfires in the camp, he hit on both of us, first Ronnie, then me." She leaned back against the headrest. "Ick, we thought he was ancient and so disgusting, even though he couldn't have been much older than thirty." She shivered, remembering. "That's how it always went in those days. Everyone was in love with Ronnie. Then once she threw a guy over or turned him down, he'd ask me out."

"That happened more than once?" I asked.

She narrowed her eyes, and I hoped I hadn't sounded accusatory.

"It was a bit deflating, but I could understand it. She was tiny and delicate, with golden curls and a bubbly personality. Guys just flocked to her; it wasn't their fault or hers."

I wasn't convinced she believed that. She whooshed out a big breath of air and pushed her door open. "Might as well do this."

I followed her to the entrance and through a screen door patched with silver duct tape that banged shut behind us. Right away I noticed a musty smell, just as Catherine had described. But underneath that was a faint rotting odor, as if all the vegetation that had been growing into and around the motel for decades had begun to rot under its own weight. There was no one at the counter. She turned around to look at me, and I shrugged. Her call.

"Ned?" Catherine called out. "Ned, are you here?" She tapped the old-fashioned bell that sat on the counter but got no answer.

From the back office, I thought I heard a faint ringing, and then a chattering noise, as though a phone was vibrating across the desk. Out on the bay, not twenty yards from the motel, the buzz of a motorboat coming closer cut in and then out. Otherwise, it was dead silence. This place was giving me the full-blown creeps.

"We may have to come back later," I said. "He doesn't appear to be in."

"Let me take a quick look," she said. "He was famous for blocking out anything he didn't want to hear, such as his wife's nagging. Or customer complaints. He may very well be ignoring us." She snickered, stepped around the counter, and poked her head into the office. After a quick glance at me, she disappeared inside. "Ned?"

Moments later, she backed out until she reached the other side of the counter with me. She was shaken and pale.

"I think there's a problem. There might be a body that could be him. And blood. Stabbed in the back." She held up the blood-tinged fingers on her left hand, looking at them as if they didn't belong to her.

"Is he alive? Is he breathing?" I asked, steeling myself to go in and check.

"Stone cold dead," she said, breaking into violent weeping.

Chapter Six

"It's a commonplace to say that food is consolation, but sometimes in McCarthy's work, food is a vivid reminder that we're all linked in the meat wheel of life."
—Dwight Garner, "Cormac McCarthy
Loves a Good Diner," *New York Times,*
December 19, 2022

I scanned the office to be sure the killer wasn't waiting for me. Then I knelt beside the man, who indeed appeared to be dead, with the handle of a pair of scissors protruding between his shoulder blades and no signs of breath. I held two fingers to his neck—no pulse—and backed out into the reception area as quickly as I could. Dialing 911 with one hand, I steered Catherine outside with the other. I pressed on her shoulder until she collapsed into one of the rusty chairs, and then explained what had happened to the dispatcher.

"We'll need to wait here," I told Catherine once I'd hung up, "but it shouldn't be long. The dispatcher thought a couple of minutes at most. One of the deputies was on patrol nearby.

They'll send an ambulance too. They'll want to be sure he can't be helped medically."

Catherine's shoulders shook as she began to sob, light years from the contained woman she'd presented as over the past two days. On the other hand, seeing a dead person—a murdered person—was a shock to even the sturdiest citizen. I heard the faint wail of a siren, and soon after, two white cars pulled up with *Sheriff* written across the sides in green and gold. A deputy in a dark green uniform got out of the driver's side of the first, and a second officer, a woman, got out of the second cruiser.

I swore under my breath.

"What's the matter?" asked Catherine, craning her head in the direction of the two vehicles, her eyes wild.

I hadn't realized that I'd said anything out loud. "I have a little history with one of the officers, not entirely pleasant. It will be fine. She's very competent and organized. Just not the touchy-feely type." I'd met Darcy Rogers last year after finding a body buried in the sand on Boca Chica Beach. She had a gruff approach to questioning that left me constantly feeling suspected of murder, bordering on accused.

I stood up to greet the deputies. "I'm Hayley Snow. Nathan Bransford's wife. We've met before." I tipped my head at Darcy Rogers. "I called the incident in, but my acquaintance Catherine Davitt is the one who found the man." I gestured at Catherine, limp and sodden in her chair.

Darcy Rogers's eyes narrowed, and I imagined the wheels starting to churn. *Hayley Snow . . . dead body . . . suspicious acquaintance.* An ambulance screeched in behind the deputy's car, and the second deputy greeted the two paramedics and filled them in. All three walked briskly into the office.

"Let's start at the beginning," said Darcy Rogers to Catherine. "Who are you exactly, and why are you here at this motel right now?"

Catherine shrunk away from her fierce questions. The paramedics emerged from the building and beckoned Darcy to join them a few yards away.

"Don't be afraid to tell her everything you know," I said to Catherine, lowering my voice and placing a comforting and protective hand on her shoulder while shooting a glare in Darcy's direction. "She's a pain, but she does know her stuff. Best not to hold back, because that will make you look suspicious, especially if they realize later that you skipped something."

As we waited, I could hear bits and pieces of the conversation between the paramedics, Darcy Rogers, and the second deputy. Crime scene investigator . . . coroner . . . protecting the area . . . interviewing guests. The deputy returned to the vehicle, retrieved crime scene tape, and began to rope off the perimeter around the motel entrance.

Darcy lasered in on Catherine when she returned. "As I was saying, what brought you to this place now?" she asked.

Catherine took a deep breath and began to tell the story, how she'd been here as a young twenty-something, met a lot of like-minded people, and returned north in mid-May of that year after her friend disappeared.

"I'm writing a book about Hemingway's lost loves," she said in a clipped voice that bordered on snotty. I couldn't blame her, as the deputy brought out the worst in me too. But the tone wouldn't help her. "It seemed an opportune time to reflect on this earlier stage of my own life. My friend Veronica's disappearance was a formative event. At the risk of insulting you, I can say that the sheriff's department did a perfunctory job of looking for Ronnie after I reported her missing. I can text or email you the clipping of what was put in the newspaper if you're interested."

"Of course," said Darcy, handing her a business card, "send that on. But it's not clear to me why you would be looking into this now. I can't help wondering how your curiosity might be related to finding the man in the motel office. It would seem quite the coincidence on the surface."

On this matter, I had to agree with her. How could it be that this woman showed up to poke into old history, and one of the men in her circle ended up dead? Then she ended up being the one to discover his body? Police officers did not believe in serendipity.

"I have no idea why this man is dead," said Catherine. "I had nothing to do with it. I can tell you that for sure. We weren't close back in the seventies, and I haven't spoken to him since. I have no idea what enemies he might have made in the interim." She lifted her chin as if to say that was all she knew and would not be bullied into saying more.

"What about enemies he might have made in the past?" Darcy asked.

"His ex-wife, some of the women he hit on randomly, people he cheated in his business, secrets he threatened to spill . . ." Catherine shrugged. "Those are directions I might go. But I can't do your work for you because I don't have the answers." She relaxed back into her chair and folded her arms across her chest, looking smug, as though she'd scored a point or two.

Darcy stiffened, looking fierce, like a bear who'd been poked. Then she lumbered closer, towering over Catherine, who was not a small woman either. "So you say. Suppose I don't believe that your happening upon this man was a fluke. Tell me exactly how you came to be here at the motel with Ms. Snow, and what your relationship was like with the deceased in the past."

Now I realized that both Eric and Nathan had been ahead of me with this situation. It seemed quite possible that Catherine knew a heck of a lot more than she had told me. Both of them kept asking the question 'why is she looking into this now?' I'd skated on the surface and didn't press her, and now someone related to her past was lying in the back office of this funky motel, stone cold dead, as Catherine herself had put it. Not that I knew how long he'd been lying there or thought we could have prevented anything, but I obviously didn't understand enough about her or her history to know for sure.

For the next half hour, Darcy Rogers quizzed Catherine in excruciating detail, reviewing the same minutia over and over. I couldn't say that Catherine's answers illuminated anything new, as she summarized her book project and then listed a few of the people she had known back in the seventies. These included Ned himself, Ginny, Arthur Combs, and Susanne, a chef, whom she had not bothered to mention to me. "The other kids who were camping weren't locals. I assume your department will still have those records, though perhaps not." She sniffed. "I can't remember the name of the deputy who came to investigate after I reported my friend missing. He's probably dead by now. He wasn't a young man then, and he was overweight to the point of obese." She paused to look the very sturdy Darcy Rogers over from head to feet. "But you'd want to speak with him if he's available."

At this point, I imagined that Deputy Rogers had the urge to reach over and choke her.

"I don't need to be told how to do my job. I know how to do my job. You do yours, which is to answer my questions." She straightened her uniform shirt, looked away for a moment and then back. "So you met Ginny at the No Name Pub, and she suggested you should talk to Ned?"

"She didn't recommend it, per se, but she mentioned he still owned the motel. She also said he'd probably end up at the Green Parrot for ukulele night. I think that's on Thursday. Obviously, he won't be there." A smirk played across her lips. "Anyway, I asked my driver if we could swing by Ned's motel since we were already here."

Her driver?

"Were you planning to go to the Green Parrot later?" Darcy asked, looking from her to me and back again. "What were you expecting to find?"

Catherine glanced at me. I frowned and shook my head. I'd been sucked in deep enough already, and besides that, I was finding her annoying and imperious.

"Hayley was kind enough to drive me up here today. We hadn't really talked about going to the Green Parrot or thought about what we might learn. As I said, it's not until Thursday anyway."

"Tell me more about this so-called writing project," Darcy said.

Catherine puffed up like a vain rooster and said, "There is nothing so-called about it. I've gotten an advance and sent in an outline. All that remains is to do a bit more research and write the pages. It's about Hemingway, of course. As I already told you." She paused.

"Go ahead," said Darcy. "Explain it again."

"The idea came to me after I'd read one of his short story collections called *Men Without Women*. The man was obsessed with war, prizefighting, fishing, boxing, and so on, all what you might call 'man's man lifestyles.' The stories reflected his obsessions. The book was published to mixed reviews, one of them describing it as a collection of 'sordid little catastrophes about very vulgar people.'"

She seemed pleased with this description.

"Anyway, it pushed me to think more deeply about the forlorn man behind the successful author, and his pathetic, needy pattern of jumping from woman to woman. Which is all very interesting, but the purpose of my book is to explore his history in order to warn today's women—hopefully my readers—away from such damaged partners in their own lives. How can we recognize the signs of toxic love before getting sucked into its vortex?" She was on her high horse now, lecturing the deputy, who did not appear to be enjoying the show.

"What toxic love affair did you wish you'd been warned about?" asked Darcy, crossing her arms over her chest to match Catherine's posture.

Touché, I thought. I wouldn't have predicted she'd be so quick on her feet.

Catherine looked like she'd been slapped, the color in her face pinking up in response to the deputy's verbal blow. "I'm not writing about myself," she said in a smaller voice. "I'm testing a psychological thesis and sharing the results with women who may need this advice."

Darcy glanced at Catherine's hands, which were clutched together in her lap. "You appear to have blood on your fingers. How did that happen?"

Catherine sucked in a big breath of air, her lips quivering. "I must have touched him. My first thought was to save his life by pulling out the scissors, so I reached for them. But then I panicked and ran."

I nodded my agreement and added, "She couldn't have been in the office more than a minute or two."

Darcy turned to look at me. "Why in the world are you here?"

I explained how Catherine had contacted me and asked for my help. "We had lunch at the No Name Pub and chatted with the waitress whom Catherine had known in the past. Catherine asked her if any of the old gang was still around. The waitress was the one who suggested that Ned would likely be playing at the Green Parrot. Catherine asked if we could stop here on our way out of town. I only went into the office far enough to confirm that there was, in fact, a body. I did not touch anything except the front door," I added, anticipating her next question. "Although I did feel for a pulse." I looked at my own fingers, feeling a little queasy. "At least I don't think I touched anything. It was a shock to see him. Those scissors . . ."

Two more sheriff's department vehicles pulled up behind Darcy Rogers, one of them a tall van with *Crime Scene Investigations* written across the side. Darcy jogged over to confer with the dark-haired man who climbed out.

When she returned, she told us the investigator would be taking our fingerprints and footprints in order to rule us out as suspects. "Any problem with that?"

"It's routine," I said to Catherine before she could wind herself up to argue. "If you don't agree, we'll have to sit here awhile until they can get a search warrant. Could be quite a while, depending on the whims of the judge."

"Fine," she said. "I'd like to get this over with as soon as possible."

The investigator returned wearing a white Tyvek suit, carrying a big black box. He quickly set up a station to take our fingerprints, followed by what looked like a small kitty litter box filled with sand to take the imprints of our shoes.

"That's all for now," Darcy Rogers said to us briskly once he was finished. She handed us business cards. "I'll need your contact information and a list of people who might have information about this present death or details about your past connections in Big Pine. I'll be in touch shortly."

She strode off before either of us could respond. We watched her go, then I rustled through my backpack to find the pack of wipes I kept there for cleaning emergencies. Once we'd brushed the black powder from our hands, I took Catherine's elbow and steered her toward the car. As she slid into the passenger seat, Catherine noticed blood on the bottom of her right sandal, now crusted with crystals of sand.

"I feel sick," she said suddenly, clutching her hand to her stomach. "Excuse me a minute." She bolted out of the car and rushed around the corner of the building into the brush. I could hear her retching. A few minutes later, she returned, her chin quivering and the color leached from her face. I handed her the pack of wipes.

"Let's get out of here," I muttered. "You can text the deputy later. She won't expect you to sit here and write out a grocery list of suspects. Trust me, she's dogged. She'll follow up until every pebble is turned over."

As I backed the car out of the motel parking lot and pulled out onto Key Deer Boulevard toward Route 1, Catherine broke down, crying hysterically. "I had a terrible feeling something bad was going to happen. We probably should never have come."

I pulled over on the side of the road and patted her on the shoulder, waiting for the sobs to subside, even though I was plenty annoyed. I could feel the tension in my jaw mounting. "I get the sense that there is more to this situation than what you've told me so far." I left it there—it was obvious she was holding back. Hopefully she'd be tempted to go deeper and tell me the real story.

She looked over at me, blinking teary eyelashes, a quivering mess. But she gave a quick nod of her head. "I can't think straight."

"We need supplies and reinforcements. We'll be home in about forty-five minutes, max, and I'll get you a glass of wine and a little something to eat."

She closed her eyes and leaned into the backrest. I punched in Nathan's phone number and pulled back onto the highway.

"What are you up to? What time should I expect you?"

He must have heard something in my voice, which sounded high and forced even to me. "Why are you asking? Is there something wrong?"

"I'm on the way home with Catherine, and there's been an incident. I'm going to bring her over to the boat because I don't think she should be alone right now. I thought you might like to meet her. She found the body of a man she used to know in a motel on Big Pine." I looked over at Catherine, who looked pale and weak, nothing like the woman I had met yesterday. I nodded at her. "My husband. He's a police officer. He'll know what to do next."

1978

Catherine

Once we heard about the unofficial campground, we packed up our stuff and headed to the mangroves, stopping first at the laundromat in the Winn-Dixie strip mall. It smelled and looked like every other laundromat in every other small town—industrial-sized machines, a soap dispenser on the wall with a choice of powdered Tide or Cheer, a small lounge area with metal chairs and a minimal selection of worn magazines and dog-eared Highlights for Children. When our clothes and underwear and socks were clean and folded neatly into our suitcases, we stopped in the Winn-Dixie to load up on supplies. She chose cookies and candy, while I grabbed a big box of Trix cereal and a bag of beef jerky. We didn't have a way to cook, so there was no point in buying meat or vegetables. At the last minute, I added two cans of Spaghetti-o's and a can opener. We could eat them cold if we had to. We'd figure the rest out once we got the lay of the land.

The farther we drove into the thick vegetation along Key Deer Boulevard, the spookier it seemed.

"It's like a horror movie," Veronica said. "Dun, dun, dun, dun . . ."

She thought that was hysterical, and I did not. "Stop it, you're freaking me out." I slapped at her hand, which she'd placed on my shoulder.

I bumped down the sandy road at the end of the pavement. We came around the corner and spotted the tents, set up in a circle around a fire pit. Between two of the bigger trees, a clothesline had been slung, now flapping with men's shorts and T-shirts. A little farther away, a Coleman cooler sat on an aluminum table.

"Hello?" I warbled once we'd gotten out of the car. "Anyone home in the camp?"

"I vote we pitch our tent now and answer questions later," said Veronica, adding her usual sly grin. She had the grin of someone who could get away with anything just by tossing her curls.

Chapter Seven

"When you're going to do a cake, you really have to have a battle plan all ready. You don't want to go out and play croquet in the middle, for instance."

—Julia Child

I settled Catherine on the deck in the awning's shade with Evinrude and Ziggy and went inside to rustle up some snacks and pour each of us a glass of wine. It was on the early side for a cocktail, but we'd both been shaken by the events of the day. As I came out with our wineglasses, Miss Gloria rattled by with her grocery cart in tow.

"Howdy," she said. "Are you having happy hour? Mind if I join you? It'll take me just a minute to put a few cold things away."

"Of course not," I said, because I always said that. She was eighty-three and a dear friend who'd grown to feel like family. She was funny and warm and loved me wholeheartedly. I wanted to cherish every moment with her. Aside from that, she'd been the one who'd encouraged me to meet Catherine, and she'd be super curious about what was unfolding. "How did you go shopping when I had your car?"

"Mrs. Dubisson drove us down to Fausto's. I didn't need a lot, but she likes the company. Now I have some good snacking cheese, plus eggs and butter and sugar and cream cheese and baking chocolate and coconut flakes, in case you get the urge to bake something over at my place."

"Did you have something particular in mind?" I asked. "Your list covers a lot of territory from chocolate cake to coconut."

She grinned, then winked at Catherine, not seeming to notice that the woman was a wreck. "I'll be right back with the other cats."

"Does she actually think she's a cat?" Catherine asked as I started to head back to the kitchen for the food and a third glass of wine.

"Maybe so," I said, grinning broadly. By the time I returned with Miss Gloria's glass and a maple cutting board containing cheese, a roll of summer sausage, okra and green bean pickles, assorted crackers, and a few token carrot sticks, my neighbor had returned and settled in next to Catherine with her cats, Sparky and T-bone. I could tell from the direction the conversation had taken that she'd already introduced herself and started quizzing my guest.

"I'm always curious," she said, "about why young people go off on sudden adventures. I got married too young to even develop such an idea, but I suppose I've made up for it by living right here." She gestured at the boats bobbing around us, a beady-eyed pelican on a post watching us from yards down the dock, the three cats who'd settled in around us, and the soothing whop-whop of the overhead fan in my kitchen. "How about you?" Miss Gloria loaded a cracker with cheese and sausage, popped it into her mouth, and looked at Catherine with her wispy white eyebrows raised. "What triggered your first trip to Key West?"

Catherine opened her mouth, then closed it again as if she couldn't figure out what to say or how much to share. "As I mentioned to Hayley, the trip took place so long ago that the details are hazy. I suppose I was tired of school, sick of bad boyfriends, ready for a change, that sort of thing." She waved her hand limply and swallowed a big glug of wine. "It's all kind of a blur."

"Interesting," said Miss Gloria. "I find that that my older memories are sharp as broken glass. It's what I had for lunch yesterday that tends to get fuzzy." She laughed out loud, looking at me. "Unless it's something special that Hayley made for me." She turned her focus back to Catherine. "What did your parents think about your junket?"

Catherine heaved a dramatic sigh. "You know how it is when you're young. You get into a rut and can't see a way out of it. My mother suggested I take time off from school. She even mentioned the Florida Keys because she and my father had honeymooned in Key Largo."

This was news to me, not at all what she'd told me yesterday.

Miss Gloria clucked. "Hayley mentioned that you two were going up to Big Pine Key today to look up old friends. How did that go?"

Catherine's lips began to quiver as though she might burst into tears again.

"It didn't go well," I cut in quickly. "We had lunch at the No Name Pub, and then we stopped at a motel to chat with an old acquaintance but unfortunately found him murdered. At least it looked that way."

Miss Gloria gasped. "Surely that was not propitious timing. Were you the ones who called the police?"

I nodded grimly. "That dreadful Darcy Rogers made an appearance and frightened Catherine half to death." I rolled my eyes. She scared me too, even though I tried to fend off her unsettling vibes.

Miss Gloria tsked. "I am so sorry that happened." She reached over to pat Catherine's back. "It must have been a dreadful shock. I suppose you've already filled Hayley in about your relationship with the deceased?"

"There wasn't much of a relationship, not then, and certainly not now," said Catherine, leaning away from my friend's touch with a horrified look on her face.

"But surely the Sheriff's Office would consider this an unlikely coincidence," said Miss Gloria. "The fact that you knew the man years ago and now here you come again to reminisce about those times and instead find him murdered. They wouldn't overlook such a possible connection, would they, Hayley?"

"Definitely not," I said. "Had you contacted the dead man before you came south? Suggested coffee or a drink or something, a chance to relive old times?"

"I had no intention of reliving old times with that man," Catherine said stiffly. "I did not come down to remember any of that nightmare. I had no idea he was still living here."

Then why had she come? More specifically, why had we gone to his motel? Up at the end of the dock, Nathan got out of his SUV and walked toward us. "Oh good, Nathan's home early."

A chime went off on Miss Gloria's Apple watch. "Oh dear, it's Mrs. Dubisson reminding me about our date. I'm about to be late for dinner and cards if I don't shower and primp right now.

I'll see you cats later." She kissed each of the animals on the head and blew a kiss to me. "I'll cede my seat to your hubby. Send my kitties home if they start to annoy you."

Nathan hugged her as she exited the boat and he came aboard, looking gorgeous as always, but a little tired.

I introduced him to Catherine and went inside to fetch him a glass of seltzer on ice with lime, as he'd said he would need to go back into the office later. He would not want to return to work reeking of alcohol, even one beer.

"Hayley tells me you've had a difficult day," he said to Catherine as he settled into the chair beside her. I handed him the glass and sat on the other side of him.

"That's one way to put it," she said. "The only dead people I've ever seen were embalmed and displayed in a coffin. Not freshly murdered and bloody. I wish you had been there to help with the inquisition." She tipped her head in the direction Miss Gloria had left. "That little woman is dogged. As was the sheriff's deputy." She fluttered her eyelids as if she needed rescuing. From a man.

Was she flirting with my husband? I felt a bubble of outrage rise from my stomach to my throat.

"How about you tell Nathan what happened, and then one of us will give you a ride back to the inn. Or we can call an Uber." I was not in the mood to include this woman in our dinner plans, the few minutes we'd have to spend alone today. Besides, she and her drama were wearing me out. I couldn't wait to send her home, and I hoped Nathan wouldn't mind taking her. I'd heard a flood of text and email chimes from my phone, probably Palamina at *Key Zest* and my mother. I owed both return calls.

"Tell me what happened, right from the beginning," Nathan said, his sea green eyes focused on her face. This was often his opening gambit because what a suspect or a witness considered to be the beginning told him a lot. Or what they were willing to say.

Catherine summarized our day, including lunch at No Name Pub, her suggestion that we stop by Ned's motel, and then her horrifying discovery of the body. Nothing I hadn't heard before, and nothing told in a new way.

"Tell me about your gang back in the seventies." He said this in such a pleasant way that Catherine seemed to relax for the first time since finding the dead man.

"It was weird," she said. "My girlfriend and I didn't know anyone in the Keys, but the group who was camped out at Big Pine accepted us right away. We ate together at night—often fish that some of the guys caught during the day. Everyone shared what they had and worked as they could to make enough money to live. We took turns cooking and cleaning up. This may sound stupid and naive, but I remember it as a dreamy, utopian time in my life."

"You were sad to see it end," Nathan said.

She looked up at him sharply. "I was. I'd never belonged to a group quite like that one."

"Was there a leader? I imagine there would have had to have been rules for living together, even in a hippie-ish setting?"

Now Catherine had a yearnful, wistful look on her face. "His name was Arthur Combs. He was tall and light-haired." She looked at Nathan, scanning him up and down. "Not far off from your size and shape, probably thinner though. He had a quiet way about him, even though everyone knew he was in charge."

"Is he still living in the Keys?"

"Apparently," she said. "Ginny mentioned that he's a local veterinarian now, and he'd probably be performing at ukulele night at the Green Parrot."

Nathan nodded. "I'm sure Deputy Rogers will follow up on that. Do you think Ned's death is somehow related to those days and those people?"

"Maybe," she said. "But I can't see how. In the end, that was many years ago, and he probably had many chances to piss people off royally in the interim."

"Best thing you can do is cooperate with Deputy Rogers. Tell her whatever you remember. Some things may come back to you that you didn't think to tell her after you'd made that gruesome discovery." Nathan got to his feet. "You could probably use a hot shower and a bite to eat. How about I run you home?"

I watched them walk up the dock to his cruiser, relieved to have her gone. It wasn't as if she'd done anything in particular; she was just exhausting. She told many versions of the same story, talking to Miss Gloria and Nathan each in a different way than she had to me. It seemed that having a handsome man in her presence, or an older woman, brought out different sides of her. While I whipped up a batch of pesto with toasted pecans and basil from our porch, I thought about her response to Nathan regarding Ned. I wondered if she had known him better than what she admitted.

Something Catherine had said to the sheriff's deputy about the project she was working on floated into my mind. She said she was looking into Hemingway's toxic loves so she could warn women to avoid this. She'd taken great umbrage with Darcy

Rogers's question about her own toxic love. What if she was looking for someone she loved? What if she had contacted some people before she came down—maybe about this man Arthur—and failed to mention this to me? Was she looking for the man she'd fallen in love with as a young woman and whom she'd thought about through all these years of failed relationships? Had something gone badly wrong with that, such that it turned sour or toxic?

Nathan returned just about the time that I was draining the pasta except for half a cup of pasta liquid that I stirred into the pesto. The hot water brought the scent of fresh basil bursting into the kitchen, along with a dash of fresh garlic and the salty tang of parmesan cheese.

Nathan said, "That smells delicious. I'm bushed after spending half an hour with that woman. Hard to imagine ferrying her around for an entire day as you did."

I laughed as I served us heaping platters of pasta and salad to carry out to the deck.

"My first impression of her was definitely wrong," I said, as we settled at the table. "She seemed completely composed to the point of impenetrable when we first met, but shortly after we found this fellow's body, she crumpled. Then she gets to our home and acts like a witch.

"Did you happen to find out whether there's anyone still in the area who was working with the sheriff's department at the time of the disappearance of her friend?"

Nathan swallowed the bite of pasta he was chewing and took a drink of water. "I haven't had a chance to ask. But considering the timing, they would've been just starting out, and they would've had a long career if they're still around."

"Exactly," I said. "Darcy Rogers wasn't a lot of help either. Poor Catherine did not enjoy talking to her, not one bit."

Nathan laughed. "No witness is going to feel like she's been rocked in her mother's arms after talking to Darcy. Not that that's her job because she's a woman, in case you were thinking I was talking like an old-fashioned, chauvinist pig." I broke out laughing again. After we'd finished supper, Nathan carried the dishes into the kitchen and then left to return to the police station.

A text came in from Miss Gloria; *How did things go in Big Pine with your new best friend?*

Ha! I texted back, and then I summarized the conversation with Nathan. *More questions than answers at this point. I'll look for you tomorrow and fill in every detail. That woman wore me out for sure.*

I took the dog for a decent walk, puttered around the houseboat straightening up, and finally got ready for bed. It was hard not to puzzle over Catherine's story. If she knew Ned better than she said she did and she needed to talk to him, why didn't she ask me to take her straight to the motel?

Another thought bore down on me, sharper this time. If we had gone right to Ned and Nora's, maybe he'd still be alive. Maybe Catherine realized this too, and that would explain her meltdown. How long had Ned been dead before we discovered him? She'd described him as stone cold dead, but that was not the same as 'stone cold.' Was it possible that Catherine had gone up to Big Pine earlier in the morning and killed him and then set me up to help "discover" him?

She'd have to be one cool customer.

A Poisonous Palate

1978

Catherine

Even though it was hot and still, and the air hung heavy and smelly like a forgotten and moldering load of wet towels, we'd both fallen asleep in the tent. We woke at the sound of conversations around us. The campers had returned.

"We should go meet our new best friends," Veronica said. She sat up and ran a tortoiseshell brush through her hair and sniffed her armpit. "Phew." She whipped off the faded T-shirt she'd had on all day, rolled deodorant under her arms, and changed into a more revealing pink tank top. "Shall we?" she asked as she crawled out through the canvas door flap into the late afternoon.

"Greetings, everyone," Veronica called out. "I'm Ronnie, and this is Kit Kat, aka Catherine if you're mad at her. We hope you don't mind us crashing the party. Kit Kat can cook and clean, and I'm the eye candy." She mugged and posed like a model. The people in the circle of chairs around the fire laughed and told us their names: Arthur, Susanne, Ginny, David, Ned, and five or six more I'd never remember.

"We're happy to have you. There are a few rules. We all pitch in at dinnertime," said Arthur. He had a deep, resonant voice and an easy smile. "Either you buy food or scavenge it or put money in the pot. You can take a shower at Bahia Honda. That's about it." He grinned, and Veronica smiled back in a way that made him blush, as with all the guys she homed in on.

*"For the new girls," Ginny said, "a little piece of advice. Don't go swimming in the Blue Hole. There's a crocodile who lives there whom we locals call Big Betty, nicknamed Always. Last year she bit off the leg of the homecoming queen when she went skinny-dipping with her boyfriend. Betty's **always** hungry, just waiting for the next course!"*

All the people around the campfire laughed.

"What else do we have to worry about?" Veronica asked.

"Don't brag about it if you come across a bale of marijuana," Ginny said. "The Sheriff's Office is looking for an excuse to bust smugglers. Just ask my father. Oh, and watch out for two kinds of poison trees, the manchineel—don't even stand under that one if it's raining. It's said to have been the cause of death for Ponce de León—one poisoned arrowhead to the chest and done." She let her chin slump to her chest, pretending to be dead. "And the poisonwood tree, that sucker will give you a rash like poison oak or poison ivy if you even touch it. In the water, Portuguese man-of-war, and sharks, and in your tent, black widow and brown recluse spiders, plus scorpions. Keep your tent zipped if you don't want visitors of the multilegged kind."

"Or even the two-legged," said Susanne. Her gaze was on a man with a goatee who looked a little older than the others. He'd joined the circle late. He was ogling my roommate, of course.

"Enough!" said Veronica, tossing a cluster of curls off her shoulder. *"We don't scare easily."* She pointed to a kid several seats over who was swigging from a bottle of golden-brown booze. *"Pass the rum, please."*

Chapter Eight

"The flavor is fantastic, bright and briny, but the firm flesh of the olive and the blobbily collapsing gelatin combine in the mouth to create a visceral texture that I loathed bodily and also immediately wanted to experience again."
—Helen Rosner, "A New Italian Restaurant Pairs Serious Cooking with a Sense of Humor," *New Yorker*, *July 31, 2023*

I woke the next morning feeling a bit drained and tired. Finding the dead man and nursing Catherine through the awkward interactions with the Sheriff's Office had punched the stuffing out of me. Nathan's side of the bed was already empty, except for Evinrude, who was splayed on his back, displaying the gray-and-black target on his belly.

"I take it you've eaten," I said as I stroked his tummy. "Otherwise, you'd never let me sleep in." He lifted his head and mouthed a silent meow. I glanced at my phone. There were the usual unhappy news headlines from Key West and New York, a few announcements of clothing sales, a reminder from my *Key Zest* boss about our staff meeting at ten, and an email from Catherine.

I poured a cup of coffee, dosed it with cream and sugar, and settled in at the banquette with the coffee and a bowl of cereal with blueberries. Fortified with caffeine and calories, I turned to Catherine's note. In a nutshell, she was devastated by yesterday's events and had a lot of work to do on her book but could meet for a quick coffee at nine to review what had occurred yesterday and any developments in the murder case, and plan next steps.

How did she manage to come across as both demanding and self-absorbed and needy in one sentence? She wrote as if I was the one who asked to meet with her, not the other way around. Part of me would have liked to wash my hands of her and her drama, but I felt like I was already in too deep. I was hooked by the story and now the murder. In truth, her suggestion would work fine since Cuban Coffee Queen was close to my office, and a quick coffee was about all I could stomach of her this morning. I messaged her back with the address, then dressed and packed up my laptop and phone to take to the office.

Miss Gloria was waiting in a lounge chair on our deck, her two cats snuggled up with her. "Good morning, sleepyhead! I couldn't wait to talk to you, but I held back from coming inside and shaking you awake."

"Thanks for that!" I laughed.

"I've been reviewing your day yesterday and wondered if you've been thinking the way I have. Do you think it's possible your friend Catherine actually killed that man and set it up so you'd "help" her discover the body?"

I clapped both hands to my head in mock horror. "First of all, she isn't my friend. Second, the thought did cross my mind, but the timing would be difficult. She would have had to find a way up to Big Pine, kill him, then race back for me to pick her up and drive her north again. She'd have to be a really cold person to pull that off. Plus, who's to say someone else wouldn't find him in the meantime?" I drummed my fingers on the railing of our deck. "Although that wouldn't be all bad, as it would take her off the suspect list."

Miss Gloria's face brightened. "In order to figure out whether she could have killed the man, you'd need to track down who took her up the Keys earlier in the day. There must be a hundred Uber drivers and cabs in this town, and you'd have to interview all of them. On the other hand, she might have had an accomplice to do the dirty work. All that sounds like police work to me."

"Yes, it does," I said, relieved to hear her step aside from playing detective for the moment.

"What an amateur *could* do, however," she said with a sly smile, "is make a quick visit to see an old friend. That Sheriff's deputy guy who supposedly threw them out of their camp years ago was known to show up at the boccie courts from time to time when Frank used to play back in the old days. His name was Ryan Lopez. I think he'd remember me, probably with some fondness." She smiled and batted her eyelashes. "You might think fifty sounds elderly, but I was quite a dish back then."

"How did you even know about him?" I asked.

"A little search in the archives." She grinned.

"What archives?"

"The Sheriff's Office has a treasure trove on their website. A gal just has to know where to look."

Hmm, her idea was kind of brilliant, but I'd been warned off, and I was too busy to follow up with this idea anyway. I blew her a kiss, shouldered my backpack, and stepped from the deck to the dock. "I'll be sure to let you know if the authorities need our help. See you tonight for dinner, right?"

Lucy Burdette

Birthdays always seemed to be a little complicated these days with my mom, her husband Sam, and me all accomplished in the kitchen but busy as one-armed paperhangers, as my grandfather's friend Angelo used to say. My mother and Sam were operating at full speed this week with a couple of small catering jobs while also preparing for a wedding feast on the weekend. No one had the bandwidth to cook up a family dinner worthy of a birthday, so we made the decision to celebrate Sam by eating out. He chose a newish Italian restaurant on the harbor called Bel Mare. Needless to say, I'd be gathering ammunition for a *Key Zest* review or roundup while I was there.

I hopped on my scooter and drove down to Old Town. Arriving at Cuban Coffee Queen ten minutes early, I grabbed a small café con leche and pushed aside a glossy rooster who was pecking at crumbs so I could settle onto a bench at one of the painted yellow picnic tables. Then I dialed up my mother, with whom I hadn't talked in the last few days.

"I wondered what you were up to!" she said. "I hear a rooster, so you must be busy at your second office." I could picture her smiling. When she first moved to Key West, I wasn't sure I wanted her invading my newly discovered island paradise. But she found her sea legs in the catering world, and I grew more confident in mine. Now, I wouldn't have traded her presence in Key West for anything. On the phone, I could hear the clanging of pots and Sam's easy laugh. My friend Danielle was getting married on Sunday, and Mom had promised to provide some of her best goodies for the rooftop rehearsal party at the Studios of Key West on Friday.

"I won't keep you long." I summarized the events of the last twenty-four hours, including the original email from Catherine, our first meeting at the Hemingway Home, and our unfortunate discovery at the motel in Big Pine Key. She exclaimed with dismay over all of it. As my mother, she hated the idea of possibly dangerous situations eddying around me.

"What did you say she's writing?" she asked.

"It's a self-help book on what women can learn about toxic love from Hemingway's wives, although his *marriages* are probably more to the point. Why should his shenanigans and failings get blamed on the women? But I suppose her marketing team can work on the right description." I chuckled.

"Who in the world would buy such a book?" she asked.

"Women with troubled relationship histories who are looking for answers. Maybe a few enlightened men? I think it's kind of brilliant because most of us probably have a relationship dud in our pasts. Chad was definitely toxic in my world," I said. "I was so lost inside my insecurities that his invitation to come to Key West felt like a solution to the problem of having to grow up and figure out who I was and what I should be doing. It's embarrassing to think back on how I behaved." I couldn't help wondering now whether one or more of Hemingway's wives had felt the same way after being swept off her feet by a dashingly handsome and talented man who'd declared himself besotted. His growing literary accomplishments would have been appealing as well as his persona. His emotional issues would have revealed themselves later when it was too late to extricate herself.

"You weren't so bad as all that," my mother said. "I suppose marrying your father had a touch of that too, though I wouldn't have described our love as toxic. I was young and needy, and he liked that attention at first." She paused, and it sounded like she was tapping a fingernail on her phone. "My father, your grand-father, was a bit distant. Certainly not abusive, but I craved his approval and affection. He wasn't an effusive man, and he couldn't give me what I wanted. I think he had the notion that children were supposed to be well-behaved and keep to them-selves; this was in their contract when they were born." She gave a quick laugh-snort. "Then I fell for your father and fell into that same pattern with him. Craving his attention, wanting more than he was able to give. His father was actually similar to mine, probably even more frozen emotionally, so neither one of us was well-prepared for a deep relationship."

"You and Sam are so lucky to have found true love the sec-ond time through. Hopefully Nathan and I are headed that way too. I think he learned a lot about how not to be married from his parents. He's really trying to share from his heart and not hold everything inside."

I described the sense I'd had last night that Catherine seemed to almost melt into Nathan. "She struck me as the kind of woman who'd brag about her independence, but the minute she had car trouble, she'd be shrieking 'We need a man!'"

My mom snickered. "Be careful with her. Don't get burned. Gotta run. One of my pots is boiling over, and my husband's rolling his eyes."

While I waited for Catherine, I sipped my Cuban café con leche and worked on drafting a piece about the No Name Pub. In a nutshell, the food wasn't the star at this establishment, but rather the local color, the Key deer, and the restaurant's history were. I found my notes on the delicious shrimp pizza and fish dip, but my food memories had definitely been eclipsed by our discovery of Ned's dead body.

Catherine rushed in fifteen minutes late and dumped her stuff on the picnic table I was inhabiting. "I'll grab a coffee and be right back," she said, adding a wink and fording past the group of tourists that was studying the big menu above the counter.

"Phew," she said when she returned. "It's a mob scene around here. I don't know how you live with these crowds." She took a sip of her iced coffee and made a face. "What do they not understand about 'no sugar'? Glad you could make it. I need to write up the notes I took on the tour of the Hemingway Home before they get stale, so I don't have a lot of time. This will be the Pauline section," she added with a sly smile. "The 'watch out because sometimes what goes around comes around' section."

I laughed along with her, though I wasn't sure I knew exactly what she meant. Pauline was Hemingway's second wife, the woman who lived with him during his Key West years. I'd be very curious to hear how she spun the facts she gleaned from those tours about the friendship between Hadley and Pauline, and the subsequent stealing of Hadley's husband. Everything Catherine said to me sounded like it had a double meaning, for the present and the past, for Hemingway's history and her own. She was wearing me out a little bit with her swings from needy to fierce. Besides, she wasn't the only one with things to do. I had a load of work too.

"How are you feeling after yesterday?" I asked. "That was quite a shock."

"Okay," she said. "It freaked me out for a few hours, but we never were close, and I hadn't seen the guy in years and years, so it's not like it was personal."

A cold thing to say. When was discovering the body of someone you knew with a pair of scissors plunged into his back not personal? "Except for the coincidence of finding him on the very day you went to the island to ask questions about your friend."

Catherine raised her eyebrows. "True, but she wasn't really my friend either. A friend would have given me some warning that she was leaving town, not simply vanished." She sipped at her coffee and shrugged carelessly. "Question is, what can we do now to figure out what happened to Veronica?"

"If it was me, I'd lay low a day or two," I suggested, beginning to seriously wonder why she was so intent on finding out what happened to this woman if she didn't consider her to be a friend. "You may have stirred up a hornet's nest, and now there's more at stake and a lot of people involved."

"I can't really lay low," she said, frowning, "because I'm only in town for a week."

"Who else were you hoping to interview?" I asked, swallowing the last of my coffee, which tasted both gloriously sweet and strong. I would never ever ask for no sugar in a Cuban coffee. Nor would I drink it cold. "My suggestion would be to make an appointment with whichever detective handles the cold cases in the Sheriff's Office." I was proud of coming up with that on the fly. It would keep her busy and out of trouble.

But she was frowning again, tapping her cup on the tabletop hard enough that the liquid sloshed onto the table. "What are the chances they'd pay any attention to my queries, never mind give me information? I searched the Internet about this. They have another cold case disappearance on their roster from 1981, and according to the newspaper reports, they have no records for that one."

She didn't wait for me to comment. "What I'd like to do some day this week is go back up to Big Pine and try to find the place where we camped. Not that anything would be left there, but maybe seeing it in person will jog my memory. Maybe I'll remember something I hadn't thought of before about her interactions with the other campers. Something might get shaken loose."

This made a little bit of sense. "Hurricane Irma hit that island hard in 2017, so much of the landscape is likely to have changed. Entire neighborhoods were wiped out, along with a lot of vegetation that hasn't recovered. You noticed that with the pine trees, remember? You might not recognize a thing near your campground."

"Understood," she said. "I did see some of that yesterday. But Ned's lousy, roach-ridden motel is still standing, as is the No Name Pub. I'm not expecting miracles, just a chance to remember."

"Fair enough," I said. "But keep in mind, we're"—I pointed to her and then me—"the epicenter of a murder investigation. They are not likely to look kindly on us getting more involved than we already are."

"How's your schedule day after tomorrow?" she asked, ignoring my protest and tapping her iPhone with her forefinger. "Maybe by then I'll have some good questions formulated. Hopefully I'll have made progress on this cursed book too."

We settled on me picking her up at 10:00 AM on Friday outside the Angela Street entrance to the Gardens Hotel, one of the premier inns on the island with its gorgeous pool and lush tropical landscape, which was expansive for Old Town. It was also expensive, even for an island where prices had grown stratospheric. She clearly was not on a normal writer's budget.

"If possible," she said, "I'd love to have you go with me tomorrow evening to the Green Parrot ukulele night too. Didn't Ginny say some of the old-time Big Pine guys hang out there? Maybe we could knock off several interviews with one stop.

"I'd like to have a second pair of eyes looking them over," she added, "before I stumble around into some other muck. This way I could hang back while you talk. I'm not ready for anyone else to recognize me. Definitely no more bodies." She found her comment amusing, but I did not.

She rustled in her purse and pulled out a faded Polaroid photograph that appeared to be vintage 1970s. "It's me and Veronica," she said, passing it across the table. "That waitress in North Carolina—the one who convinced us to drive south to the Keys—took the picture."

The two girls leaned against a yellow two-door Dodge Dart with a black vinyl top and interior. This must have been hellishly hot in the Florida sun. The back seat of the car was packed to the roof with their belongings. I tried to picture them emptying that back seat in campgrounds or rest stops so both girls could sleep in the car for the night. I didn't think there was much chance that somebody meeting her today would recognize Catherine as the lanky, buxom girl in the picture with the long legs, black hair, and bangs that hung in a fringe over her eyebrows. They were the kind of bangs that a mother would be desperate to trim. Looking at those two girls with their hopeful faces, I felt unaccountably sad. "You two were gorgeous. Why is it that young women don't understand how much they have going for them?" In truth, I was talking about myself as a younger person as much as her.

She looked sad now too.

"Okay. I'll do it."

She flashed a wide smile. "Thank you for helping. I knew you would, even before we met."

Chapter Nine

"Almost every family has a secret they never discuss. Ours is this: We were taste testers for Pop-Tarts."
—Laura M. Holson, "Confessions of a Pop-Tarts Taste Tester," *New York Times*, October 6, 2023

I fired my empty coffee cup into the trash and walked two blocks to the *Key Zest* office. Once again, I felt baffled by the many moods of Catherine. How could one person be simultaneously imperious and grateful?

Palamina and Danielle had already gathered in Palamina's office. My boss, Palamina, moved down from New York to Key West a few years ago to take charge of *Key Zest*, and she still struggled to adjust to the slower pace of island life. Danielle had worked at the e-zine as a receptionist almost from its inception. She was a native Key Wester—a Conch—who had embraced her engagement and upcoming marriage to a Key West police officer with the same ebullience she brought to her job and her friendships. At the moment, Palamina wore the expression of a cold-snap-stunned fish, so I suspected Danielle had been regaling her with the last-minute details of her Sunday wedding. She practically grabbed my hand to pull me in. "What do you have for us for next week?" she asked.

"I was thinking of a short piece on Big Pine Key eateries, which we've never done before. Part of it could be about how the island has managed to recover since Hurricane Irma's devastating blow. I'm also planning a review of Bel Mare on the harbor, and possibly Antonia's on Duval Street. That way, we'd have something old and something new." I winked at Danielle, who was gazing lovingly at the diamond rock on her left ring finger.

Palamina was a lot more enthused about the possibility of a foodie piece on Big Pine Key than I would have predicted, making me wonder if she only wanted to get us out of her office quickly. I told her that I'd already been to the No Name Pub and started a review.

"It's not exactly a foodie hot spot," I said.

"That's okay," she said. "Not everyone cares as much about food as you do. Meanwhile, I've gotten some negative feedback that we are too Key West–centric, so this will throw those people a bone."

We ran through the other articles for next week's issue, including Danielle's exuberant report on where to get married in Key West and her rundown on the best wedding vendors, and then I retreated to my nook to work for a few hours. I wondered if Palamina regretted offering Danielle a trial run as reporter. I thought it was a brilliant idea, as my friend had a lighthearted point of view that we'd been missing in our e-zine, and she came up with ideas that might interest island residents, not just the tourists. Plus, she was responsive to edits and produced rewritten versions that were head and shoulders better than her initial drafts.

"Hayley, any new non-food ideas from you?" Palamina was tapping her lip with a pen, eyes narrowed.

"I'm noodling over something along the lines of how to look under the surface of our island legends. The surface is absolutely fine for tourists who are visiting for a day—in fact, it would be hard to absorb more than that. However, those of us lucky enough to stay longer or visit more than once, or even live here, can go deeper." This was one of Palamina's frequent critiques of my work—that I skimmed the surface in my writing—so I thought she'd love that addition. As long as I could figure out what the heck it meant.

"Give us an example," she said, leaning back in her chair.

"Hemingway," I said. "Scratch the surface of the stories about him as a macho, cat-loving, super writer, and you might find an insecure boy-man who searched his whole life for a woman who could quiet his inner demons." Next, I described to Palamina and Danielle the book that Catherine was research-ing, then said, "With any luck, I could land an interview with her well before publication."

"I like it," said Palamina. "Carry on." She snapped her chair up straight, slapped her datebook closed, and stood up. "When can you get me a draft?"

"Um, maybe by the weekend? Or Monday, in case I can't schedule the author right away. Plus, we do have a wedding to attend." I winked at Danielle and went to my own office cubicle to work.

At lunchtime, I popped home to the houseboat to eat and to walk Ziggy. Holy yikes, I'd gotten myself into deep water by proposing an article about Catherine's work. I had no idea whether she'd be willing to disclose parts of her juiciest research well before the book was published. When Ziggy and I returned from our expedition over the Palm Avenue bridge, Miss Gloria was waiting again on my houseboat.

"Not to be a pest," she said, "but I have some news for you. Do you know the old sheriff's deputy I mentioned, who I might possibly have a connection with?" She didn't wait for my answer. "I emailed him this morning. He still lives on Big Pine, and he's open to a visit. I told him you were writing an article about cold cases on Big Pine Key."

"Cold cases?" I squinted at her, emphasizing the plural on cases. She always pushed the limits. "What does that mean?"

"I assume you know that Catherine's friend wasn't the only girl who disappeared from that island. A young woman, a mother of two, vanished in 1981. Her daughter's been searching for her ever since, but the Sheriff's Office has no information on the case prior to 1995."

This sounded like the case that Catherine had mentioned. "And you happen to know this because?"

"Dr. Google told me!" she exclaimed, looking pleased with herself. "We have a perfect reason to go talk to this retired officer, and I might have suggested to him that this afternoon or sometime tomorrow could work. You know, he's much more likely to talk off the record to an old pal than to put something in writing."

"Give me a minute to think this over," I said. At the staff meeting today, Palamina had also instructed me that if I was going to write about food in the middle Keys, I needed more venues. I'd been browsing the food possibilities on Big Pine Key, and the Good Food Conspiracy seemed like a reasonable option. Billed as an organic juice bar and deli with vegan options on the menu, it wouldn't appeal to everyone, but it wouldn't hurt anyone either.

If we did visit the retired sheriff's deputy, I wanted to do it without Catherine. In my limited experience with her so far, people changed their stories around her, and she changed hers with every wind blowing through as well.

"Let's go up for lunch tomorrow," I suggested. "Maybe you could find out if he's available for a visit either before or after? Now that I think about it, we could grab an early bite, then visit the sheriff's deputy and maybe drive around the area that Catherine described. Then we'll stop at the Square Grouper on the way home." This restaurant on Cudjoe Key was well known for its seafood, exotic cocktails, and inventive everything else. Cudjoe was not exactly Big Pine Key, but Palamina hadn't been that explicit, and honestly, she wouldn't know the difference. I doubted that she'd ever set foot out of Key West proper and into the wilder regions of Monroe County.

Miss Gloria was grinning and clapping her hands. "Road trip! Road trip!"

Feeling very sleepy, I decided to take my laptop to the library for a change of scenery. Sometimes snoozing on the deck with the animals was too tempting, whereas I would be too embarrassed to fall asleep in the Florida History Room. I parked my scooter in the lot behind the pink stucco library and went inside. I wanted to understand more about Catherine and her history and the subject of her book before we talked with the former sheriff's deputy. Thinking that perhaps her book subject would provide clues, I began by skimming through old photographs of Hemingway with each of his wives. With every marriage, the earliest photos shone with happiness and hope, all of which dimmed as life with Mr. Hemingway unraveled. Had they understood before they married him that their relationships were doomed? At least several of the wives had known the woman whom she replaced in his affections. Had they been thinking 'that happened to her, but I am different'? Did they truly believe that his love for her was stronger and purer than for his other wives?

Next, I did an Internet search on how to deal with toxic people. On the first results page, I found an article on how to look for signs of a toxic friend or partner. Moodiness, manipulation, showing several versions of the self and confusion about which is real—these were some of the warning signals. I wondered how many of these Hemingway had shown his wives both before and after they were married.

My next thought was that this list of attributes pretty well described Catherine.

Chapter Ten

"Fernand Point famously held that in order to master a dish you must cook it 100 times. He was as fastidious as he was fat. 'Look at the chef,' he advised. 'If he is thin, you will probably dine poorly.'"
—Wendell Steavenson, "The Rise and Fall of French Cuisine," *The Guardian*, July 16, 2019

Birthdays were super important in my family. We took care to celebrate each birthday person and toast his or her presence in our lives. However, my mother and Sam were very busy this week with a couple of catering jobs, and they were also preparing for Danielle's wedding rehearsal party. They were on food preparation overload, and knew I was busy too, and so had made the decision to eat out. Sam chose a newish restaurant situated on the Key West Bight called Bel Mare. This sounded like a wonderful celebration of Sam: Italian food that no one in our family had to cook, plus a fancy cocktail while admiring the harbor. It would be a nice break from everyday life. In addition, I could take notes and photos for next week's review.

At the appointed time, Nathan zipped home to pick up Miss Gloria and me and drove us across town to the old harbor, aka the bight, which bustled with visitors enjoying music, happy hour beverages, and food. With his usual good parking juju, he found a space within easy walking distance to the restaurant.

"This brings back memories of the ill-fated tiki boat cruise," said Miss Gloria, gazing out over the water. "Though all's well that ends well. Those scone sisters were amazing, weren't they? I miss those ladies. They're going to FaceTime me this week from somewhere in the Midwest—Omaha, I think."

"They were such good sports," I said, grinning and offering my elbow to assist her up the steep stairs.

"I'm good," she said, waving me ahead of her.

"Of course you are," I laughed. "Give them my love."

We climbed up to the restaurant on the second floor and joined my mother and Sam at a round corner table covered with a crisp white cloth. Our view overlooked boats bobbing in the harbor.

"If a person has to get older, this is a grand way to do it," said Sam, grinning widely and gesturing at us. "All of my favorite people gathered together and a view to die for. We ordered a bottle of prosecco to start things off. Hope that's agreeable."

"It's your day, old fella," said Miss Gloria, clapping him on the shoulder. "We'd drink kerosene if you ordered it."

Everyone laughed.

"We should go around the table and have a check in," said my mother, wiping tears of laughter from her eyes. "I know Hayley's up to her neck with a new adventure, but I don't know about the rest of you."

"You start," I told my mother, thinking this would give me a chance to figure out how to spin Catherine's investigation with Nathan. I always told him the truth, but sometimes there were sins of omission or slight shadings of plain facts.

She and Sam described the two luncheons they were preparing for this week, one at the oldest house on Duval Street, and the other at the Truman Little White House. "Some of the hors d'oeuvres are a little fussy, such as tiny sandwiches, savory cheese cookies, and so on, but we're right on schedule," said Sam. "My colleague is an expert at preplanning." He picked up my mother's hand and gave it a smooch. "As for Danielle, she's easy to work with, as far as brides go, anyway."

"What kind of food will we be eating for the main course?" asked Miss Gloria.

"Fortunately, we're only cooking for the rehearsal party, but I heard from a reliable source that they are serving surf and turf," said my mother. "She's the only child, and her parents adore her fiancé and didn't want to spare any expense. There will be a phalanx of police officers at the party since her guy is on the force, and she's seen what they can eat." She winked at Nathan. "I helped her think through the menu, and she decided that everyone should get a Florida lobster tail dripping with butter and a small filet mignon. Luckily, they also hired a phalanx of waiters and cooks to do the work on-site, so we'll be able to enjoy the party without responsibility."

"They should make sure someone guards the van," I said, raising my eyebrows. We'd had one disaster several years ago, when a murderer pretty much spoiled a major wedding with a kidnapping in the catering van. After several hours of observing the couple as we prepared for the party, in our collective opinion, the bride and groom had been a horrible match anyway. But that was not true of Danielle and her beau, Jeremy.

"How about you, Nathan?" asked Sam. "No wedding drama in your life, I hope?"

Nathan shook his head. "We're focusing on disaster simulation scenarios this week," he said. "Unfortunately, it gets more and more important to make sure everybody in the community is ready, including our law enforcement personnel. We're lucky that we haven't experienced a mass shooting, but we're not immune. So, I'm spending most of the week up the Keys in training along with personnel from the Sheriff's Office. It's called Exercise Citadel Shield—Solid Curtain."

"That's a mouthful," said Sam. "What does it mean?"

"It's a two-week program conducted as a joint exercise on Boca Chica Field. It's a way for all local law enforcement agencies to work together using realistic scenarios to plan for response to threats." He could probably see the faces around him growing worried. "Nothing has happened, but we are planning in case these scenarios occur. We are rehearsing how to react to things like active shooters, unauthorized access to restricted areas, suspicious packages, unmanned aerial surveillance, and so on." He turned to me. "Speaking of disasters, have you had any more interactions with that strange woman?"

I nodded, pausing to let the waiter fill our water glasses and deliver our flutes of prosecco.

"We have a few specials on the menu today," the waiter said, catching a moment of silence while we all sipped. "Chef has prepared a seafood stew with a mild curry flavor, and the fish today is black grouper. I'll give you a few minutes to make your selections."

"I think we're ready right now," my mother said, smiling up at him. "We always look at menus ahead of time and have a pretty good idea of what appeals." We went around the table, choosing chicken cacciatore, butternut squash ravioli, black grouper piccata, wild mushroom risotto, and a ribeye for Nathan. He avoided meeting my gaze before announcing his selection, probably figuring I might try to talk him out of two steaks in one week. "Plus, Caesar salads all around," my mother added.

As the waiter left with our order, Nathan turned to look at me, so I answered his dangling question. "I had coffee with Catherine this morning. She wants me to take her back up to Big Pine Key the day after tomorrow to try to find the area where they pitched their camp back in the seventies. She's thinking it will jog her memory about those early days. We could also take the opportunity to stop at the Cudjoe Sheriff's Office and speak to the officer on duty about the murder case. I figure if we go directly to the horse's mouth, we can't get in trouble for interfering in an active investigation. Maybe it will all be sorted out by then anyway."

"Plus, Hayley and I are going up tomorrow to eat at a few places and talk with one of my old pals," said Miss Gloria. "To be accurate, he was Frank's old pal from his boccie days. He happens to be a retired sheriff's deputy."

"Here we go," Nathan muttered. To me, he said, "I think you should leave the actual present-day police work to the professionals."

I gave a quick nod. "I know my limits as a civilian, and we will be super conservative."

"I did some reading on cold cases today," said Miss Gloria, ignoring Nathan's comment. "If the evidence is circumstantial, the cops need a mountain of it to make a case. If the body and or the weapon are missing, as they appear to be in this situation, the case is even more difficult. In the case of a missing person, such as Catherine described, this probably wouldn't be an active case. Hence, it will be useful to talk to my old friend, who was *actually there* at the time the girl went missing." She smiled sweetly at Nathan. "I believe there was a kerfuffle before this fellow's retirement, so it's likely he'd cooperate with me and Hayley rather than the official channels. He did not leave on the friendliest of terms. That was the rumor, anyway."

"I promise we won't interfere with the murder case," I said to my husband, "but you can't blame me for being curious since I was second on the scene, after Catherine."

Nathan smiled. "I never blame you for being curious. I suspect you were born that way."

"Back to the mystery of Catherine," Sam said, "My ex-wife's brother-in-law worked as an editor with a publishing company in New York. He told me once that most authors tend to write the same story over and over. They keep pecking away at the same themes, even if they're writing fiction. Something to do with their childhood traumas, I suppose. Makes me wonder about whether and why Hayley is perennially hungry. Did her mother not feed her?" he asked innocently as if it was a real question.

I glanced at my mom, and we burst out laughing.

"One thing is for sure: my mother fed me very well and still does."

"And I am here to testify that Hayley also feeds the people around her," said Miss Gloria.

"Emotionally hungry, maybe. When I moved down here, I was," I said. "It's not so easy to be a young woman without real direction in her life."

I was thinking, of course, about Hemingway's wives. And Catherine. What had driven her and her friend to wander down the Keys when they were in their twenties, beyond the superficial explanation she'd offered—bad relationship, boring job, etc. What exactly brought her back to look for answers now? After all, she'd waited a long time to return. I did not have a handle on the answers yet.

1978

Catherine

We drank ourselves stupid that night. Billy had managed to snag two bottles of just-good-enough-to-drink rum from The Lost Weekend in Key West, and Ginny had lifted bourbon from her father's liquor cabinet. There was going to be no stopping until the bottles were empty. They started to talk about party games.

"I know. Since we are just getting to know you, let's all say how we ended up in this campsite. You start. Then you choose the person who will follow you." Veronica pointed at Susanne.

Susanne fidgeted in her seat, first looking annoyed, then resigned. "Have you ever spent a winter in upstate New York? I couldn't take it anymore. Plus, my mom died last fall. It was too sad in the house. Every night my dad wept while he sat in her Barcalounger watching the shows Mom loved. There wasn't a thing I could do about it." She pressed on her cheek bones as if to push back tears. "Now Arthur." She gestured at him.

"Nothing deep here, just the usual. Too much sex, drugs, and rock 'n' roll. I needed a chance to think about my life, regroup as it were." Arthur grinned, glanced around the circle, and pointed at me.

Nobody was really reaching too deep inside to reveal their inner demons, so I followed their lead. "I get what Susanne's saying about winter. School was boring, I needed a break. My sister is the golden child who always does everything right. I needed a break from that too." I dipped my chin, passing the torch to Ginny, the girl next to me.

"Big sigh," she said. "I'm a local and can't wait to get out of this place, away from my parents. In the meantime, while I'm waiting, at least you guys are cool." She was looking at Ronnie, her eyes shining with admiration.

Veronica fidgeted silently with a little smirk on her face while some of the other kids talked about trouble at home, flunking out of college, getting fired, and ugly breakups. Finally, Billy pointed at her.

"Mommy issues here, for sure," she said when it was her turn. "One day I was sick of her trying to control me and tell me what to wear and how to behave and how I wasn't studying enough and on and on and on, and how nobody would want me unless I shaped up.

"'Want me for a wife, you mean?' I finally asked her. 'Like Daddy loves you?'" Veronica laughed out loud, *looking around the circle. "Ha, that kind of dried-up relationship was the last thing I wanted. She knew exactly what I meant. She was so mad. That shut her up right away.*

"That night I met Catherine at the town pub, and we decided on a road trip."

Chapter Eleven

*"I never want to shave white truffles on to asparagus for
someone from Toronto ever again in my life."*
—*David McMillan, as quoted in* Bill Brownstein,
"Brownstein: Renowned Chef David McMillan Throws
In Apron After 32 Years," *Montreal Gazette,*
November 25, 2021

On the way up to Big Pine Key the next morning, Miss
Gloria and I talked over the facts of the case. "Have you
been able to track down any of the others who were staying at
the compound back in the seventies?" my friend asked. "As far as
I'm concerned, that young lady is an unreliable narrator."

"Young lady? Catherine?" I chortled. "She's got to be sixty-
five if she's a day. Probably older."

"It's all in your perspective, ma dear," said Miss Gloria, patting my hand and mimicking her Scottish friends' lingo.

A great buzzing began to emanate from my friend's large hand-
bag. She pushed my backpack aside to rustle around in her bag.

"What in the devil is that noise?" I asked as she shifted the
contents of the bag from side to side.

Miss Gloria rolled her eyes. "It's probably that silly Apple watch. Frank and James bought it so they could keep track of me, but it feels kind of clunky on my wrist, so I usually tuck it into my bag." She finally pulled the watch from the bag, then held up her slender arm, and ringed her wrist with her thumb and middle finger, demonstrating its delicacy. "I've figured out how to turn off the tracking, and then I ask them questions and act dumb as a rock when they call to grill me about why I'm not walking anywhere. They're frustrated, but they don't bug me because they still believe I'm an impaired old woman."

I laughed out loud, reminding myself not to baby her and to keep an eye out for the ways she might be snowing me. "How are you supposed to be using the watch?" I asked.

Her face brightened as she explained that it was particularly good at tracking exercise. She explained about the rings of movement. "If I don't close my ring, which happens when I've reached my goal, I pace back and forth in the houseboat until I reach the correct number of steps for the day. Obviously, I have an easier time racking up the steps if I'm giving a cemetery tour that day. Unfortunately, the stupid machine won't let you carry over extra steps. You have to start fresh every single morning."

"So, in other words, if I see you pacing out there, it's not because you've lost your marbles or are sleepwalking. You're just short on the day's performance."

She giggled. "In truth, it could be any of the above. But the main reason why the boys want me to wear it is because it alerts people if you fall. It also checks for irregular heartbeats, panic attacks, blood oxygen levels, and sleep patterns. I sleep like a stone anyway. As I mentioned, they like to know exactly where I am too. But the watch can't report these things if you aren't wearing it." She snickered again, leaving me to guess that she took it off on purpose half the time to keep them on their toes. She stuffed the watch back into the bag at her feet. "If you don't mind, I'm going to rest my eyes for a few minutes."

"Not at all," I said. As I continued driving up to Big Pine, I mulled over the fact that it was hard to get a handle on this island and this community. There had been so much turnover because of the damage wrought by Hurricane Irma, and probably Wilma before that, that it was difficult to find people with roots. I thought about talking to the local librarian, but he'd recently arrived from New Jersey and was likely not yet intimately familiar with the cluster of homes and people on the island. The Key deer, of course, had been here forever, but they weren't likely to say much to me. The main economic engine appeared to be fishing and water sports. Maybe I could find some old fishermen to talk to.

After driving what seemed like miles and miles of narrow Route 1, with turquoise water dotted with mangrove islands on either side, we finally approached Big Pine Key. It wasn't built up with ugly box stores and strip malls like Marathon or Key West, but on the other hand, there weren't that many restaurants or shops. Our first stop was a small health food store on the right-hand side of the road called the Good Food Conspiracy. Miss Gloria sputtered awake like an old but trusted engine as soon as I parked.

We got out of the car and wandered in. It resembled the natural foods store Sugar Apple in Key West. The shelves were crammed with potions and tonics and dried herbs and organic canned food. The sandwich and smoothie menus were hand-written, and surfaces were plastered with notices of local events, such as community yoga, music, and art. Two pleasant-looking women were bopping to the music of Bob Dylan as he sang about getting stoned.

"This isn't your usual restaurant beat," Miss Gloria said, looking around with a grin on her face.

"Nope, but I heard they make a good wrap." After studying the menu for a few minutes, I chose a hummus and avocado wrap, and my friend ordered the tuna melt and a fruit smoothie. A sign on the outside window said the shop had opened in 1982, too late for Catherine and her friend to have frequented. However, the women would certainly have heard about Ned's murder, and at least one of them looked old enough to have heard about the girl's disappearance in the 1970s.

"Such a shame about the awful murder," I said while I paid. "Has anyone been arrested?"

"Not yet, and we're all a little jumpy, as you can guess," the cashier said. "Are you visiting?"

"Up from Key West for the day," said Miss Gloria. "Can you imagine my friend here has lived in the Keys for close to five years now and has yet to see a Key deer? I told her there's no time like the present. Plus, we heard about your sandwiches."

The cashier beamed. "Have a seat if you like, and we'll bring the food when it's ready." She gestured at a table pushed into a small cranny near the front window. Miss Gloria read the news to me from the posters in the window.

"That botanical garden Grimal Grove is now producing distilled spirits made from breadfruit. However, we missed the open house. We also missed community paddleboard yoga— now that one's a little hard to picture, though I suppose it's good for both balance and a belly laugh." Then she began to read bumper stickers. "Nothing could be finer than to be a Big Piner," she read, which made us both smile. "If this place wasn't here in the seventies, it sure has that vibe," she added.

The woman who'd taken our order arrived with our plates and my friend's smoothie.

"Did you know Mr. Newman?" I asked.

"Everyone knew Ned," she said. "I have to be honest. He wasn't universally beloved even though he's lived here forever and had that motel for almost as long. My neighbor's niece stayed there once with some girlfriends, and she said it was a pit, not even fit for a sorority party on a shoestring budget. He didn't seem to want to put a dime into its upkeep, but he kept raking in the tourist dollars. All those girls—almost a dozen of them—spent the weekend on my living room floor. I think my water bill almost doubled. But they said they couldn't bear one more minute in that motel because of the bugs and the odor." She let loose a peal of laughter.

A scent-memory surged into my mind, the combination of must and rot and a metallic smell that had turned out to be the dead man's blood. I set down the sandwich that I'd been so eager to tuck into the instant the server delivered it, and took a few deep breaths to push the memory away.

* * *

Retired deputy Ryan Lopez lived on a rural lane that opened into a small neighborhood near the water. His home was perched high on concrete pillars—a must on this island since it was so prone to storms and flooding. He had a carport and what looked like a workshop underneath. Several of the near neighbors we'd passed by had pools in their yards and lots of tropical shrubs and fruit trees and palm trees. His front yard was mostly poured concrete, with a jungle of vegetation crowding the turquoise-blue home on both sides.

"This is it," Miss Gloria said. "Not the most welcoming approach I've ever seen."

We heard the whine of a saw coming from the room under the home. "Either he's doing some carpentry or cutting up a body," said my friend.

I burst out laughing. "Let's go with option number one. If he played boccie with your hub, he's got to be a good guy, right?" However, I wasn't as sure of that as I made it sound. Because why had he been canned as she'd heard instead of retiring with accolades and dignity? Law enforcement folks were known to take care of their retiring members. We got out of the car and started toward the house. A distant gong sounded as we breached the perimeter of the carport, and a sturdy man wearing a blue cap emerged from the shed with a large wrench in his hand.

"Can I help you?" he asked brusquely.

My first impulse was to retreat, but Miss Gloria started toward him with her hand outstretched. "I am Gloria Peterson. You might not remember me, but you'll probably remember my husband, Frank, with whom you played boccie."

His face relaxed into a smile. "Of course I remember you, though we've aged a bit, you and I." He patted his stomach. "Some of us have doubled in size."

Miss Gloria laughed. "It's not quite that bad. This is my next-door neighbor, Hayley Snow. She was one of the women who discovered Ned Newman's body the other day."

I wished she hadn't said that since we had pretty much promised Nathan that we'd stick to the history rather than nose around in the present. On the other hand, I was convinced that the two were connected.

"Actually," Miss Gloria continued, "we are interested in an older case involving a young woman's disappearance."

"Come upstairs," he said, nodding, as if we'd passed a critical test. Or else he was super curious about what we were up to. "I can't offer you lunch because I already ate it, but how about some sweet tea?"

As we followed him up the outside stairs, I whispered to Miss Gloria, "If you don't mind, I'll take it from here, unless you feel like he's not telling me as much as he would tell you."

She shrugged. "Whatever floats your boat and gets the best information, that's all I am after."

He settled us on a porch furnished with white wicker, flowered cushions, ceiling fans, and jalousie windows, which had been cranked shut against the afternoon heat. He disappeared into the kitchen and returned with a tray containing three glasses of tea and a plate of Thin Mint Girl Scout cookies. "I always stock up on these, and I'm happy to share." He patted his stomach again. "My wife would never keep them around the house, but she's not here to nag me now, is she? Tell me what it is you are really after."

I took a sip of the tea, which tasted like he mixed it up from powder. Still, it was a shot of caffeine and sugar, and that never hurt in the middle of the day. I explained that Catherine had reached out to me and that Miss Gloria and I had grown very curious about the incident that had occurred back in the late seventies.

"You were there at the time, so you probably remember more about the circumstances than most anyone else. We wondered what you could tell us about that commune, what the conditions were like, how the young people were getting along." I stopped talking to see what thread he might pick up.

Miss Gloria piped up. "We also wonder how the locals and the authorities reacted to having these kids camping in their wilderness."

He rasped his fingers over the stubble on his chin, his eyes narrowing. "I wouldn't call them kids. They were more like extremely immature adults. There was only me on patrol at the time. I had a lot of territory to cover, so I couldn't do everything. I did try to keep a close eye on that crowd. There were a lot of drugs floating about, fortunately not as lethal as the ones being passed around today. They shared sex and drugs without a thought. The sheriff advised us deputies that he didn't mind them being there so long as they didn't get involved with anything illegal or bother the locals or trash the island. Eventually, they crossed every one of those lines."

"That's when you asked them to leave." He nodded. "Do you remember the girl who disappeared?" I asked.

"I couldn't pick her out of a lineup forty years later, but I do remember that her girlfriend was quite hysterical. She waved me down on the main road to report her missing. I guess she was on the way to our substation when she spotted my cruiser. I drove her back to the office, but it took a while before I could get a straight story."

"Poor girl. I imagine she was worried about what happened to her friend," Miss Gloria said.

"Either that, or she put on a good show."

"Meaning?" I asked.

"Meaning I didn't trust any of them further than I could throw them. I was the law, and they were the lawbreakers." He frowned and swiped at the beads of moisture his glass had left on the coffee table.

"How did the department handle the issue of the missing woman?" I asked.

"We informally interviewed most of the people in the camp, plus her employer."

I mentally filed that away—I hadn't thought about her job. "Were the other campers worried?" I asked.

"Not terribly. People came and went. From the interviews I conducted, the friendship between the two women had started to fray. Sleeping in a tent with someone for months with the heat and humidity and bugs building to unbearable levels might do that," he added with a laugh. "I always suspected she hitched a ride back north and didn't bother to tell anyone."

"Did you make phone calls?" I asked. "Did you try to reach her parents?"

"Nobody seemed to have that information on them. Remember, these kids were society dropouts. They weren't calling home every Sunday like normal people. Several of them told me she had a lousy relationship with her family and hadn't stayed in touch. Since Veronica was over eighteen, we weren't going to treat the case like we would have if she'd been a missing child. There certainly weren't any traces of a crime."

Note to self: despite his claims that he barely remembered her, he recalled her name perfectly well, along with many details about her case.

"You must have gotten to know these kids while you were working," said Miss Gloria. "How much time did you spend with them?"

"Like I said, I was the main deputy patrolling this part of the Keys. We worked twelve-hour shifts. If there was nothing else going on, no other more pressing calls, I'd circle around to check in on them and make sure nothing was going awry. I didn't drink with them, if that's what you're thinking." He'd kept his voice level, but I noticed a flush of red creeping up the back of his neck.

"Honest to goodness, we weren't thinking anything. We're just trying to figure out what happened to that girl." I smiled in an ingratiating way. "What was she like? Did you get to know her separate from the group?"

"Everybody got to know her," he said, a grim ghost of a smile playing across his lips. "Not so much in a carnal way, though I suspect there was plenty of that. But she was everybody's fantasy, everybody's lost love. She was the ringleader when it came to games." He shook his head as if to shake himself out of an unpleasant dream.

"Between us, I always thought it was Ned who either killed her or, more likely, drove her off. He was mad for that girl, and she wouldn't give him the time of day. He followed her around like a lost puppy dog, but she never chose him. I can't imagine she ever would have. He wasn't young and handsome like the others."

His voice had a wistfulness to it that I hadn't heard from him before. Maybe Ned was not the only "older" man who followed her around like a lost puppy. Now I was very curious about the games he mentioned.

"What kind of games?" I asked.

"More sophisticated versions of spin the bottle, basically," he said.

"Where did she work?"

"It was a restaurant/bar on the main drag. Maloney's. I'm pretty sure they went out of business and left the keys not long after." He paused for a moment, as if considering what else to tell us, and then he continued. "If you go to the No Name Pub, there are some pictures posted from across the years, regulars at the bar and visitors too. I'm still a regular. Almost every morning, I grab a coffee with my buddies. Some days, we stay for lunch too, whether we need it or not. There are some photos of the group from that time in the seventies." He looked a little sheepish. "I might even be in one or two. You can kind of get the idea of what they were like."

If he'd had trouble with his superiors, I was beginning to understand why. I wondered if he had merged with his suspects, if that was the right word for them, almost like a jailer who falls in with the prisoners. This wouldn't surprise me, because he was probably only a few years older than the campers—maybe even younger than some of them. How odd it must have felt to have had a job in law enforcement in which sticking to the letter of the law was the main point, while these other young people were playing by no rules at all. Maybe he wished he could be one of them because their way of life looked a little simpler and more fun.

Until it didn't.

"Anything you can tell us about Ned Newman's murder?" Miss Gloria asked. "Do you think it's possible his death was related to this old disappearance?"

"I can't see how," he said, now sounding grumpy and standing up to signal the interview was over. "But I'm not privy to the details of the case. As you're well aware, I'm retired."

Chapter Twelve

"Buried under this cloudy pork-based broth is a tangle of noodles so thin and reedy, they look like they might break under questioning."
—Tim Carman, "Seven Restaurant Soups to Transport You Far From Home This Winter," *Washington Post,* November 11, 2022

I started the car, backed out of his driveway, and began to wend my way through the neighborhood looking for Watson Boulevard. As soon as we'd driven away from the deputy's house, Miss Gloria asked, "Did you see his police scanner? It's a lot fancier than the one the girls gave me last year for my birthday. I bet he can pick up calls in Miami."

I laughed, partly at the idea of her scanner envy, and partly at her calling her elderly friends "the girls."

"I'm not buying for a minute that he doesn't follow the comings and goings on this island," she added.

I should have known she was thinking about more than the superiority of his equipment. I nodded. "Agreed. Plus, he seemed irritable there at the end, as a person might if you were getting uncomfortably close to something secret."

Now she positively vibrated with excitement. "I bet he was desperately in love with the girl who eventually went missing. When he realized he couldn't have her, he murdered her and buried her body. Now he's freaking out inside because we're stirring things up."

I glanced over at her and laughed. "I hadn't taken it that far, though I suppose anything's possible. That might be a stretch for a guy who took an oath to protect and defend, don't you think? It would also put us in pretty serious danger, right? From my perspective, it makes more sense that Ned killed the girl."

"Maybe, but then who killed Ned? And what's next?" she asked.

"I think we should stop over at the No Name Pub again and see if we can talk to Ginny. Maybe she'll confess to knowing something more than she was willing to say when Catherine was with me. Surely the woman remembers more than what she told us." I glanced over at my friend again. "No offense, but I'm going to ask to be seated inside so we can look at those photos the deputy mentioned. We're going to have to order another lunch."

"Not a problem," she said. "Willing and ready to take one for the team. Frank always told me I had a hollow leg for snacks and fun. Why would I take offense to that?"

I retraced the route to the pub, and we parked and went inside, blinking in the sharp contrast between the sunny day and the pub's dark interior and its odors of beer and food past. This felt like the old bar version of Proust's madeleine, the cookie that unlocked his rush of old memories, though this definitely smelled less appealing than a delicate French wafer.

Ginny approached with a smile on her face. "You again! We don't often see such enthusiastic repeat customers. Nice to see you. Inside or outside?"

"Inside, please. My grandmother's a bit elderly, as you can see. She doesn't do well in the heat. In fact, she wilts." Miss Gloria made a face, as if she'd just now realized why I thought she might take offense.

"We can't have that," said Ginny with a laugh, beckoning us forward. "Where's your other sidekick?"

"I'm sure she's working," I said.

As we followed her to a table in the corner, Miss Gloria poked me hard in the ribs. "Are you saying your grandmother's decrepit?" she hissed.

I snickered, then squeezed her thin shoulders with one arm. "I warned you that I had to tell her something. Why else would we want to eat in the dark on a perfectly glorious day?"

After we had ordered soft drinks and a few appetizers, Miss Gloria went off to find the restroom and I made a beeline for the wall of photographs that the deputy had mentioned. Most of the wall and ceiling space in the bar was plastered with dollar bills left by visitors, but the staff had also posted photos of customers hailing back to the earliest days of the pub.

Ginny came up behind me with our drinks in hand. "The more things change, the more they stay the same. At least on Big Pine Key." She chuckled. "We all looked so young back then, didn't we?"

"Are you in one of these photos?"

She set our drinks down and tapped on a faded Polaroid photo with eight young people hamming it up, arranged around a table outside this very restaurant. I squinted to try to make out the faces. It had been a blurry action shot that had faded over the years, even in the dim light of the bar.

"This was me." She pointed at a slender girl with long hair almost to her waist who stood just outside the group. "I never felt exactly like an insider, but I loved these guys so much. I wanted to be them when I grew up." Now her voice held a melancholy tinge. "As you can imagine, my parents weren't all that thrilled. They were fighting with each other about everything in those days, but they could agree on that."

"I can imagine," I said, trying to picture my own stern father allowing me to join a bunch of hippies in the woods every evening. "My father would've had a cow."

She winked. "I got pretty good at climbing out of the window, shimmying down the tree outside, and dropping to the ground like a cat burglar."

"Who is the tall guy in back?" I asked. "He was very handsome."

"That's Arthur Combs. Handsome and smart and a little bit full of himself." I swore she straightened her shoulders as she said his name. "He was pretty much the fearless leader, even though Ned might've challenged him about that."

"Oh, I thought Catherine said Ned was an outsider?"

She shrugged. "He wouldn't have thought of himself that way. He was always hanging around, though he didn't live there like most of the others. He was a little older than the rest, and he'd been married. Or maybe he was married at the time, but his wife had left by then. I can't quite remember the details. Not that I could blame her for calling it quits. He was kind of a creep."

So, he was a lurker, from the sound of it. Could something he did back in those days have resulted in his murder in the present? "How did everyone spend their time?" I asked.

"Most of the campers had a job or even more than one, and others went out fishing. And everyone chipped in for the communal dinners. I remember one night Veronica and Catherine declared they were going to fix a midwestern hot dish casserole, which turned out to be cutting up franks and opening cans of beans. They added a little mustard and Worcestershire sauce and cooked it in a pot over the fire. Obviously, we didn't have ovens." She laughed. "They were so pleased with themselves. But nobody cooked anything gourmet except for Susanne." She pointed to a petite woman standing next to Arthur with pale blond hair and an apron. "She loved dumpster diving, and she'd come home so excited about the perfectly good things she'd found that other people had discarded. Then she'd make something unusual from those ingredients and give it a fancy name, like 'vegetables and rice a la garbage.'" We both laughed.

"She's the chef at the Square Grouper these days. I'm certain she's gone more upscale," said Ginny. "During those times, the group was kind of retro. The women cooked, for the most part. The guys had set up a raised tank that collected rainwater where we did dishes and so on. But they all took showers over at the state park. Everyone would gather at night at the campfire. Sometimes there'd be other town kids hanging around. The group welcomed everyone and anyone so long as they brought booze. Some high standards, right?"

Miss Gloria returned from the restroom and came over to see what we were looking at. "Ginny was showing me Catherine's gang and reminiscing about the good old days."

"If that's the right description," Ginny said sharply. "Give me a firm mattress and a working bathroom and a stove with an oven these days. No communal decisions either."

"It's almost like you guys were living a dream for a while though, right?" I asked.

"For a while they were," she said, though she was frowning. "Your food should be out shortly."

She wheeled away before I could ask her about the games that the deputy mentioned. I would have liked to hear more about communal decisions too, but I thought she was pretty much done with hashing over the past with a couple of nosy ladies. Why had she acted as though she didn't remember Veronica when Catherine first brought her up? Today, she was full of memories of those days. To be fair, maybe seeing Catherine had jogged them loose.

* * *

On the way home, Miss Gloria and I talked about what we'd learned about the case.

"I wished we'd pressed Ginny on what she thought happened to Catherine's friend," said Miss Gloria. "Don't you think she must have a theory?"

"I don't think she was going to tell us anything more," I said. "She was getting annoyed with all my questions, like Deputy Lopez did. Do you want to go with me to the Green Parrot tonight?"

"Absolutely," she said. "But first, I do have to talk with my boys, and I need a nap."

"Got it. We'll pick Catherine up around eight."

Chapter Thirteen

"She rubbed a hand over her tousled white curls until they stood up in peaks like the meringue on my recent banana cream pie."

—Lucy Burdette, *A Clue in the Crumbs*

While waiting to visit the Green Parrot, I wrote up my notes about the restaurants where we'd eaten over the past two days. I knew from experience that if I didn't, all the dishes I'd tasted would start to run together. Plus, it was only through writing that my opinions and recommendations would begin to solidify in my mind and then on the page. In this case, I most enjoyed writing about our birthday visit to Bel Mare for Sam. The twinkling harbor through the window, the white tablecloths, the cheerful but efficient waitstaff—all this had contributed to our pleasure while downing those yummy dishes. My mouth began to water at the idea of re-creating the chicken cacciatore that my mother had ordered.

After walking the dog, feeding both animals, and eating half a sandwich, I took a quick shower and dressed in a clean white T-shirt and a swingy skirt. I left a note for Nathan that we were headed to the Green Parrot but wouldn't be late. "It's uku-lele players, not rock stars tonight!" I added with a heart emoji.

Out on the dock, Miss Gloria was chatting with our mutual neighbor, Mrs. Renhart. She was watering the flowers in her window box with a small plastic can. Her elderly cats watched her carefully, hoping that she might dislodge a gecko.

"Mrs. Renhart was telling me that her schnauzer Schnootie has been ill. Of course, the moment she made an appointment for the vet, she perked right up."

"She's eating like a horse and drinking well too. I suppose I should take her anyway," said our neighbor with a big sigh, "but it's such a production to try to get her into the travel crate. Even if she's at death's door, she fights me tooth and nail. I guess I'll call and cancel in the morning."

"What vet do you use?" I asked. This was a perennial topic of conversation with pet owners in our town. It was not that easy to find someone whom the animals tolerated and the owners liked, who was also available for emergencies.

"Dr. Combs," she said, almost simpering. "Arthur Combs. He's very kind and easy on the eyes."

We all laughed, and I noticed Miss Gloria's steady gaze focus on our neighbor and then switch to me. She rubbed her chin and frowned. "You know, I'm embarrassed to say this, but T-bone has not been to the vet since he left the humane society. I know I'm behind, but Sparky hated the other vets so much that I couldn't force myself to do it. And T-bone is like your Schnoo-tie; he hates being crated. Maybe he thinks I'm taking him back to the pound. Which I would never do, of course! But the point is, if you don't want the appointment, and you like Dr. Combs, I would be happy to go with my cat."

"Sold," said Mrs. Renhart. "It's at ten o'clock tomorrow morning. I'll call and tell them you'll be coming."

We walked out to the parking lot. "That was serendipity at its most brilliant," said Miss Gloria as she slid into the passenger seat of her big Buick. "Arthur Combs has to be the handsome commune guy, right? The one who was in the photo on the pub wall that everyone said was the leader of the pack in the old days. This way we can take him by surprise and ambush him while he is admiring my kitty and then scolding me for being late with the inoculations. Maybe if the doctor is distracted, he'll tell us more about those old times than he might have otherwise." She slammed the door and grinned at me. "By the way, I lied to her a little. T-bone is not that far behind."

I would have protested about her getting too involved with the Big Pine murder case, but honestly, the plan was flawless.

I drove the short distance to the Gardens Hotel to pick up Catherine and found a parking space on Simonton.

"I'll wait here," said Miss Gloria. "I never did reach Frank Jr." She held up her phone while punching in her son's number.

Catherine was not waiting for me out on the sidewalk as we'd agreed. Big surprise? Not. I walked through the Angela Street gate and up the stairs, through the white door flanked by tall turquoise planters hosting lush plants. The reception area inside was paved with brick-colored floor tiles and featured rotating ceiling fans and hanging plants everywhere.

I'm here, I texted, but there was no response. I huffed in annoyance and walked through the vestibule to the interior gardens and pool, thinking she might be finishing up a drink at the little bar in the courtyard. Wrought iron café tables were sprinkled around the pool area, along with large turquoise umbrellas, and an octagonal structure with lace curtains and a cupola at the end. I watched the visitors floating in the pool with drinks in hand—this was truly an island paradise. But no Catherine.

The guest rooms were scattered around the exterior of these gardens, and Catherine had told me where to find hers. I walked in that direction thinking that she might be on her way out since she still hadn't texted back. No dice.

When I reached her room, I knocked on the door. It swung partway open, and my heart rate picked up. I gulped, praying I wasn't about to find another body.

I poked my head in. Should I call the authorities immediately before even looking around? That felt like an overreaction. "Catherine?" I called out. "Catherine, are you in here? Is everything okay?"

There wasn't any answer. The only thing that came to mind was the shower scene in *Psycho*. Against my better judgment, Miss Gloria had insisted I watch that movie last month as part of my education in the vintage films of her era. It had haunted me ever since. Having barely survived seeing the scissors in Ned Newman's back, I did not want to find this woman bludgeoned and bloodied behind her shower curtain. Now that I was in this far, how could I not look? My heart thundered. I grabbed my phone and pulled up the keypad, my finger on 911 to call the troops the instant I determined they were needed.

But the room was empty, and the king-size bed was made. Some of Catherine's belongings were folded neatly in the suitcase, and more stuff was hanging in the closet. I paused for a moment to look around the suite, with its vaulted roof line, lazy straw ceiling fans, and a leather couch with a tray of liquor on the table in front of it. How could a struggling writer afford a place this nice? The small white plastic brick that I assumed was for charging Catherine's phone was still plugged in by the nightstand. A paperback had been left open and upside down as though she'd return to finish reading at any moment. She'd only gotten a quarter of the way through the book, but it had about a half dozen dog-eared pages. Next, I peered into the bathroom. No sign of her there, except for an array of pastel-colored beauty potions, a hairbrush on the counter, and a toothbrush in the glass next to the sink. There were droplets of water on the glass door of the shower as if it had been recently used. I checked my phone again to be sure I hadn't missed a message. Nada.

I walked back into the bedroom, stopping to linger over what Catherine was reading. Ernest Hemingway's *Men Without Women*. Something that never happened in his own life, I thought. He bounced from one wife to the next, and this pattern had caught Catherine's attention in a powerful way.

I wondered if I should call the office or even the police to report her missing. But was she really missing if her stuff was still in the room? Was she simply blowing me off? Maybe she'd forgotten that we were supposed to meet, or perhaps she'd decided to go alone. I would leave a note on her desk, I decided, and then wait to see if she either called me or we ran into her at the Green Parrot. In the top drawer, I found a notepad with the Gardens Hotel logo across the top, along with a matching pen.

It's Hayley, I wrote. *I thought we'd planned for me to pick you up at eight, but maybe our wires got crossed. I will stop in at the Green Parrot to see if you're there. Give me a buzz when it's convenient.*

As I leaned over to position the note under the circle of light thrown off by the desk lamp, I noticed a crumpled page in the wastebasket. I pulled it out and smoothed the crinkles so I could read it. As the Sheriff's deputy had requested outside Ned's motel, Catherine appeared to have made a list of people she remembered from her former days camping on Big Pine Key. What could it hurt to take a photo of that list? After snapping the picture, I crumpled the paper up again and replaced it in the trash, thinking all the while that I hoped this room wouldn't turn into a crime scene.

My fingerprints would be all over it.

Chapter Fourteen

"I'd always been fascinated by food but this was new: I had discovered that food and memory are deeply intertwined."
—Ruth Reichl, "Refrigerator Psychology," *La Briffe*,
December 30, 2022

"What took you so long?" Miss Gloria asked when I returned to the car. "Where's Catherine?"

I sat in silence for a moment, second-guessing myself about whether I should have gone to the front desk to report her missing. But there really hadn't been anything out of order, other than the fact that the latch wasn't caught when she left the room. Plus, she was a grown woman with a mind of her own—if she chose not to meet us and to leave her door open, wasn't that her business? I explained all of this to my friend.

"Most likely it was a misunderstanding, and we'll find her at the Green Parrot. If she isn't there, we'll figure out what comes next." I glanced over at Miss Gloria. "How was Frank?"

She heaved a great sigh. "I don't know when my sons are going to realize that I'm perfectly capable of taking care of myself, and that I have built-in nagging right there on the pier if the day comes that I need more guidance."

"Nagging? Surely you don't mean *moi*?" I asked, pretending outrage.

She fluttered her eyelashes and snickered. "Other than that, he reports that Michigan is finally starting to show signs of spring. His wife's unhappy with her job, but what else is new with that? They swear they're coming to visit after hurricane season but then say, by the way, why don't I come up there for a couple of months and skip the drama of deciding whether to evacuate or stay in the path of the storms? I said I was busy at the moment, but we would discuss this later in the summer."

Hurricane season was a regular topic of discussion for homeowners and long-term renters on our islands. Some residents got tired of evacuating multiple times over the late summer and early fall, often without due cause because storms had minds of their own and frequently veered from predicted paths. What might look like a direct hit on Key West could turn out to be only a brush-by. Many of my friends had determined that next time they would hunker down like the rest of the braver locals. Others hightailed it up the Keys at the first mention of a category 2 or higher. The problem was, storms were getting stronger as the air and water got warmer, and predictions were not always accurate. I was sympathetic to Miss Gloria's sons worrying about her. Nathan was not able to leave because of his position in the police department, but maybe if our island was predicted to be in the path of the next big storm, I would drive north with her and my mother and Sam and all our pets. To be continued . . .

I found a parking space on Whitehead Street a couple blocks from the bar and managed to jockey Miss Gloria's car into the smallish slot without drama. The Green Parrot bar, a musical icon in Key West, was founded as a grocery store in 1890 by well-known Key West folk artist Mario Sanchez's grandfather. Over the following decades, it morphed from a Navy gathering place to an open-air hipster watering hole in the seventies, and now to a casual haven for music lovers, both locals and visitors. I could imagine that Catherine and her pals might have made road trips from Big Pine to the Green Parrot when they grew tired of slow and buggy nights camping in the mangroves.

The wooden flaps that covered the windows when the bar was closed were propped open to the sidewalks on Whitehead and Southard Streets when the bar was open for business. If a popular band was playing, partiers spilled out onto the street. Ukulele night appeared to be not quite so popular, although eight o'clock was early for Key West nightlife.

I stood in the doorway looking for Catherine, but as far as I could tell, she hadn't yet made an appearance. So where was she? Even if she'd walked over from the hotel, it wouldn't have taken her long. The place was not so busy that I thought I would miss her.

At the bar, I ordered two beers and picked up a cardboard container of free popcorn drenched with salt and butter as I returned to our seats. Miss Gloria had hoisted herself onto a stool with her back to the wall and a good view of the stage. I perched on the stool beside her and sipped my beverage slowly, scanning for Catherine and any trouble that might follow her. A three-man band performed several classic rock songs, ukulele style. A man playing the bass and singing in a very deep voice sat on the stool at the back of the stage. He had long wavy hair and a woolen cap that seemed way too warm for the season.

The leader, a tall and handsome man wearing a weathered blue shirt and Birkenstock sandals, reminded the crowd that this was ukulele open mic night. "We'll be clipping the chords for each song onto this frame so you can play along." He smiled broadly and gestured at what looked like a clothes drying rack. "Anyone who wishes to perform should come up and put their name on this list." He held up a clipboard. Several people in the audience with ukuleles on straps around their necks approached the stage.

I hadn't spent a lot of time in this bar lately, so I wasn't sure whether this was the usual crowd. It shaded more hippie than tourist. The lead musician returned to the microphone. "Welcome to the Green Parrot. My name is Arthur Combs. The ukulele is not known as the ideal instrument for playing a dirge. Truth be told, those mournful tunes might be best left to the fiddle. I always think of Niel Gow's classic 'Lament for the Death of His Second Wife.' But we've lost an old friend this week and wanted to honor him with something slow and sad and sweet, something that might bring our minds and memories back to old times, better times."

He began to strum, and I recognized the opening notes of Bob Dylan's "Forever Young." "Those of you who are regulars here know that Ned never missed a ukulele night. This Dylan tune would have suited him. Tonight, we're singing it for our friend. Ned was a searcher, always on a quest for a place he could feel happy. I only wish his story had had a happier ending."

As Arthur sang and played along with the two others in the band, I watched him carefully to try to understand what his true relationship with Ned might have been like. If pressed, I would have said he didn't play a false note: he looked and sounded honestly sad.

110

Miss Gloria leaned over to whisper, "He's very good-looking, isn't he, and he has some undefinable charisma. Imagine when he was forty years younger. I can very well see that he must have been catnip to the lady campers. Even I feel a little thrill in my nether parts." She knew that would get a giggle from me.

Once the song was finished, the band continued with more cheerful music, and several amateur players from the audience came up onto the stage to pick and strum and sing. Arthur Combs announced that a few ukuleles were being auctioned off to raise money for children's classes at the Bahama Village Music Program, courtesy of the guitar shop in town. "We will take a short break and be back with you in about fifteen minutes. Don't forget to add your name to the clipboard if you wish to play us a tune."

Miss Gloria was looking sleepy, probably overcome by our travels today, as well as the beer and popcorn, which she'd polished off quickly. I felt worn down by the events of the last two days as well. "Why don't you wait here," I said. "I'll take a spin around to be sure that Catherine isn't tucked away in a corner, and we didn't notice her. Then we'll go home." I didn't really think I'd missed her—the bar was still not that crowded. I was beginning to worry, as I knew she'd been planning to come.

Miss Gloria nodded. I circled the bar that took up the middle of the main room, then walked around the area where the ukuleles were up for auction. Arthur Combs was deep in conversation with another man, and I pretended to admire a ukulele in the shape of a banjo so I could listen in.

"Stabbed right in the back with a pair of scissors," Arthur was telling him.

"Have they arrested anyone yet?"

"Not yet," he said, "though the sheriff's deputies have talked to just about all the residents of Big Pine, along with the rest of us who knew Ned."

"What's your theory?" the second man asked.

Arthur Combs sighed. "You know, I loved the guy and knew him for a long, long time, but he wasn't easy to live with or do business with. It could have been anyone, maybe one of his four ex-wives? He pretty much made a sport out of avoiding alimony and child support payments over the past forty years."

The second man frowned. "Surely he's not still paying child support? At our advanced age, he should be rocking on the front porch and watching the grandchildren play with geckos in the yard."

Arthur looked rueful. "Believe it or not, his youngest son is five. The boy and his mother, Arden, live in a real nice house on the water on Sugarloaf Key. Ned was complaining about her bloodthirsty tactics at our last practice. He claimed that she drained almost everything left in his bank account." He shrugged gracefully and ran his fingers through his blond hair. "I didn't know her well enough to judge whether that was true—the marriage barely lasted a year after the kid was born. Then he returned to his cot in the back room of that dreary motel."

Before I could catch his eye to chat him up, he excused himself to return to the stage. Probably just as well to talk with him tomorrow during T-bone's vet visit. We could take him by surprise and have all his attention.

Chapter Fifteen

"Food plays a central role in our reaction to tragedy, to death and grieving. It's why casseroles appear on the doorsteps and countertops of those experiencing it, why we feel the urge to roast chickens or assemble lasagnas when the news is grim."
—Sam Sifton, *New York Times Cooking* newsletter,
May 26, 2022

The next morning, I got up early to spend a few minutes with Nathan since he'd come to bed when I was already asleep the night before. He told me how well the joint law-enforcement exercises were going, and I told him how Catherine had failed to appear at the bar.

"We went to pick her up at the Gardens Hotel, but she never showed. Her room seemed fine though. There were no signs of it being tossed or her fleeing town."

He looked alarmed, his shoulders stiffening. "So, how were you in her room if she wasn't there?"

I patted his hand. "Don't worry. I didn't break in. The door was left cracked open. I was afraid she'd maybe fallen in the shower or something, so I felt it was my duty to look around. But she wasn't there. I did, however, find a list on her desk." I grabbed my phone and pulled up the photo I had taken, which I'd forgotten to look over when we returned from the Green Parrot. "Truthfully, it was not on the desk but in the trash." Nathan narrowed his eyes at me, then took my phone. There were five names on the list, with a line drawn through the first one.

~~Ned Newman~~
Arthur Combs
Deputy Ryan Lopez
Susanne Howe
Virginia XXX

After those entries, she'd added both her own name and the name of her missing friend, Veronica. At the bottom, she'd scribbled *Call the PI.*

"Suspects?" I asked as Nathan passed my phone back.

"Maybe," he said, scowling. "We know the line drawn through the first name means the guy is dead. Let's hope it doesn't mean she is planning to work her way through the list. Killing people, I mean. Please keep in mind this could go either way. Either she's in danger or she's dangerous." He glanced at his watch and then back up at me with a concerned frown. "What are your plans for the day?"

"I was planning to take Catherine back to Big Pine, but since she's missing in action, I'm thinking I will go by myself. I'd like to stop by the Sheriff's Office on Cudjoe Key to see if they have any more information about the old case, other than the little bit we've heard."

He nodded slowly. "They probably won't tell you anything except keep your nose out of law enforcement business. Which is not bad advice."

I laughed. "I know how to handle that—say yes, sir, and then ignore it. I'm also taking Miss Gloria and her kitty T-bone to the vet. He happens to be Arthur Combs, the number two man on Catherine's list."

He glanced at my phone again. "Will you please be careful?" he asked as he stood and gathered his phone and keys. "Talk to people, fine, but then tell the authorities what you've learned and let them handle the rest of it."

"Absolutely," I said, blowing him a kiss.

* * *

Dr. Arthur Combs's office was located in a strip mall on Kennedy Boulevard, a street that connected North Roosevelt Boulevard with Flagler Avenue. A covered porch ran the length of the strip mall, which included an Asian restaurant, a pet store, and several other shops. A sign on the door instructed patients to call the receptionist to let her know they had arrived and then take a seat on the porch. I imagined that this was a leftover practice from pandemic days, but it also worked to keep the animals at a distance from one another since the waiting area looked tiny. It had been a bit of a struggle to get T-bone into the cat carrier, which we'd strapped into the car's back seat during the drive. He paced and yowled the entire trip. He would not do well mixing with other people's pets.

"It's okay, buddy," said Miss Gloria, pressing her finger into the mesh to stroke him. "It's all for your own good, and who knows? It may help us solve a murder."

Fifteen minutes later, the vet himself came out onto the porch. I recognized him from the Green Parrot. Up close, the lines around his eyes made him look sad and wise. He squatted down on his haunches to meet T-bone at his own level—quite a graceful move for a man who had to be in his sixties. "I'm Arthur Combs. What brings you here today?" T-bone hissed. Dr. Combs laughed, then patted the top of the crate and shifted his gaze to Miss Gloria, his expression questioning.

"I'm embarrassed to say that I got this kitten from the FKSPCA, and I'm a little late for his inoculation updates," she said. "Maybe three months overdue?"

"That's within the cone of respectability. Let's get him inside into one of the examination rooms, and we can take care of that right away. Is he having any problems otherwise? Is he eating and drinking okay?"

"He's in top-top shape," she said as we followed him inside. "He does everything perfectly as a cat should and poops like a champion too."

Dr. Combs chuckled. His office looked and smelled like many of the places I'd visited over the years with my own pets—a not-unpleasant combination of animals and disinfectant. Once ensconced in a small examining room, Miss Gloria unzipped the carrier, and T-bone sprang out.

"Isn't he handsome?" she asked the vet. "I'm especially fond of his half orange, half white paw." She pointed across the room where the cat had jumped onto the counter by the sink and begun batting loose items to the floor. "As you can see, he's not a lap cat. He's his own man, and that's that."

"He's very handsome, and it looks as though he's landed in a very good home." He smiled at Miss Gloria, then scooped the cat up and set him on the metal table. A vet tech came in with two syringes while Dr. Combs examined the cat, running his hands over the sleek orange body, peering into his ears and under his tail and inside his mouth. "He looks good. His fur is shiny, and he's not overweight. How are you doing with brushing his teeth?" He ran his hand over T-bone's back, and the cat arched and purred.

"Not very well," Miss Gloria admitted. "I keep meaning to do that, but when night falls, we all just want to tumble into bed. I swear I'll try harder." She flashed a winning smile.

After the exam was completed and the shots were given, the vet asked, "Any other questions?"

"My friend Hayley Snow has a question," said Miss Gloria, holding her hand out to invite me to speak.

He raised his eyebrows, and his foot began to jiggle. I had seen from the other people and animals waiting on the porch that he had a busy day ahead of him, so I got right to the point.

"I was one of the people who discovered Ned Newman in his motel office several days ago," I said. "We are very sorry for your loss."

He nodded solemnly but still looked puzzled, so I hurried on.

"Has Catherine Davitt been in touch with you, by any chance? She asked me to bring her to the ukulele night last evening, but she didn't show up. I'm certain she wanted to speak with you."

"Catherine's back in town?" His voice cracked a little.

I tried to decide whether he sounded astonished or concerned. Or was he acting, in either case? Had she already talked to him but didn't reveal that to me and now, neither was he? If so, why? "She came to the Keys to work on a writing project, but she also wanted to try to figure out what happened to her friend Veronica years ago. I understand you were part of that gang back in the seventies. She wanted to speak with you about that. But now Ned is dead, and she's disappeared."

"We're worried," Miss Gloria added, clutching her squirming kitty to her chest.

"Is there anyone else who belonged to your group still living on the Keys?" I asked.

He took a few steps back to lean against the counter, no smile left on his face. "Explain again how you're involved. Are you with the police?"

"Not really," I said. I'd thought a lot this morning about how to approach this question that I was certain he would ask. Hoping I'd come up with a reasonable explanation, I told him about my connection to Catherine and Ned's murder, and then asked him my questions. "I have a feeling that both her disappearance and the murder are related to the old days. That makes me wonder several things: What brought them to the camp on Big Pine Key back in those days, and what went wrong before Veronica disappeared? Finally, what provoked Catherine to return to this place now?"

These seemed exactly like the kind of questions that a shrink would ask during a first meeting: What brings you here today? There had to be more to what motivated those girls than just running away to have fun. They couldn't have been just teenagers going on a sudden joyride. What were they running away from, and how did they fit together? These were the things I wanted to find out.

He neatened a stack of papers on the counter and threw away the crumpled packaging that had protected the syringes.

"Catherine and Veronica were an odd couple. I never would have placed them as the best of friends. Ronnie, I think, was running away from her home, especially from her father. She felt dominated and restricted, and once she broke loose and ran away, there were no rules large enough to contain her. She was darling—elfin and curly-haired and always laughing." His face softened at the memory of her. "Catherine, on the other hand, was tall and gawky and awkward. I think she envied how loose her friend was, how comfortable she was in her body, and her way with others. Maybe if she hadn't met Veronica, she never would have embarked on this trip."

"She said that?" I asked.

"Just my observation. She didn't quite have the guts to pull it off the way Ronnie did." He rubbed his chin and looked directly at me. "We were all half in love with her. If we'd stayed much longer, it was going to get ugly. Uglier. I should have stopped it sooner than I did."

"Though you weren't actually in charge, were you?" I asked. "What could you have done? What would you have stopped? I get the sense it was an unruly crowd."

"I tried a couple of times to calm things down, but not hard enough. I took Veronica aside and told her that people were taking advantage of her, that she shouldn't give herself out like Halloween candy." Now he looked so sad. "That made her laugh and laugh. I remember her reaction so clearly. She asked if I'd been the kind of kid who liked apples and toothbrushes in my trick-or-treat bag." He paused. "She said she had some candy for me too, if I was hungry."

I paused to see if he'd add anything else—such as how hungry he had been—but he didn't. He seemed embarrassed about already saying too much. "What do you think happened to her?" I asked. "What is your theory?"

He was silent for a moment. "For the longest time, I hoped she finally had had enough and took off on her own. But when I think back on that last night before she disappeared, I think that can't be true."

"Are there any other locals still in the area with whom we should speak?"

"Susanne's still here," he said, "but she won't know anything more than I do."

Susanne had to be the chef that Ginny had mentioned.

"Did you tell the Sheriff's Office everything that you knew when they came to investigate?"

He narrowed his eyes. "Of course I did. But one of theirs was more involved with them than he should've been."

"Deputy Ryan Lopez," said Miss Gloria.

Dr. Combs nodded.

It took everything I had not to gape.

Chapter Sixteen

"Chef got the eggs from an old lady with cataracts upstate. Chef foraged for the mushrooms in a thicket near the Tappan Zee. Chef counsels a bite from the ramekin on the left, then a sip from the shot glass on the right, then a palate-clearing curtsy."
—Frank Bruni, "You May Kiss the Chef's Napkin Ring," *New York Times*, January 24, 2007

"That girl Veronica must've been hot stuff," Miss Gloria said on our way back to the car with the cat. "Dr. Arthur Combs was gaga for her, don't you think?"

"I agree, though I can't tell whether they actually had a romantic relationship. Sounds like he tried really hard to do the right thing with her. After all these years, he still feels badly about what happened." I strapped T-bone's carrier into the back seat and slid behind the steering wheel.

"What did happen? That is the question," Miss Gloria said. "Nobody's exactly told us what occurred that last night. What was it that tipped the Sheriff's Office over the edge so they felt like they had to clean the sewers of the rats?"

Stopped at a traffic light on North Roosevelt, I looked over at her and grinned. "That's a little harsh, but probably on point. Are you hungry? Once we drop off the kitty, we should cruise up to the Square Grouper and grab a bite to eat. Maybe if we fawn all over the lunch, we can persuade the chef to come out and talk with us."

"Chef Susanne," she said. "Yes, I'm in."

*　*　*

The Square Grouper restaurant didn't look like much from the outside—a plain white building with a red roof and awning, decorated with a square blue fish. But inside we saw an attractive, polished wood bar, and beyond that, two rooms full of eager eaters. In the center of the room floated an aquarium, lit by blue lights, that featured a faux square grouper (aka marijuana bale) in the center. Beautiful black-and-white lionfish swam around the grouper, the coral, and the rocks. Lionfish were a much-maligned invasive species that I understood were delicious, though I had yet to get my nerve up to try them.

Our waitress came over with menus and water. "Our special today is fried chicken and waffles."

"Sold," said Miss Gloria, slapping the menu on the table.

I perused the blackboard posted on the far wall that listed all the specials, having found over several years in this job that the specials showed the true love and artistry of the chef. Now I was very curious about what made Susanne tick.

"I'll have the bacon, artichoke, and cheese soup, and the panko-dusted yellowtail," I said, smiling up at the server and handing over my menu.

"Sorry," said Miss Gloria after the waitress left with our order. "If you need me to try something, we could call her back. But that waffle was singing a very powerful siren song."

I laughed. "No problem, as long as you'll let me try one forkful," I said. "I'm going to wash my hands and check out the other dining room."

The walls of the back room were painted a deep blue, dotted with vintage photos of the Keys the way they used to be. Several showed the authorities bringing in bales of marijuana on boats—the square groupers after which the restaurant was named. After I'd visited the ladies' room and returned to the table, our food was delivered.

Miss Gloria's waffle dish was slathered in butter and maple syrup and topped with a crispy fried chicken cutlet. I persuaded her to share a bite in exchange for a taste of my flaky yellowtail and a sip of the rich soup.

When the waitress came around to check on us, I asked, "Is Chef Susanne cooking today? Could you let her know the food is outstanding and that if she has a minute, we'd love to meet her?"

After a few minutes, a sturdy woman in chef's whites with a long blond braid streaked with gray approached the table. Her face was friendly and weathered, probably by years spent in the hot Florida sun, or years in the kitchen, or maybe hard living.

"This is our first time visiting, and we wanted you to know that we adored your food," I said.

Miss Gloria showed her the empty plate that had arrived overflowing with chicken and waffles. There was barely a smear of syrup left. "This was divine. How long have you been cooking here?"

She rubbed the back of her hand over her forehead. "It must be close to twenty years. Before that, I was at Louie's Backyard in Key West. I learned so much there, but when I heard about this new place with so many opportunities, I jumped." She smiled. "Seems like yesterday."

I remembered that Martha Hubbard had worked at Louie's too, though I wasn't sure about the timing. I was about to ask if Susanne knew her, when Miss Gloria asked, "Where were you from originally?"

"Upstate New York," she said, flashing another smile, not quite as broad this time. "I couldn't wait to get away from winter."

I was afraid we'd lose her back to the kitchen, so I got to the point, hoping that she might tell us the truth if I was direct. "We're very curious about a woman who disappeared around Big Pine Key some years ago. Her name was Veronica. A friend, Catherine Davitt, asked me to help her look into this, but now she's gone missing, and Ned was murdered. We're worried that things are spiraling out of control. Arthur Combs mentioned that you knew some of the key players and spent some time in the mangrove camp back in the late seventies."

A shadow crossed her face, mirroring the sudden tight clench of her arms over her chest. "We thought those times were so easy, but they turned out to be more complex than we'd imagined. Put a bunch of early twenty-somethings and teens together who didn't know who they were or where they were going in life, then add a lot of booze and drugs and no rules, and what you get is an ugly mess."

Miss Gloria asked, "How long did you camp out there?"

"A couple of months, maybe? Those were the days that the Moosewood cookbooks were so popular. They featured lots of complicated vegetarian recipes, mostly. I fancied myself an earth woman, the mother figure, always taking care of the ones with the hangovers and such." She chuckled, but not in a happy way. "I tried to get people to eat deliciously seasoned vegetables, not just fried junk and hot dogs." She looked around the restaurant, where people were still finishing up their lunch. "I guess I'm still doing the same thing."

Miss Gloria made a guilty face. "Do waffles count as vegetables?"

We all chuckled, and the tension was broken.

"How well did you know Catherine and Veronica?" I asked.

"Pretty well," she said, "though I wouldn't say I was close with either one of them. I was a little shy, and Veronica certainly was not. Catherine kept her own counsel, though I think she was getting tired of the whole scene. Maybe a lot of us were. Maybe it was the natural end of whatever we had there, a manifestation of the circle of life."

"Do you think Veronica was killed?" I asked.

"Oh no," she said, looking horrified. "I think it ended only because some of us realized we weren't going to find ourselves by smoking pot and drinking in the woods. It was time to move back into the real world and figure out how to be adults." She began to edge away from our table.

"I know you must be so busy, but I have a couple more questions. What do you remember about that last night, the night before Veronica disappeared and the sheriff's deputies came to clear out the camp?"

"That was a very long time ago."

"For sure," I said, nodding with sympathy. "But on the other hand, it sounds as though it was a big turning point for many of you. Sometimes a moment like that lodges in our heads and never lets go." I nodded again, smiling as if inviting her to share more. "We wouldn't push except for the fact that a man is dead and one of your friends went missing that night."

"I wouldn't have called her a friend," Susanne said. "She wasn't the kind of person who was easy with other people. Everything she did was transactional or for effect. She wanted to be the most sexy, the most in demand. She tried to act like she was interested in learning to cook from me, but really, she wanted to be closer to Arthur. Looking back, I'm surprised she was there at all. We weren't fancy enough for her, and we didn't have that much to offer. Why would she come looking for herself in a camp in the mangroves?"

"Those days meant a lot to you, though," Miss Gloria said gently. "You must have some powerful memories of that last night."

Susanne closed her eyes and sighed. "I was kind of out of it," she said, now looking steadily at my friend. "I'd worked a busy morning shift at a restaurant on the highway, and then they asked me to stay through lunch and set up for dinner. I was exhausted. When I got back to the camp, Veronica told me to go take a shower at Bahia Honda beach. She said I looked and smelled like a dead fish. Fried dead fish. She could be harsh like that. I said I needed to start dinner, but Ginny piped up and said that she'd decided on campfire food that night and didn't want or need my help. She was preparing hot dogs on sticks and baked beans from a can. I think she idolized Veronica, and this was almost the same menu that she'd served a few weeks earlier." She paused to think. "A bale of marijuana had washed up onshore that morning, and many of the campers had been smoking all day. It was kind of hard to be around . . ."

"Because?"

"Because you could feel the tension building. It was so hot and still, and the bugs were getting worse and worse. The only ways to get some relief was by zipping yourself up in a tent or huddling around a smoky fire. Or by swimming, of course."

"Tell us about the tension," Miss Gloria said. "Who was there that night?"

"The usual crowd—Arthur and Ned and Catherine and Veronica and some kids from town that Ginny had brought along. Richard and Jimmy had gone out fishing, and they'd found the marijuana and dragged it onto their boat. Arthur wanted them to turn it over to the cops, but the others were against that."

"Ned was there too?" I asked, all innocence. "Someone said he was married."

"Oh, he was, but not for long." Susanne gave another grim chuckle. "Those guys were all in love with Veronica, and she played them against one another. Nothing obvious that you could call her on, but some of us could see what was happening. I think Ned's wife must have figured it out. It wouldn't take a genius since he was at the camp most nights and went home smelling of beer and pot. And probably girl."

She shook her head and pointed. "I need to get back to work. I hope you find what you're looking for."

We watched her braid swinging all the way to the kitchen door.

Chapter Seventeen

"The first bite, the first sip: what power they had sometimes, especially, she now realized, when you'd left the beaten track of your life."
—Spencer Quinn, *Mrs. Plansky's Revenge*

"Did you trust her?" Miss Gloria asked as we climbed back into the car and drove off.

"Honestly, I don't know who to trust," I said. "I liked her, if that counts for anything. Certainly better than Catherine. You?"

"I wanted to trust her," my friend said. "Her waffle was divine, and surely that means something." She snickered. "The way she tells it, it seems more likely that one of the men fighting over Veronica would have disappeared, rather than Veronica herself."

As we turned off Key Deer Boulevard onto Watson, we saw a mass of black birds picking at something on the road. Miss Gloria gasped, and I slowed the car down to a crawl.

"I hope to God it's not a body," she said.

We drove close enough that I could make out the shape of what they were pecking at. "It's a deer, not a person. They're turkey buzzards. Nothing to be afraid of. They eat dead creatures—it's their contribution to the circle of life, as Susanne might say." I grinned at her. She would know this, of course, but I wanted to sound reassuring and normal.

Miss Gloria still looked worried, and I rolled the car forward until we could see the wrinkled red skin on the birds' heads and necks and their sharp yellowish beaks.

"You know what they call a group of vultures?" she asked. "And don't tell me a committee of politicians."

I laughed. "Not really."

"A wake of vultures," she said. "That's what they call a group of birds feeding. These creatures spend their whole buzzardly lives devouring flesh. This gives me a very creepy feeling. It's a sign."

I reached over to pat her leg, and then honked the horn until the birds took off with a great flapping of wings. Then I drove around the carcass in the road. "I wouldn't worry about it. It's just nature. It has nothing to do with what we're working on."

"I wouldn't be so sure," she said, looking and sounding glum. "How do you plan to approach Ginny this time?"

"I think we have to be direct with her and tell her we have some new information, then ask if she remembers anything more about those times. I even wonder if it might be a good idea to mention that we've spoken with Arthur and Susanne. Or is it smarter to wait and see what she comes up with? The main thing is to see whether she tells us a different story than the one she told when I was here with Catherine. Once we let her know that Catherine's disappeared, she may come out with more. Somebody's hiding something, but I don't know why."

"Or she may snap shut like a harvested clam," said Miss Gloria, sounding even more gloomy. It seemed like the weight and sadness of the old story was starting to work on her mind. Next time I was poking into a depressing case, maybe I'd come without her.

I parked in the back lot, and we both got out and walked around to the front door. No one was sitting at the yellow picnic tables in front of the restaurant; it was just too hot.

"You again," said Ginny pleasantly once we moved inside to stand by the hostess podium. "You can't stay away from our pizza?"

"Not exactly," I said. "Could we speak for a couple of minutes? We won't keep you. I know you're working." Ginny shrugged, moving a step closer to the podium.

"Catherine has disappeared, and we're a little worried."

"More than a little," said Miss Gloria, patting my shoulder. "When we went to her room at the hotel, this one here freaked out like we were all extras in the *Psycho* movie."

"I covered my eyes during the shower scene," Ginny said, shivering.

"Exactly," I said. "My friend here loves horror. The scarier the better. You haven't seen Catherine since that day she and I came for lunch, have you?"

Ginny shook her head. "But we've been super busy, and I had yesterday off. So, if she stopped in here, I missed her."

"We've grown quite curious about the campground where Catherine and the rest of your group stayed back in the seventies. Can you tell us exactly where it was?" I asked.

She rubbed her nose and then pulled the order pad from her apron pocket. "Better still, I'll draw you a map," she said, and began to sketch. But then she added, "Don't be disappointed if you don't find anything there. There is no there there. The authorities drove a front loader into the bushes after everyone left. They plowed it all down."

This matched what the deputy told us about the campers leaving a lot of junk behind. It would have long since rotted or rusted at the bottom of the dump. I considered asking where the dump was, but then what? I would end up digging through a mountain of trash, some old, some repellently new. Ginny showed us the primitive map she'd sketched, including a path reaching from the end of Key Deer Boulevard into the brush at the end of the island. "They camped here, toward the water." She tore the sheet off the pad and handed it to me.

"Thanks. What do you remember about the last night in the camp right before the Sheriff's Office shut everything down?" I asked.

"It was a big party," Ginny said. "Some of the guys had scored a bale of marijuana, and everyone was celebrating. Everyone was so happy. But my parents had caught on to how much time I was spending there and moved my curfew back to 10:00 PM. So, I missed most of the action." She shrugged. "In the end, they were right. That was no place for a high school kid."

No place for a kid—what exactly did she mean? Drugs and booze, I assumed. She was looking antsy, so I squeezed in one more question. "What can you tell us about Arthur and Susanne? What were their relationships like with Veronica? And Catherine?"

"Like I said, everyone loved Veronica. Kit Kat, not so much. She was a little sour back then, and from what I saw the other day, that hasn't changed much. Susanne and Arthur acted like the parents of the group. Arthur was kind of an Eeyore and Susanne was a little self-righteous and goody-goody. But they slipped up sometimes too." She flashed a sly smile. "They wouldn't have been there in the first place if they were perfect. I've got to go back to work. I've got a table of customers who're going to be unhappy if I deliver cold food."

Miss Gloria and I waved our thanks and walked back outside into the oppressive heat. A swarm of no-see-ums descended, and as I batted them away, I caught a whiff of the dead fishy odor of seaweed washed ashore at the end of the road. The combination of heat, odor, and bugs might have been exactly what Catherine and the others experienced forty-something years ago.

"What did you think of the interview?" I asked Miss Gloria as I started the car.

My phone buzzed with an incoming text from Danielle. I knew instantly what it would say: *I'm going to see you on the rooftop at 4:00 pm, right? I'm really, really super nervous about everything going well, and you said you'd help me make sure no one forgets the last-minute details. Can you call me?*

I texted back. *Wouldn't miss it. On the way.*

"Darn," I said to Miss Gloria. "I forgot all about Danielle's rehearsal party. We're not rehearsing tonight, but the groom's family wanted to put on a party. Weren't you supposed to be going with me? I was hoping we'd be able to swing by the old campsite, but we better head south in case there's traffic."

"I need to mop off some sweat and put on some party duds too," said Miss Gloria. "Do you mind if I take a little catnap on the way home?"

"Have at it," I said. "I better give Danielle a call and see if she needs pasting together."

Chapter Eighteen

"If you put this sauce on a two-by-four, you'd gnaw on the wood."
—*New York Times Cooking*, July 26, 2023

Back at the houseboat, I took the dog out for a quick pit-stop, promising him a good walk in the morning. Ever since Catherine had appeared and sucked me into her mystery, everyone else in my life had gotten the short shrift on attention. I fed both animals, showered off quickly, and pulled on the apricot-colored sundress that I'd selected for the evening that brought out my auburn highlights. Then I pinned my hair up in a messy knot, with a few loose curls framing my face, and put on a bit of makeup and a pair of dangly rhinestone earrings.

"What do you think?" I asked Evinrude, who had jumped up onto the sink to sip water out of the faucet. He was non-committal. I texted Miss Gloria to tell her I was ready to go, and then I texted Nathan to remind him to meet us on the roof.

The Studios of Key West was a gorgeous, white stucco art deco–style building only two blocks off Duval Street. With the strong support of the arts community in town, the building had been completely renovated to include gallery spaces, artist studios, a stage, a bookstore, and a stunning rooftop bar that could be rented for private parties. Danielle's rehearsal dinner party was taking place on this rooftop.

As a nod to Miss Gloria's age, we took the elevator to the fourth floor instead of the stairs. Every available pole and the blue railings all around the roof had been strung with twinkly fairy lights, with the skyline of Key West spread out behind. There were café tables set up around the space, which were covered with white tablecloths and gorgeous tropical flower arrangements. We moved over to the buffet spread, where I recognized my mother's signature leek and Gruyère triangles made with buttery phyllo pastry, a giant platter of Key West pink shrimp on a bed of ice with spicy cocktail sauce alongside, and a plate of antipasto skewers, layered with olives, artichokes, marinated mushrooms, roasted peppers, salami chunks, and mozzarella balls on a short bamboo skewer. I was practically drooling over the amazing display of appetizers. We took plates and loaded them up, and then moved to stake out chairs along the side of the roof. It had been a long day for both of us, and if I was drooping a little, I knew Miss Gloria had to be tired.

"Be right back with drinks," I said. "You guard the food." I winked.

Halfway through our food and wine, Danielle approached with her fiancé, Jeremy, and his parents. I stood up to hug the happy couple and compliment Jeremy's parents on the upcoming marriage and the excellent party. Danielle explained to them that the caterer was my mother.

"Have you seen the crab cakes with the avocado and mango salsa? Have you tried them?" Danielle asked me. "Your mother is incredible."

I grinned. "We already gobbled those down. She is amazing. How are you holding up?" I knew the answer to this because she'd kept me on the phone going over every detail of the planning all the way home from Big Pine to Key West. Honestly, she was dangling by a thread. But then most brides ended up in this state, from what I'd seen and experienced. I hoped she'd be able to tamp down her anxiety enough to enjoy the festivities.

"I can hardly believe this is happening," she said. She leaned in close to me until I could smell her expensive perfume and a whiff of equally expensive champagne. "Talking to you helped a lot. I realized that I've never been so happy. Is Palamina here?" she asked, craning her head to look for our boss. "She promised she would come even though she insisted she's not a cocktail party, chat-with-strangers kind of woman."

"Everybody on the island is here," said Miss Gloria. "We made a beeline for the food and the bar," she added. A big grin spread across her face as she patted her belly. "Now that we're fortified, we can chat and visit." She explained the connection between us and Danielle's family. "Hayley's hubby is in the police department too, like your Jeremy. She met him when she was a murder suspect, and he was the investigating detective. As you can imagine, it wasn't exactly a *coup de foudre*."

"She means a bolt of lightning," I explained. Danielle's mom had the glazed look on her face that Miss Gloria's chatter sometimes brought, so I hugged Danielle again and released them to make the rounds. We did the same, circling the rooftop, talking with our neighbors Connie and Ray, who were reveling in a night out without kids, our good pals Eric and Bill, my boss Palamina, plus Chief Sean Brandenburg and Steve Torrence from the police department. The party was thick with law enforcement types since Danielle's fiancé was a popular patrol officer.

"Did Nathan make it yet?" the chief asked. "He was outstanding today in our joint exercises. He was the only one who didn't get sick in the Blue Angels flight demonstration, though I think he passed out twice."

That stopped me cold. I tried to join the chief and our friend Steve Torrence's laughter with my own weak ha-ha. "That sounds like my husband."

Nathan hadn't said a word about flying in a jet until he passed out, probably because he knew how much I'd worry. But he was desperate for the promotion to operations captain in the police department, which would make him second-in-command, in charge of planning and directing the activities of the department. These joint exercises would be a test of his skills, especially communication. If he was asked to fly in a Blue Angel jet, he'd certainly do it. The promotion question aside, he would love an experience like that.

Was the chief telegraphing a message to me about his chances for promotion? Before I could decide whether it was a good idea to pursue this, someone gripped my elbow. Darcy Rogers. I froze, feeling the tight squeeze of her fingers on my arm. This was the first time I'd seen her out of uniform. As a nod to the occasion, she'd worn black pants and a white shirt, and her hair was out of its usual tight ponytail. She still looked utterly fierce.

Too late to duck away, I launched into inane chitchat about the night, the food, and her connection with Danielle's husband-to-be.

She ignored all of it but at last loosened her grip on my forearm. "I keep hearing whispers that you aren't minding your own business. May I remind you that we have an active murder investigation on our plate?"

Whispers from who? I wondered, deciding quickly not to allow her to tweak me into a lather. "My business is reviewing restaurants," I said pleasantly, baring my teeth in a wolverine grin. "This week I've been focused on venues up around Big Pine Key." I leaned in closer to whisper. "My boss has been a little concerned that we are too Key West–centric. On the other hand, I'm worried about whether we should review every place we visit, whether it's great food or mediocre. I'd hate to recommend a place and have readers end up disappointed with their dinners and upset about spending hard-earned money on something that's not excellent. Do you have an opinion about that?"

Still ignoring her question, I continued to blather on about food, which was an automatic response when I was nervous, but it also happened to be one of my superpowers. Maybe it would distract her from scolding me. What I really wanted was to ask questions about the investigation, but I was sure she wouldn't tell me anything that wasn't already public.

She looked very unhappy. "You told me that your friend Catherine arrived in the Keys last Monday."

"Umm, I don't remember telling you that. She approached me by email on Sunday, and I met her at the Hemingway Home on Monday afternoon. I did say that much because it's true. I was under the impression that she'd arrived the day before, because how else could she have started right in to work? Why do you ask? Is that incorrect?"

Darcy Rogers had her lips pressed together in a grim line. "We went to the Gardens Hotel to follow up on some questions about Ned Newman's death. She was not there, and the staff at the desk said they hadn't noticed her coming or going in several days. However, they don't keep tabs on their guests for reasons of privacy. They also informed us that she checked in last Friday, not Sunday or Monday as you told me. We've had the opportunity to look at the calls made and received by the deceased in the days leading up to his murder. Ms. Davitt had phoned him several days before she arrived in town."

I felt shocked—and dumb. If what Darcy Rogers said was true, I'd been taken for a fool, and acted like one too. Good gravy, Catherine could well have made plans to murder Ned if she was here a day or two earlier. That would explain her disappearance too. Somehow, I couldn't quite believe this was the truth.

"No way," I said. "She didn't even know Ned was in town. We only stopped by his motel after Ginny mentioned that he still lived in the neighborhood." Another realization hit me. "Are you suggesting that I'm the one who's lying?"

"Either that, or your friend took you for quite a ride and then left you holding the bag."

She wheeled away into the crowd, leaving me feeling confused and queasy. What the heck was Catherine's game? Had she already been in contact with her old friends before we had lunch and then failed to mention that to me? This would change everything.

Across the room, I spotted Nathan emerging onto the rooftop. I knew he'd be looking for me, and maybe he'd want to share news about his day. He'd be worried about telling me he'd flown in a jet, and I had to decide whether to tweak him a bit by pretending to freak out or tell him I knew already and was glad he enjoyed the ride. That aside, this was Danielle's big evening, and I was doing a lousy job of supporting her. I needed to put all my niggling worries aside—including the annoyance that was Darcy Rogers—and try to enjoy the evening.

Chapter Nineteen

*"The cook can stir and adjust seasoning but is basically little
more than a witness to the adagio of a low flame nipping
the underside of a big pot, working a slow alchemy."*
—Molly O'Neill, "A Simmer of Hope,"
New York Times Magazine, January 30, 1994

Once we arrived at Houseboat Row and had walked Miss
Gloria safely to her home, I told Nathan about what Darcy
Rogers had said. "In other words, Catherine might have lied to
me right from the beginning. It seems I'm a great big sucker," I
added with a sigh.

"A sucker with a great big heart," said Nathan. I punched
him in the shoulder, and he grinned. "Keep in mind that it's
not a personal vendetta with Darcy Rogers. You're a civilian and
she feels it's her duty to keep you safe." He hesitated a minute,
looking very serious, and then burst out laughing. "Besides, she's
pretty sure you'll muck up her case. I'll call the Sheriff's Office
tomorrow and see if they'll tell me anything new."

I followed him and the animals into our bedroom to get
undressed for bed. "Thank you. Speaking of telling, what's this

about you passing out in a jet?" I asked, as I hung my dress in the closet.

He looked sheepish as he described how he'd volunteered to be one of the passengers in the Blue Angels' F-18. "They taught us this cool maneuver to help us breathe when the force of gravity got too powerful. I may have passed out more than once, but I was the only one who didn't throw up."

"Congratulations, I think," I said, kissing him as I slid under the covers. Because really, what else could I say? He was so excited about it, and my nagging wouldn't change his mind one bit about the level of danger involved. Just as he didn't try too hard to keep me from solving the mystery of Catherine.

*　*　*

In the morning, I determined that I should look back over the notes that I took while having lunch with Catherine last Monday. Among those scribblings, I found that she'd definitely mentioned the name of a private investigator, Simon Landry. After a few minutes of searching, I uncovered that name in Birmingham, Michigan. I tapped it into the Google search bar and came up with a few newspaper stories about cases that he had solved or contributed to solving. He also had a rather simple website, which bordered on primitive. In fact, it looked like it had been taken from a stock website for private investigators, if such a thing existed. It was decorated with a close-up photo of an eye, and a magnifying glass that had been laid across a fingerprint card. Clichés galore. There was a small photo of a tall, thin man whose face looked grimly confident and weathered. He had listed his experience in military, retail, and private investigation, assuring potential customers that he would handle their business in a discreet, professional, and extremely confidential manner.

"Every case is important to me," he was quoted as saying, "because behind each problem, there is a troubled family or individual needing help. No case is too big or too small."

Across the bottom of the page, it was noted in red that Mr. Landry was REtired, with a capital R and a capital E. I guessed that if he was in his seventies, he might be more responsive to a phone call than an email, so I dialed him up.

"Landry," he answered, his voice thick, the kind of raspy sound that came from a lifetime of cigarettes.

I explained our connection. "I'm calling about an old case you worked on with Catherine Davitt. I have lots of questions about the case, which are made more urgent by the fact that there's been a murder on Big Pine Key, right near the original disappearance. This occurred after Catherine came to Key West and asked me to help her look into the old case. Since then, Catherine herself has vanished. I wondered if you would be willing to talk to me about whatever you remember about your work on the case. Catherine said that your trail ran cold once you left the Keys, but maybe you have a different perspective. If you prefer to look me up online before chatting, that would be fine too."

Finally, I took a breath and gave him a chance to respond.

"I already checked you out while you were talking," he said with a gruff laugh. "You probably better tell me more about yourself so I can decide what to share. If anything."

I figured he'd be more interested in crime solving than restaurant recommendations, so I focused on that, beginning with the first time I'd been pulled into a case. "It all started with a poisoned key lime pie," I said. "It's been downhill from there—or uphill, depending on your point of view." I summarized a few of the situations that I felt most proud of helping to solve, including the murder clues I'd found in an old Key West Woman's Club cookbook.

"You're married to a police officer? Is he involved in this case too?"

The marriage would be public record, so I wasn't surprised or alarmed by the question. "He's not. The murder happened north of Key West in greater Monroe County, so the responsible agency is the Sheriff's Office rather than the local police department. But Nathan certainly knows what happened. He always worries if my inquiries stray into law enforcement territory, but honestly, this time I did not go looking for a mystery. Catherine came looking for me. As I mentioned, she's disappeared. I'm positive she would approve of my asking for your help."

He was silent for a moment. "Tell me what your questions are."

I reviewed Veronica's case and explained the current situation. "Catherine emailed me out of the blue at the beginning of the week because she said she'd read about my involvement in other cases. I am not a private investigator or a detective of any kind," I hurried to add. "I suppose I might be more curious than most people, and I found that if you pay attention to what's around you, you notice things that other people might miss."

"Exactly," the man said. "It's not rocket science, is it? Tell me more about why Catherine contacted you."

"I got the sense that her friend's disappearance has always haunted her. It was a time in her life when she was at loose ends, searching for direction. The book she's working on about

Hemingway and his wives stirred those old memories up, reminding her of this missing piece. Visiting the Keys again probably brought back memories. That's what I think, anyway." I paused a moment. "It sounds kind of goofy, but I have an inkling that the disappearance is related to toxic love."

He gave a grunt of agreement. "I do remember this. It's one of the cases that haunts me as well. What is toxic love, anyway? People throw that term around these days, but I couldn't give a definition even with a Glock to my head."

"I think it means a relationship in which you feel demeaned or attacked, where a person professes to love you, but your emotional well-being is threatened by this person. The relationship seems to be based on love, but the support and understanding is not there. There's a lack of empathy." Now I realized I wasn't sure exactly what Catherine meant, so I was struggling to describe it to him. "Hemingway's relationships are the hook she's using, but I think the topic felt personal to her as well. I just don't know how it all fits with the past."

He was silent for a moment. "This was a frustrating case. Everywhere I searched, I found misdirection and dead ends."

"What kind of misdirection?" I asked.

"I interviewed as many of the former camp residents and visitors as I could find, but each claimed not to know Veronica's plans and inner thoughts intimately and pointed me to someone else who might. The consensus was that she was impulsive enough to head north on her own without telling anyone."

"Catherine called you for help once she returned to Michigan, right?" I asked, nudging him for more details. "Around the end of May or early June?"

"Yes."

"I know this happened a long time ago, but do you remember what she sounded like? Was she upset about her friend? As she talked about her with me, I got the sense it was a love-hate relationship. I think maybe she was jealous of Veronica, so remaining her friend was not easy."

"Yes," he said. "Let me pull my notes from the file. I'll be a minute." Once he returned to the phone, he said, "Veronica appeared to be a favorite of many of the young people in the commune, while Catherine herself was not so popular. Or so she said, and that was borne out in my interviews."

"Was she envious of her friend?"

"Probably. You know, there are some people who bob along easily on the currents of their lives, collecting friends without a thought and discarding them just as easily. Veronica was one of those."

This made me think of a new angle on Catherine's Hemingway book. Was Veronica the female version of the famous writer? "Catherine struck me as somewhat awkward, even now as a grown woman," I said, nodding vigorously even though he wouldn't be able to see that. "She didn't say anything about a partner or children. I wondered, but I didn't ask because it felt intrusive and didn't seem relevant.

"I don't want to ask you to break confidentiality if you're not comfortable doing so, but if it's okay, I'd love to hear about how Catherine approached you and how you went about looking for Veronica."

He cleared his throat, then began to speak. "Well, she came the first time accompanied by Veronica's father. He was furious about the whole situation. He wanted it solved. Now. He was actually the one who paid for my services in the beginning.

I think he blamed Catherine for encouraging Veronica to run away in the first place and for not looking after his daughter while they were in the Keys."

"She didn't spell out who encouraged who, but I would have bet on Veronica as the instigator of the adventure," I said.

"Her father kept saying, 'How is it that you went to Florida as two people but came back as one?' The whole time, he was jabbing his finger at Catherine, with this ugly, angry look on his face. I suspect that he also contacted Catherine's family, blaming her for the disappearance and for acting irresponsibly."

"What was Catherine's reaction?"

"Catherine finally spoke up and told him that he was being unfair and that he didn't understand how difficult and impulsive his own daughter was. I remember she said, 'You're the one she ran away from.' Then he said, 'We're done here. Either she'll come home or she won't, but I'm done footing her bills, and I'm absolutely done with you.' Then he stormed out of the office."

"What happened after that? Gosh, you must have been shocked."

He laughed. "In my business, I see plenty of people throwing snits. Sometimes the emotions seem genuine, and other times, they might be covering up their role in the problem. For him, I was betting on the second option. He mostly didn't like that someone might be on to him. Once he left, I asked Catherine if she still wanted me to look."

"Did she?"

"She did, though she didn't have his resources. She insisted that his accusation that she didn't care about Veronica was wrong. After all, she was the one who contacted the Sheriff's Office to report her missing. Then she added that if anyone in the group should take the fall, it should be Arthur. Arthur Combs. I gathered he was the unofficial leader of the group, and she seemed to think that Veronica reacted strongly to something he said right before she disappeared. I looked for him, of course, but he'd already left the state, and none of the other campers knew where he was headed."

"I can tell you that," I said. "He went to veterinary school, and now he's a practicing vet in Key West. He seemed very kind, hardly the sort of man who would cause a young woman to disappear. Did you suspect that Veronica's father was abusive?"

"Emotionally, at least. From what Catherine described, Veronica made intense emotional connections, but serially, and usually overlapping. Then she would break them off, leaving the exes bewildered and sometimes angry. But this was all done in a fishbowl in front of all the kids. Campers, whatever you want to call them. I'm no psychologist, but I believe this pattern had something to do with her relationship with her father. It was as though she was proving to herself and the others that she was worthy in a way she hadn't felt with her father. She also showed them that she could end relationships on her own terms."

"What did you do next?" I asked. My head was spinning while trying to figure out the psychology of a girl I only knew by hearsay.

"First, I tracked down Veronica's mother. The parents split up right before she and Catherine went on their road trip. I thought maybe the two girls had had a falling out and she'd returned home without telling Miss Davitt her plans. The mother had not seen her in months. I got the impression Veronica had worn them all out over the years with her antics. But she definitely blamed her ex for the situation.

"Then I traveled down to the Keys to look at the so-called scene of the crime." He chuckled. "There was not a lot left to see, as the camp had been scraped bare of their belongings. It's so bloody hot down there in the summertime, and they have a terrible rainy season too. Between the moisture and the heat, the vegetation had sprung back up. It was as if no one had ever been living there."

"But you poked around, right, just in case the Sheriff's Office might have been hasty and left important things behind?"

He gave an audible sigh. "Of course I did. I didn't travel all the way there to take a cursory look. Then I interviewed Deputy Ryan Lopez, who had been closely connected with the commune as well as instrumental in closing it down."

"Yes," I said. "We've met with him as well. He's retired now, but he didn't have any problem remembering those days. I got the sense that it wasn't easy to be close in age to the others but be in law enforcement, light-years away from their reality. He may have suffered from a lapse in judgment because of that." I paused, hoping he would have something new to say about the deputy and a possible lapse. He didn't. I sighed, thinking that would have been so helpful. "Do you think it was really a commune?"

"Not in an organized fashion," he said. "But it was a group of hippie-ish young people. Lost souls. The deputy informed me that there were two strikes against them: a good amount of drug use that they knew of, and the fact that they were camping on private property. Apparently, they shared resources and tasks, until the group began to fall apart."

"Do you mean there were troubles inside the group?"

"I'm sure that was true. Plus, the neighbors had begun to complain about the noise and the drug use, and the camp attracted the local young people. The squatters were not deemed to be a good influence. Gypsy trash, they called them. And then Catherine reported Veronica's disappearance. The Sheriff's Office found no signs of foul play, but this complaint along with the neighbors' complaints drew the situation to the forefront, and they had to act. By the time I arrived in the Keys, only a few of the former camp residents remained in the area."

"Did you get the sense that the officials looked hard for Veronica?"

"I did not," he said. "They did interview the remaining campers, but when no one had any insight, they cleared out the camp."

"Have you heard more recently from Catherine?" I asked. "It might have made more sense for her to contact you for help rather than me."

"Nothing recent," he said. "But I'm retired, and you are free." We both laughed.

"Did you end on good terms?"

He sighed. "For me, good terms depended on solving the case I'd been hired to solve. However, this young woman seemed to vanish into thin air. Then Miss Davitt ran out of money and enthusiasm, so we called it quits." He hung up after assuring me that he'd call or text if remembered or learned anything new. "Not that I'd expect news after this many years."

Chapter Twenty

"Audiences fell in love with Julia Child not because she was technically the best French chef, but because she made us feel like we too could make beef bourguignon."
—Amy McCarthy, *Eater Newsletter,* July 23, 2023

I gathered up my computer and papers and headed to the office to discuss my articles for the week with Palamina. Danielle wasn't there, of course—she'd be hip deep in the final details of her wedding. I reminded myself that I was supposed to show up for a facial and massage with the other bridal attendants at 4:00 PM. With champagne, of course. Danielle wanted to do things differently for her wedding than most brides managed. Instead of cramming the night before with an extravagant party for anxious relatives meeting for the first time, she'd planned an event with her best girlfriends, followed by a special dinner alone with Jeremy. "This way, no one's too wound up to enjoy the big day," she'd told me, wearing a big grin. "Especially me. And we can remember why we got together in the first place."

Palamina was sitting at Danielle's desk in the tiny space we called the reception area, pecking away at her keyboard. Her normally perfect wavy hair was scrunched on top of her head with a rubber band and a pen stuck through it, and she was muttering to herself.

"I'm not cut out for this," she said when she saw me come up the stairs. "My secretarial skills are nil. Thank God you're here, so we can retreat to my office."

Once seated, I reviewed what I had so far on Big Pine Key for my boss. Honestly, it sounded a little thin. But then a new idea sprang to mind. "Last night at the cocktail party, I had an interesting conversation with a friend about the ethics of restaurant reviews." Darcy Rogers was not what I'd call a friend, nor had it been much of a conversation, but Palamina didn't need to know either of those facts. "I wondered if we should consider hosting a survey about our reviews. Do readers want to hear about places that we feel neutral or negative about, or should I attempt to find something positive about every place I try? I'd hate for people to spend hard-earned money on mediocre food because of my overly positive reviews. On the other hand, people in the restaurant business have to make a living—it's still a small town, and my words could have a big effect on their bottom lines. I don't know the answers, but maybe readers would appreciate weighing in."

"How would you say you handle a review now for a restaurant you haven't enjoyed?" she asked.

"I do my best to find something to like. Maybe the view is fabulous, or it's in the busy part of town and therefore super-convenient for tourists, or I liked certain dishes. Even one dish. One thing I try to avoid is sounding snarky at the restaurant's cost. I hate when people show off in book reviews, and I don't like restaurant critics who do this either. But it might be interesting to find out what our readers would find useful."

"I like it," she said. "Perhaps a quick survey, and then a place to leave comments. We could include reader opinions in follow-up articles. Maybe set up some interviews with the owner/manager of a couple of restaurants too." She closed the notepad that lay open on her desk and slapped her pen down on top of it. "Anything else? I have to tell you, I'll be glad when this wedding business is over. The honeymoon too." She smiled to soften the comment a bit. "We'll be okay as long as Danielle doesn't turn up pregnant. Or you." She furrowed her brows as though this had only now occurred to her as a possibility.

"No plans along those lines," I said, because she looked so frazzled. But, honestly, there weren't any plans. Neither Nathan nor I felt the least bit ready to turn our lives over to raising kids. For now, marriage and careers and friends and family were more than enough.

She nodded with relief. "What else are you working on?"

"For the future, I'd love to write a story about the real Hemingway. With Hemingway Days coming up in July, this might be an interesting twist."

"We already cover that event, don't we?" she asked.

"We run photos of the Hemingway lookalike contest and write about the marlin tournament and the silly running of the bulls down Duval Street, sure. But that's surface stuff. Because of the tours at the Hemingway Home, everyone knows about his time here with his second wife, Pauline, and how she spent his money on that pool—although I think really she was the one with the money in that marriage. It's also well known how he used the lighthouse to guide himself home when he was too drunk to see, and how all writers crave his adorable office that's reached by a spiral staircase and a catwalk. But most of us don't know the real story of his wives—what their family histories were, what drew each of them to him, and him to them. I'm imagining this as something more serious. I want to examine the psychology of Hemingway and his wives and their connections, rather than the myth."

As I talked, I wished Catherine would reappear, because with her study of toxic love, she would be an amazing resource for a piece like this. The parallels that might exist between Veronica's disappearance in Big Pine Key all those years ago, and the people she gathered close and discarded just as easily reminded me of Hemingway's history. Hopefully, she wouldn't feel that I was stepping on her toes by writing on this subject, assuming she reappeared.

"Get me an outline," she said. "I'd like to have input before you write the whole thing."

I gathered up my notes and headed back to my office. With all of this talk about Hemingway and the mystery of Big Pine Key in mind, I suddenly felt like I could do a more insightful job of interviewing the people who had known Veronica. I couldn't talk to Ned because he was dead, but I could talk to his ex-wife. I also could go back to Susanne and Arthur with questions that were shaped by this theory. And Ginny too. She was certainly a front-row witness to those days.

But first, a visit with my friend Eric would help me make sense of the psychological connections. I texted him quickly. *I'm about to run home and pick up Ziggy to spend half an hour at the dog park. Any chance you could meet us?* I added that I had an interesting psychological puzzle that I hoped he could help me with.

See you in 15! he answered.

I buzzed home on my scooter, scooped up Ziggy, and headed over to the White Street pier. Inside the dog park, Eric was waiting in a plastic chair in the shade. With the snowbirds gone north, the crowd of dogs and owners was reduced, and neither we nor the dogs had to fight for space. Ziggy trotted off purposefully toward the chain-link fence to check out the denizens of the big dog park, with Eric's Chester and Barclay close behind.

"So, what's up?" Eric asked.

I explained that Catherine had gone missing, then told him about my conversation with the private investigator and described what I'd been reading about Hemingway's wives. He listened carefully.

"Catherine was writing a book about Hemingway and toxic love. I've begun to wonder if her interest in the topic is related to something in her own life, probably from the period of time in the late seventies that she spent in Big Pine Key."

"Do you see Catherine as the Hemingway figure?" he asked.

"No." I shook my head. "The woman who went missing, Veronica, was entrancing and infuriating, from what I hear. She had serial relationships and many flirtations. The private investigator told me that he had a feeling her father had been emotionally abusive and that's partly why she ran away to Florida."

Eric sat back in his chair, looking sad. "I'm sure I've told you this many times, but when people don't understand their family's psychological history, it lingers with them. The trauma gets repeated over and over in their current lives. I cannot tell you how many times I've seen this in my office, and how astonished patients often are to recognize the patterns in themselves. So, your theory makes perfect sense to me."

Chester came up and leaned against Eric's leg, and he ruffled the brown-and-white fur on his dog's head. "Tell me more about the connection to Hemingway's wives."

"Take it with a grain of salt because I haven't had time to do serious research. I turned to Dr. Google and Mr. Wikipedia." I grinned but then felt the smile fade away as I considered the tragedies in the Hemingway legacy and in his marriages. I pulled out my phone so I could read off the notes I'd made.

"First, you've probably heard this part, but Hemingway was dressed in girls' clothing and long hair like his sister during his first three years." I paused to look at Eric. "What was up with that? Later, according to Hemingway biographies, he professed to hating his mother. Let's start there. If he hates his mother, what would that mean about the wife he is searching for? Next, while he was working as an ambulance driver during World War I, he was injured and nursed back to health by a woman he thought he would marry. He was devastated by the news that she was marrying someone else. Biographers state that, ever after, he abandoned wives before they could abandon him."

"Except maybe for Martha Gellhorn," Eric said. "She didn't quite fit the mold."

"Right," I said. "His first wife, Hadley, had money and a nurturing instinct, both of which Hemingway needed in order to write. I think the incident where she lost his suitcase full of manuscripts on a train was a tipping point in their marriage. He could no longer trust her to take care of him.

"He became involved with Pauline Pfeiffer, allegedly Hadley's best friend. During this period, he learned that his father had killed himself, a tragedy that would befall him at the end of his life as well. While he was working as a journalist, covering the Spanish Civil War, he met the woman who would become his third wife, Martha Gellhorn. She was a very talented and fierce journalist herself, and by all reports, she did not cater to Hemingway the way his previous wives had. She grew fed up with his bullying and neediness, and demanded a divorce, and he quickly married Mary Welsh, his fourth wife."

Chester hopped up onto Eric's lap and butted his hand until he began to stroke the dog from nose to tail. "You have traumatic family-of-origin relationships, possibly mental illness, overlapping dependent relationships, alcohol abuse, and a history of suicide. That last is a tough one," said Eric. "It's not that there is a biological underpinning to suicide, but once it occurs in a family, it presents itself as a way to opt out of what appear to be intractable problems." He rubbed Chester's ears, and the dog settled against him with a satisfied groan. "If you're wondering about the parallels between Hemingway and Veronica, have you noticed those same factors in your interviews about her?"

"Traumatic family of origin, check. Overlapping relationships, check. Substance abuse, most likely. Not suicide, at least not that anyone's mentioned." I stopped for a minute, horrified by the thought. "Oh my gosh, do you suppose that's what happened to her? But wouldn't they have found a body? Or a note?"

We chatted for a little longer, then I thanked Eric for listening and we set off our separate ways. After dropping Ziggy off at home, I decided to take a quick trip back to the Gardens Hotel. I kept thinking—hoping—that Catherine would resurface and not just disappear into thin air. If I could find her, I could ask these questions directly rather than traveling all over the Keys interviewing reluctant witnesses.

Chapter Twenty-One

"Those of us who tend to eat with others simply want a fun way to think about eating alone, however feral or photograph-ready the meal may be . . . No one meal is 'girl dinner' nor is 'girl dinner' a prescriptive thing since 'girl dinner' depends on the girl."
—Bettina Makalintal, *Eater*, August 27, 2023

I parked across the street from the Gardens Hotel and hurried up the steps to the entrance hall. Spotting a desk clerk in an office on the right-hand side, I took a deep breath, trying to get my story straight for myself before I started blabbing.

"Hello!" I warbled. "I'm Hayley Snow, and I am a friend of Catherine Davitt. She is one of your guests here, or she was one of your guests. The thing is—I hope you don't think this is intrusive or weird—but I'm very worried about her. She was supposed to meet me here two days ago, and she never showed up. Perhaps you've heard about the murder up in Big Pine Key? She and I discovered the body."

The desk clerk gasped.

I nodded dolefully and kept going, thinking that I might have a chance at winning her sympathy. "I assume the police have been here looking to talk with her. She told me that she had checked in on Monday. Or maybe that was my mistake. Maybe she didn't tell me that and I just assumed. But I guess she got here several days earlier. I'm just wondering, and I understand this is probably not appropriate, but could you confirm when she arrived? Have you seen her since? She hasn't checked out or anything, has she? As I said, I'm terribly worried."

I felt my lips tremble, and I realized I *was* worried. I didn't know her well enough to be as sad as I would be if a dear friend had gone missing, but I had a sinking feeling that something bad had happened. Like it or not, I had sunk into her story and her problems up to my eyebrows.

The clerk glanced to the right, then to the left, and leaned across the counter. "The police were here, and I did inform them that she had checked in on Friday. No, she hasn't checked out, and I personally have not seen her during any of my shifts. Obviously, I'm only here about a third of the time."

This information told me essentially nothing, except it did confirm that Catherine was gone and that her disappearance was probably not planned. "Have there been any calls from people asking to be connected to her room, or perhaps visitors looking for her?"

"Not that I'm aware of," the clerk said, her jaw tightening. She leaned closer to whisper. "You don't suppose she was murdered as well?"

"I don't . . . I hope not . . . that's a big jump." I shrugged my very tense shoulders and let them drop. I, of course, had had the same awful thought. "The truth is, I have no idea what's going on."

She leaned across the desk again to whisper. "I can tell you that she did ask about hiring a local driver."

"You mean like an Uber?" I asked, thinking everyone who had a smartphone and traveled would already have that app downloaded. This information would not be all that helpful.

"No. I did suggest that, but she wanted one reliable local person who could take her several places." She rustled in the desk under the counter and handed me the business cards of two drivers. "I gave her these."

"Thanks. When was this conversation?"

"The day she checked in. Friday."

"Is it okay if I go to the garden and sit for a minute to pull myself together?"

"Of course," she said. "The bar is open to the public when we have events like wine tastings and piano bar performances, so I don't think anyone will mind you relaxing for a moment. I'm so sorry about your friend."

I thought for a moment about asking her if she would let me into Catherine's room, but I hated to put her in that position. She surely would say no. She *should* say no. Instead, I wandered through the vestibule and into the garden area, which had a pool surrounded by tropical foliage on the left and the open-air bar off to the right. I did not see a bartender on duty, nor was it a good idea to start drinking this early in the morning. Instead, I poured myself a glass of cool water with slices of cucumbers and limes floating in it and sat in the shade to think things over.

Had any of the people who knew Veronica back in the day noticed an underlying depression? If her relationship with her father had been abusive, then I imagine she would have felt that way whether she recognized it or not. My conversation with Eric had underscored how little I really understood about the young woman. For that matter, I didn't understand Catherine very well either.

Catherine had disappeared in the middle of a quest that she seemed devoted to. Why?

Possibility one: she was Veronica's murderer. With all the questions about the past stirred up, maybe she recognized that she was in deep, deep trouble. Maybe someone was on to her. Perhaps she had to kill Ned because he knew too much or realized he knew more than he thought he did, and he had decided to talk about it? Maybe Ned even blackmailed her? This wasn't out of the question given that she had lied to me about when she had arrived. Because of the extra fingerprints the crime scene investigator found, she must have been in Ned's office well before she and I stumbled in, allegedly to discover the body. In that case, I'd been set up as a kind of stooge. Maybe she'd already killed him when she talked me into driving up to Big Pine so we could "find" the body. But then why in the world would she get me involved rather than simply fleeing?

Was it also possible that all the other people we'd interviewed had lied? Maybe she'd talked with Arthur, Susanne, and Ginny before we visited them one by one? None of them had confessed that. I glanced at the cards the clerk had given me. I phoned each to see if one remembered ferrying Catherine around the Keys. No one answered either line, so I left messages asking for a call back.

Going down another rabbit hole, why would she or anyone else murder Ned now? Perhaps the secret of what happened to Veronica had been well buried—until recently. What if the person responsible for her disappearance (and I was beginning to believe her death) had begun to panic? This wouldn't be the first time that a second murder was committed in an attempt to disguise the first.

I wished I knew more about Ned. So far, Ginny's description sounded one note: miserable, lecherous, and cheap. Catherine had pretty much concurred. But Arthur had given what appeared to be a heartfelt tribute to him at the Green Parrot's ukulele night. Who was covering up or stretching the truth?

A text came in on my phone from Lorenzo, my tarot-card-reading friend, reminding me that we'd planned to meet for an early lunch at The Café on Southard Street. *Yes!* I texted back. This would be a relaxing break in an otherwise hectic day and week.

I called Miss Gloria to see if she was interested in taking a quick ride up to the neighborhood on Sugarloaf Key after lunch, where Ned's latest ex, Arden, lived with her son. She eagerly agreed, and we made a plan to meet up at Houseboat Row at one. That would give me time to swing by Williams Hall to chat with chef Martha Hubbard, who would have known Susanne in the past. I would also be able to see Lorenzo. I texted Martha to ask if she was working, and when she replied affirmatively, I headed in her direction.

A set of double doors led to a nondenominational chapel in a beautiful white building that housed not only the renovated church's nave and chancel but also rooms for activities such as dancing and sewing classes. Martha's gorgeous kitchen was upstairs. I would never again be able to visit this room without picturing Violet and Bettina Booth manning the quadruple ovens for the first taping of *UK Bakes! Key West Edition*. Although that week had turned into an old-fashioned rhubarb, with no wannabe home bakers rising to the occasion, Miss Gloria and I hadn't missed an episode of their popular baking show ever since. Martha was busy cooking at the stove behind the long counter, and the scents of her ingredients were amazing.

"Good morning!" I called. "What are you making?"

"We're serving a Mediterranean-flavored dinner tonight," she said. "Poached salmon on a bed of arugula with lemon chili sorbet, grilled pork tenderloin with fruited couscous, and an olive oil and orange cake."

"I'm swooning," I said, peering into a pot that bubbled softly with herbs and spices. "I can't ditch Danielle's bridesmaid party, but I'd be here in an instant if I could."

She grinned and pointed at the big pot. "That's for poaching the salmon later. I'm about to start the cake. What's up?"

"It's more like what's not up," I said. "I have two questions for you." I had decided in advance to get her opinions about restaurant reviews—the good, the bad, and the ugly—and then move on to the murder case. She'd have an insider point of view about what it was like on the receiving end of a flurry of reviews from diners, both happy and unhappy. Then maybe she'd talk about the past.

I described what I was writing and how I'd love to get a quote from a chef.

"Honestly," she said, as she began to zest oranges on a stainless steel microplane, "cooking is like any of the other art forms. A serious chef puts her heart and soul into a menu. It's devastating when it translates poorly to the diners, whether that's because it's a bad idea to begin with, or it's poorly executed by the sous chefs, or something's off with the ingredients. There are lousy chefs, of course, and chefs who have lousy nights. Some of them run out of steam and lose interest and rely on a reputation that's no longer deserved. I suppose people should know about those. That's only fair. On the other hand, sometimes it's not the chef, it's the diner. Don't try to trash the reputation of a restaurant or a chef because you chose your dishes poorly or you're having a fight with your spouse. Especially don't show off at someone else's expense."

"Exactly!" I said. "I knew you'd give me something pithy."

She bowed, her grin spreading even wider. She studied my face again. "But there's more, right?"

"Always." I sighed and launched into a compact rundown of Catherine's request for help and the disasters that had unfolded since. "To keep it short, one man is dead, and Catherine herself is missing. Of course, I can't keep myself from sniffing around; you know how I get on the trail of a mystery."

"Do I ever." She grinned and shook her head. "How can I help?"

I explained about the encampment on Big Pine Key and how I'd been canvassing the people who lived there during the time Catherine's friend went missing. "One of them is Susanne Howe, the chef at the Square Grouper. She said she worked at Louie's Backyard for a time, and I thought you two might have overlapped."

"We did," she said as she brushed the orange zest into a pile and scraped it into a small bowl. "She was the *garde manger* when I was hired, responsible for salads and cold vegetable dishes and garnishes and such. I worked on the line, preparing mostly fish and steaks. She'd been there a good ten years, I think, before I took the job."

"Salads and vegetables sound exactly like her jam," I said. "Do you remember why she decided to leave?"

"We both recognized that there isn't much turnover in that restaurant, and they keep their menu steady and traditional. People go there for the waterfront setting, of course, but they've grown to expect the shrimp and grits, the fresh catch of the day, the beef with horseradish crust, and so on. In other words, we'd have to keep looking if we wanted to spread our wings and run our own kitchen." She juiced the zested oranges, set the liquid aside in a second bowl, and began to measure out flour and sugar.

"Did she ever talk about those early days in the mangrove camp? She was there when the young woman went missing."

Martha swiped at her forehead, leaving a smear of flour behind. "Remember, a restaurant kitchen is a busy place and gets frantic if the front of the house is full. But . . ." She paused and I imagined she was deciding how much to say. "I was a little bit in awe of her because she was so sure that vegetables were her calling." I couldn't help laughing, and she snickered too.

"It sounds silly, doesn't it? But I loved her stories about eating at the Moosewood restaurant in Ithaca and working there once she was old enough. She loved the local, sustainable food angle and the collective atmosphere at that place. I think she always regretted leaving before it really bloomed and not getting the chance to work on those cookbooks."

Martha waved at her shelves, overflowing with books. I recognized the tall paperbacks with hand-lettered titles that had come out of the Moosewood restaurant. "She talked about how much she enjoyed cooking for the campers. Her signature became using repurposed food that others had thrown away."

"Dumpster diving," I said, grinning. "Any other impressions?"

Martha nodded. "She seemed very gentle and kind and earnest, very earnest."

"Not the sort of person who might murder someone by plunging a pair of scissors in their back?"

Martha looked horrified. "Not in the least."

"Do you know anything about her personal life?" I asked.

"I don't think she ever married," Martha said. "Not that wedded bliss is perfect for everyone. But she seemed sad whenever the topic came up, as if maybe she'd planted a seed of love that had grown up stunted and didn't bear fruit."

1978

Catherine

There was a run-down hippie cabin not far from the altar. Arthur told us not to go in because it wasn't safe. It could collapse any moment, and besides, it belonged to crabby Mr. Silverton, who would have us all evicted in an instant if he caught one of us there.

But sometimes I had to get away from Ronnie, from all of them, really. I'd sneak over through the brush and climb up to the second floor and take a nap. That afternoon, I woke up hearing rustling down below. I peered out the window. Susanne was kneeling in front of the altar of love. She was crying. She placed something on the surface of the slab of stone that one of the guys had propped up between driftwood logs, fashioning a rough table. I was too far away to identify what she'd delivered.

Then Ronnie burst out of the bushes, laughing. She snatched up the item that Susanne had placed on the stone and held it over her head. "You know he slept with me, don't you? He adores me. I wouldn't bother with this if I was you. Even black magic isn't going to win him over to you."

Ronnie could burst anyone's bubble of hope, even sweet Susanne's.

Chapter
Twenty-Two

"'The secret,' she'd tell me as I helped her measure, 'is the quality of the cocoa powder and the depth of your love.'"
—Lucy Burdette, *The Ingredients of Happiness*

At The Café on Southard Street, Lorenzo was already seated at a table by the window. He was wearing a pink checked shirt that brightened his face and made his dark curls and blue eyes stand out. He looked refreshed and happy. The waitress came by before I could inquire about his life, so after a quick skim of the menu, I ordered the falafel sandwich. I found the description irresistible: crispy balls of fried and spiced chickpeas in fresh pita, with a side salad that included hummus and tahini dressing. Night owl Lorenzo, who was on his breakfast to my lunch, chose the fresh fruit Belgian waffle. "Extra whipped cream, please," he said with a sparkle in his eyes. I must have looked a little surprised.

"Sometimes a guy has to splurge. I think I'm worth it."

I reached for his hand and squeezed. "I think you are too. You look lighter today. Do you have good news?"

"Pluto is finally dipping into Aquarius. It's a big relief after years of dragging through Capricorn. Can you feel it?"

"No, but I believe you can." We both laughed, and he most likely realized I had only the vaguest idea of what he meant but trusted him anyway. "If you feel lighter, I do too."

"But you don't look light," he said, his brow furrowing with concern. "You're carrying something. Something heavy."

As always, he was right, of course. I gave him the summary that had grown so familiar over the last few days—email from Catherine, murder on Big Pine, finally Catherine's disappearance, mirroring Veronica's disappearance in 1978. The waitress delivered our food—my steaming falafel and Lorenzo's gorgeous, fluffy waffle. I took a few bites and then said, "I don't know what to worry about more, who killed that poor man that we found in Big Pine, or where Catherine has gone."

Lorenzo wiped a dab of whipped cream off his upper lip. "I don't suppose it would help to say that none of this is technically your responsibility?" He looked hopeful. "I hate to see you weighed down by outside problems. Like, shouldn't solving the murder be the Sheriff's Office's responsibility?"

"Technically, yes, but I was there on the scene. Catherine and I found him. This might sound strange, but finding a murder victim feels like that old Chinese proverb about saving a life—once you're involved, you're responsible forever. Or in my case, at least until the killer is caught." If anyone would understand that kind of thinking, it would be Lorenzo.

"That makes sense to me." He nodded and pulled a pack of tarot cards from his pocket. "Do you have time for a quick reading?"

"Please," I said. "Four cards? Or maybe three." Usually, I loved any guidance from my wise friend, but I was anxious about this whole case, both the past and the present. I hoped he wouldn't see more than I felt I could manage. When we'd finished eating, we pushed our dishes aside.

He meditated over the cards for a moment, then had me shuffle the deck and choose a pile. From that stack, he dealt out the ten of swords, which showed a man lying face down with swords stabbing the length of his torso; the three of swords, which had a big red heart pierced by three swords; and the moon.

He studied the cards and then glanced up at me, his brow again lined with worry. "Hmm, there's a strong theme of betrayal and fear here. No surprise, from what you've told me. The ten of swords is the ultimate card of betrayal. The person in the card is pinned by the swords, symbolizing—and not subtly—that one person has betrayed another, and this has or will destroy their relationship."

I put an elbow on the table and parked my chin in my hand. "None of this is subtle. Ned was stabbed in the back, and all the people in the old camp sounded as if they were on the verge of betraying one another. It's a matter of finding out what really happened before someone else gets hurt. Who would act violently in the face of a betrayal?"

"I'll say it again. It's not really your job, though, right?" He smiled gently and moved on to the second card, the three of swords. "More betrayal here, but this is matters of the heart—lying, unfaithfulness, stone cold dumping." He tapped the third card, the moon, which showed a gorgeous yellow orb with a sad face inside, two angry dogs barking, and a lobster. "Danger, deception, fear of the unknown," he said.

"What about the lobster?" I asked. "That seems a little bizarre."

"That symbolizes us moving out of our primordial igno-
rance toward a higher light. Lobsters change by molting their
old shells. You may be experiencing change as well, but the card
warns you to be careful about what's influencing you to move
in a certain direction. As always, with the cards, take what feels
useful and set the rest aside."

As he gathered his cards together, my phone beeped, alerting
me that it was time to pick up Miss Gloria.

"I don't have to tell you to be careful, do I?" he asked, his
whole face shaded with worry.

"Nope." I gave Lorenzo a big hug and my thanks, with
promises to sit together at Danielle's wedding the next day.
He wouldn't know a lot of the police officer types in atten-
dance, and we'd enjoy his company. He always liked visiting
with Eric and Bill and my family. I buzzed home to freshen
up, take the dog out, and collect my friend. I would have to
mull over the meaning of Lorenzo's reading when I had some
downtime. I was so confused about the primordial lobster.
I'd already suspected that betrayal was a huge theme for this
group of campers in the past, but maybe it applied to the present too. My time with Lorenzo hadn't been as relaxing as I'd
hoped.

* * *

Most people living in Key West have very small yards, ranging
from postage stamp–size to nonexistent. There wasn't enough
real estate for the people living on the island to spread out. Several of the other islands up the Keys, on the other hand, had
more space. Homes were less expensive outside of Key West,
and thus more property could be acquired. I found Ned's ex's

address in the notes the PI had given to me and punched it into my phone's map app.

"Now what's the plan?" Miss Gloria asked once we were in the car. "I assume you've already been in touch with her about a visit?"

Actually, I hadn't. I hadn't had time to figure out the details. "No," I said. "We're winging it. I'll introduce us and tell her that I was one of the people who found Ned, and then hope she invites us in."

Miss Gloria made a face. "That's not much of a plan. How about you call her and tell her that we're driving through and that we've been involved in Ned's murder case. Ask her if she will talk with us for a few minutes."

I had to admit she was right. The homes on Sugarloaf Key were off the beaten track, not the kinds of places you could drive up to and pretend you had been happening by. An appointment would be better. I scrolled through the information I'd been collecting on my phone and dialed her number.

After explaining how I'd been the one to find her ex, and that I'd been asked to look into a woman's disappearance from the old days, I ended with a plea that she give us a few minutes to talk to her. "We're looking for background information, mostly, from someone who knew him well, the good and the bad. No one seems to have leads on his murderer, and others are now in danger."

She didn't sound happy about it, but she agreed to see us. Miss Gloria pumped her fist once I hung up. "Yes!"

Arden's home was located not far off the main road, tucked into a little peninsula. I knocked on the door and took a step back. A woman of indeterminant age answered, blond and well-kept, wearing subtle makeup that brought out the green of her eyes. I would have guessed early to midforties. Ned had been close to seventy.

I introduced the two of us and held out my hand, which she shook firmly. "Thank you so much for agreeing to see us. It's been a difficult week all around. I am certain it has been for you too."

"Yes," she said, "especially for my son." She ushered us into an open living space with soaring cathedral ceilings and ceiling fans everywhere.

"Oh my goodness, your home is stunning," said Miss Gloria.

"Let's go sit on the porch," she said. "We can catch a breeze off the gulf. Can I interest you in a glass of lemonade?"

"We'd love that," I said.

She pointed us to a sitting area overlooking the water. There was a boat launch behind her property where two motorboats were tethered, a pool with an umbrella inside of it for shady paddling, and an outdoor kitchen and dining area covered by a tiki roof. Closer to the house, there were lovely clay pots of herbs and vegetables, along with a key lime tree, a mango tree, and other tropical vegetation that I could not identify. Fifteen or twenty orchid plants had been wired onto the palm trees nearest the house. There were lounge chairs around the pool with blue cushions that matched the color of the water, and more places to sit or visit or read than I would know what to do with.

"I love my little houseboat," Miss Gloria said, "but this open space tugs on my heart. I bet she doesn't hear one siren, ever." She sighed and sank back into the cushions. "Luckily, I am not a greedy person."

"No, you are not," I said with a laugh. "You are the least aspirational person I know. Besides, think about how far you'd have to drive to see your friends or even pick up groceries. And how much time you'd have to spend cleaning instead of playing mah-jongg. Who would take care of the grounds and the pool? Neither one of us knows how to drive a boat."

She was laughing hysterically by the time I finished my list of chores. I blew her a kiss and turned to gaze at the kitchen, which had pale quartz countertops below blue cabinets, an enormous double stainless refrigerator, and a six-burner gas stove. Never mind the boats and other water toys, it was big kitchens that I pined for, even though I loved my houseboat kitchen completely.

"You could cook for an army in there," Miss Gloria whispered. "I hope she entertains."

The woman returned with a tray of lemonade and a small plate of sugar cookies. "Don't get your hopes up too high. I don't bake," she said, adding a polite smile.

"Thank you." I took a sip of the lemonade and settled the glass on a coaster. "We were hoping you might have some insights into Ned, and possibly how he ended up dying in the tragic way that he did."

"I don't know that I can help. Ned and I weren't married that long, just long enough to produce my son. As you know, that can happen quickly." She flashed a faint smile. "We lived together a couple more years after he was born. It was long enough to realize we would be miserable staying together. So, I can't really answer questions about the good old days, which I don't think were all that good in the end." She gazed out at the horizon. "The wife that came before me invited the four of us

173

exes to lunch about a year or two ago, once it became clear that my marriage to Ned wasn't going to work out either."

Miss Gloria nearly choked on her drink. "Yowsa. What was the point of that?" she asked. "Were you going to share poison recipes?" It took everything I had not to burst out laughing.

Arden looked hard at her, but then her glare softened into a tentative smile. "You're not far from the truth. Once we began talking, I regretted having gone. All it did was stir up the worst memories and confirm that my judgment was suspect. Ned wasn't a terrible person, but he was limited. He knew how to give a lady a rush of attention, but once he had what he'd gone after, he got bored. He was a lot better at thinking about himself than thinking about the people he supposedly cared for. I felt a little bad about sending him back to that ramshackle motel, but not bad enough to change my mind."

"I'm sorry," I said. "What a disappointment." I couldn't help but wonder if this lovely home we were sitting in had been bought with his money or hers. He couldn't be making too much money from the motel. Why in the world had she married him in the first place?

Arden was studying my face. "In case you're wondering why I'd marry a man with such a lousy track record, the answer is I wanted a child. He was all for it at first, because he wanted me. But he hadn't learned much from his experience."

"Four wives is a lot," added Miss Gloria. "Didn't Mr. Hemingway have four as well?"

"He was hardly a Hemingway," Arden said. "He was a very bright man with a lot of musical talent who hadn't used any of it well. He lusted over what others had, and he always wanted to be younger than he was. His first wife, Nora, threw him out because he spent so much time with a bunch of teenagers, smoking pot and drinking beer. Probably angling to get laid. He was always so sorry when he got caught, but then it happened again. And again. I may be hopeful, but I'm not stupid."

"Uh-huh," said Miss Gloria, wagging her head in sympathy. "Were there more infidelities while he was married to you?"

"He was shameless," she said.

"When you heard about his murder, did you have any thoughts about who might have been that angry with him?" I asked.

"Not really," she said. "The sheriff's deputies asked the same thing. His modus operandi was more death by a thousand cuts.

"Nora was probably the most enraged of all of us, but I can't fathom why she'd stab him now. She wasn't going to get any more money from him, and she certainly wasn't in love with him anymore. He broke her heart years ago. At this point, I'd say her rage is more embers than flames."

"Was it because of someone from Big Pine Key camp?" I asked.

"Apparently. According to Nora, all the men—including our Ned—were in love with one girl. She must have been something."

"Probably Veronica," I said, glancing at Miss Gloria. "The girl who went missing." I paused for a moment, wondering whether to push her. She did not seem fragile. "Do you think Ned himself was capable of murder?"

She looked out through the screens to the water, watching a large fishing boat glide by toward the Straits of Florida. "I can't imagine that," she said. "He was kind to our boy, when he bothered to spend time at home." Her eyes glistened with tears. "I've sent him up to stay with my parents in Miami for a few weeks so he doesn't have to deal with me or the gossip about Ned."

"We should leave—we've intruded into your grief long enough," said Miss Gloria. She stood up, slugged down the rest of her lemonade, wrapped two cookies in a napkin, and tucked them into her pocketbook. "These are delicious, by the way. I would never undersell what I serve to company—not everyone can cook like our Hayley." She was smiling kindly, like a wise elder statesman advising a youngster. "Do you mind if I hit your powder room on the way out?"

"Of course not. It's the second door on the left."

"She's a pip, isn't she?" I said as she disappeared down the hall. "I've lived next door to her for years, and she's still full of surprises." I paused, thinking we hadn't gotten much from Arden. I made one more try. "Do you remember any of the exes mentioning a girl named Catherine? Most likely, his first wife might know her name because she orbited that camp. She was connected to those people whether she wanted to be or not."

Arden shook her head and stood up. "Sorry, the name isn't familiar."

Maybe this was a dead end. After all, maybe his death had nothing to do with Catherine or Veronica or any of them.

Miss Gloria came out of the powder room and stopped in front of a display of photos on the wall that I'd not noticed. I stood as well, and we walked over to join her.

"This must be Ned, with your son," Miss Gloria said. "Both so handsome and happy. Oh, and look at this one," she added. "Your husband was a musician!"

"Yes," Arden said. "He played the ukulele before the ukulele got cool. Everyone and his dog took it up over the pandemic."

I nodded and leaned in closer. "So this is Ned, and this fellow is?" Of course, I knew exactly who it was, but I wanted to hear what she would say.

"That's Arthur Combs. I suppose you could call him Ned's closest friend. He's a veterinarian now, and he was part of the original gang. The leader of the pack, I think."

"Was there any conflict between them?"

"Not that I knew of," she said. "He seemed to be a good influence on my husband."

Then I noticed Susanne lurking in the background of the picture looking kind of googly-eyed at Arthur.

"Who is this?"

Arden said, "That's Susanne. She was part of the original gang too. She's a chef now. She was a soft touch. Ned always said if you wanted to know something secret, you would go to her because everyone told her about their heartbreaks and hopes; and yet, if somebody pressed on her the least little bit, she spilled it all."

Miss Gloria peered at the next photo, which was faded and a little blurry. There was Arthur again, and Susanne, but this time Catherine, Veronica, and Ginny were included. Susanne and Catherine were gazing at Arthur. Ginny gawped at Veronica. Veronica looked straight at the camera.

"The middle two are the missing girls," I said, tapping the frame.

Arden squinted at the details but shook her head. "I never met either of them, sorry."

"Is that a bale of marijuana I spy in the background?" asked Miss Gloria.

"Probably," Arden said. "These islands have always been a haven for drug running, both back in those days and now. Ned never was opposed to using what washed ashore. Or selling, for that matter. It was a constant source of disagreement between us, once our boy arrived."

Then she added, "He really wanted to be one of those kids. Even in the past few years, it sometimes felt like being married to a fifteen-year-old boy—all hormones and no sense of responsibility. Something back then was the tipping point. He seemed clueless about what exactly it was, but I don't think he was surprised that the deputies came in and cleared everything out."

We thanked Arden again for meeting with us and exited to the car. "I think we have time to nip up to the Square Grouper, if you have it in you," I said to my friend. "I'd like to chat with Susanne again. I want to ask her about what the private investigator told me, that Arthur Combs should take the fall."

"Oh, I do have it in me," she said.

As we buckled our seatbelts, I couldn't suppress a niggling worry that Miss Gloria might be starting to lose her marbles. I should expect it, as she was in her eighties, but I didn't welcome it.

"You probably think I'm losing it," said Miss Gloria as she leaned back against the passenger headrest. "But there's a method to my madness. I noticed the wall of photos on the way in, but I couldn't think how to study them and then quiz her without appearing intrusive. That's when stuffing the cookies in my pocketbook and using the powder room occurred to me. Who could say no to a demented old lady?" She snickered, glancing over at me.

"Amazing," I said, shaking my head. "You are amazing."

Once we pulled into the restaurant's parking lot, I wondered aloud, "Should we go through the front of the house or go around and knock on the kitchen door?"

"Back door," said Miss Gloria, grinning. "You're always going to get a better look at what's really happening by going in the back door."

I parked, and we walked around the dumpster behind the restaurant and knocked on the screen door. The smells of fish and rotting onions wafted toward us from the trash while we waited. Susanne appeared at the screen, looking surprised to see us and not at all pleased.

"I know you're getting ready for dinner tonight, and we won't keep you, but I thought of one important question that I forgot to ask. Could we possibly come in for a minute?"

She glanced behind her where four people in white aprons were chopping and frying. Then she stepped outside to stand on the stoop.

Okay, she felt more comfortable not being overheard. That was important information right there. "I keep going back to the night before Veronica disappeared, wondering whether there was something everyone missed. You described a little about that night, but what about the next morning? Did anyone act different? Were people worried about Veronica? Did anyone else disappear, perhaps a friend who decided to go north with her?"

"I already told you. There'd been a lot of drinking, even more than usual, so everyone was hung over. I can't remember whether it was that day or the next that the deputies showed up and told us we had to go." She sighed and brushed at a red stain on her apron. "I was relieved, to tell you the truth. Maybe I wasn't alone in feeling that either."

I studied her face, wondering how hard we'd have to push before she told us something new. She hadn't said anything about the night in question. "I've been in touch with a private investigator who was hired to look for Veronica once Catherine returned home to Michigan. He remembered her saying that the whole mess was Arthur's fault, and so he should take the blame. Do you know what Catherine meant by that?"

The chef looked sick to her stomach. "I have absolutely no idea. I have a kitchen full of dinners to prep." She spun around and stepped through the screen door, which banged hard behind her.

"Well," said Miss Gloria as we headed back to our car, "so much for her being a pushover."

"She's must've played a part in the incident, though, don't you think? She acted too strange. Either she had something to do with Veronica's disappearance or—"

"Maybe it was Arthur," Miss Gloria interrupted. "She could be trying to protect him because she's always been in love with him, even though her adoration never was returned on his side. Oh, he was very fond of her, for sure, and he admired her earth mother qualities. And my guess is that they did sleep together, but the sparks did not continue to fly once Veronica arrived. He fell hopelessly in love. Or lust, anyway."

I laughed, sliding into the driver's seat. "You should write one of those breathless romance series, or a Hallmark movie. How surprised your readers would be to find out you're eighty-something years old."

"What?" Miss Gloria asked, straightening her shoulders. "Old ladies can't be sexy and yearn for love?"

I flashed her a grin. "The problem is, we need to talk to Arthur again, but I don't think we can get away with another emergency pet vaccination story," I said. "Besides, this is Saturday. No self-respecting veterinarian works on a Sunday."

"Maybe it's time to turn everything you know over to the authorities and assume they're as smart as we are," said Miss Gloria as she drifted off into a catnap.

1978

Catherine

Deputy Ryan Lopez had a lot of questions after I reported the disappearance.

"Did your friend have any enemies?"

"Not exactly, but sort of."

"Meaning?"

"Meaning she was a tease, and she flitted from guy to guy. Of course, some of them got upset when they were dumped. She was so beautiful and so much fun." I hated that I was starting to talk about her in the past tense.

"Is it possible that she had decided to leave of her own accord and not bothered to tell anyone?"

"It's possible," I said, "but not likely. Her stuff was all scattered around our tent, including the rabbit."

"The rabbit?" he asked.

I remember laughing. It was something she'd had since she was a kid, a lucky talisman. She would never leave it behind. In fact, that ugly thing sat in the front seat between us as we drove south. The fur was worn off so that only the bare leather was left, and one of the ears was missing. The eyes were nothing but balls of brown thread. It smelled to high heaven. But she slept with that thing every night. Every night that she was in the tent, that is. I explained that she would not have left the bunny behind. She could come across like a mean girl, but deep inside she was soft like everyone else. I started to cry again.

"I'll be in touch if I have more questions," the deputy had said.

Later that night after dinner, Arthur asked me where I'd gone when I got home from work. His face was hard like he was angry, and he knew exactly what I'd done. Susanne was standing behind him, wringing her hands and looking worried.

'I went to the Sheriff's Office and told the deputy that Veronica is missing. I don't know what happened to her. I have a terrible feeling about this.'

Almost exactly two hours later, four Sheriff's Office cruisers pulled up around the entrance to the camp, shining their headlights into the camp. The deputies got out of the cars, looking fierce, their belts bristling with guns and tasers. Deputy Ryan Lopez had a megaphone. He cleared his throat and then put it to his lips.

"You people are trespassing on private property. Per the sheriff of Monroe County, you need to pack up and move out. You are not the kind of people that we want on our island. You have twenty-four hours to gather your belongings and clear out. Meanwhile we will be interviewing all of you about the missing girl."

Then they moved into the campground and spoke with people individually.

Chapter
Twenty-Three

"Beryl sat down next to me and bent in to smell the cin-
namon roll. 'That's a good scent, isn't it?'
'Yes,' I said. It was the fragrance of love."
—Barbara O'Neal, *The Starfish Sisters*

Danielle had arranged for a late afternoon of beauty for her bridesmaids and maid of honor at the Pier House Spa. That meant facials, massages, and a group yak session with champagne and snacks around the pool. To be honest, I would have liked to spend these hours at home relaxing, but I was sure I'd enjoy the event once I arrived.

The receptionist greeted me, pointed me to the ladies' lounge, and gave me a gift bag containing sample-size beauty potions, a robe, and slippers. After I changed, an aesthetician cleaned my face with a key lime salt scrub and applied a thick paste of something that smelled like blueberries.

"It'll take five years off your skin, so you'll look dewy and glowing in the wedding photos," she promised after she'd painted on the final touches of goop. She directed me toward the indoor dipping pool to join the others. I shuffled out, dressed in a white terry cloth robe and with blue paste on my face, exactly like the rest of the bridal attendants.

After greeting everyone, I perched on a lounge chair and scrolled through my Instagram feed while listening to the ladies chat. Danielle removed a slice of cucumber from her right eye and said, "Hayley, you're so quiet. Is everything okay?"

I smiled with reassurance. "Sorry. I've had a busy day and I have a lot to think about."

"Oh, the murder," Danielle said. "Jeremy is a little disappointed that he'll be off duty next week. He really wanted to be in on the solution."

"He won't want to skip his own honeymoon, though," I said with a chuckle. Danielle had chosen spring in Paris as her dream destination, and I'd helped her make reservations for a special dinner every night. Choosing restaurants, after all, was one of my superpowers. "Has he said anything more about the case?"

"Only the usual, following all leads, etc., etc. He realizes that I'm with the press now, so he has to be careful about what he shares." She let loose a peal of laughter.

I snickered too at this description of her role at *Key Zest*. I wasn't sure Palamina would agree.

"I'm pretty sure they think the murderer is the woman who disappeared from the Gardens Hotel," Danielle added. "Did you know they found her fingerprints all over the crime scene?"

I knew, but I couldn't wrap my mind around how it had happened or when she could've gone up the Keys to do it. Would she have asked an Uber driver to wait ten minutes while she plunged the scissors into the man's back? One question nagged at me: Why would she kill Ned? I was getting increasingly annoyed that Catherine had dragged me into an ugly and confusing situation and then evaporated completely.

Brooke, Danielle's best friend from high school and her maid of honor, piped up. "I know, let's all give our best advice about what makes a good marriage. Hayley, why don't you start? You've been married the longest. I bet it feels like forever, right?"

I took a deep breath and let it out slowly, transitioning my thoughts from murder to marriage. "I still feel like a newlywed," I said, grinning. "But it has been a couple of years. With ups and downs, of course." I rolled this over in my mind for a minute, wanting to offer something real and useful to my friend. "The biggest mistake I made at the beginning was to take up *everything* with my Nathan. Why was he a little late? How did he feel about such and such? Why didn't he want to spend more time with my mother? And on and on."

I took Danielle's hand and gave it a squeeze. "Remember to give the marriage time to breathe, and your guy too. Give him some air. Looking back, I think that we had some struggles because we were both nervous about deciding to get married. Maybe we had unrealistic expectations about spending every minute together." I laughed. "That was true for me, not necessarily him."

"Ooh, such good ideas," said Brooke. "Anything else?"

I thought back to the advice I'd been given before I got married. I hadn't always taken it in that moment, but I'd remembered it. "One more thing. My psychologist friend, Eric, always tells couples to remember that it's not only one marriage, but it's a series of marriages that change over the years as the couple does. The important thing is to nurture your love all the way through and adjust as needed. Come to think of it, Steve Torrence, the minister who married us, said the very same thing."

"Thank you," said Danielle, blowing me a kiss. "That brings tears to my eyes."

Brooke giggled. "Wow, your advice is so deep," she said. "Mine's a little simpler, and we've only been married a year. My hubby likes it if I greet him at the door from time to time wearing a roll of Saran Wrap and nothing else. I never warn him in advance, so it keeps him on his toes."

The women burst out in hysterical laughter and chatter. The busyness of the week was catching up to me, so I closed my eyes and almost drifted off to sleep. We were called back into the spa to have our blue beauty masks removed. While the other women were tussling over where to go for dinner, I got dressed, hugged Danielle, and headed home.

On the way, I had a text from Nathan; he was still at the bachelor party with Danielle's fiancé. ETA 8:00 PM. "Go ahead and eat," he said. "I'll forage later."

I took care of Ziggy and Evinrude, then collapsed onto the chaise lounge on the deck with a glass of wine, thinking about the events of the week, ticking through the various possibilities yet one more time. I checked my phone. Still no return calls from either of the drivers whose names I'd gotten from the clerk at the Gardens Hotel.

Then I began mulling over the marital advice that Brooke had given. What would Nathan think if I showed up at the door in a roll of Saran Wrap? First, Houseboat Row was crowded with floating homes and other boats. Pretty much everyone knew everyone else's business. News of my see-through outfit would spread like a norovirus on a cruise ship. Second, I could only imagine Nathan thinking I had lost my marbles. He was passionate, for sure, but also very, very private.

My stomach rumbled. I'd nibbled on a few hors d'oeuvres at Danielle's party, but not anything you could really call dinner. My mind drifted toward waffles. I'd salivated over them twice in the last two days: Miss Gloria's waffles and fried chicken, and Lorenzo's Belgian waffle. The universe was trying to tell me something. I thought it would work out better to meet Nathan at the door with waffles rather than Saran Wrap. That was more my style. His too.

I found the waffle iron that we'd received as a wedding gift several years ago tucked at the back of a low cabinet. I pulled it out, along with ingredients for cottage cheese oat waffles. The recipe would make too many, but I could freeze the leftovers so we'd have them for breakfast or a last-minute dinner. I would skip the fried chicken this time, instead choosing yogurt and strawberries with a swirl of maple syrup as a topping. Dinner and dessert all wrapped up in one sweet but high protein package.

Ziggy rushed to the door woofing when Nathan arrived home a little after eight thirty. I greeted him too, then poured a half cup of batter into the hot iron and pulled the yogurt from the fridge. When the waffle was golden and fragrant and loaded with toppings, I settled the plate on the small table in the kitchen and sat across from my husband.

"You look tired," I said.

"It's been a long week," he admitted. "I probably shouldn't have had the second beer either. How was your night?" Nathan asked.

"Pleasant enough," I said. Then I told him how the brides-maids had shared a few words of marital advice, ending with

Brooke's suggestion. We both started to laugh. When I stood up to collect his plate, he pulled me close and gave me a good kiss. "But you could try me one day. Right now, what I need most is a shower."

After I'd cleaned up the kitchen, I looked into the bedroom. Nathan was sound asleep. Not quite ready to turn in myself, I took my laptop out to the deck. It was still warm and humid, but a slight breeze had kicked up, so the mast on the sailboat up the row clanked, and Mrs. Renhart's wind chimes tinkled. I could not keep the questions about Catherine, and Ned's death, and Veronica's disappearance back in the seventies out of my mind.

For sure, Susanne knew more than she was willing to tell us. For sure, Arthur should be interviewed again. I would also like to talk to Ginny, the waitress. She saw a lot from her place on the sidelines. I guessed that she'd been too young to have Veronica's confidence with men, and since she didn't actually live there, she'd probably not been involved in the worst of times in the camp. Whatever those might have been. But she would have noticed a lot. I wished I had time to go back to Big Pine Key to interview her again, even though she hadn't been that forthcoming up to this point. Pointing a finger at her about Catherine's disappearance or Ned's murder would not help.

Deputy Ryan Lopez was another person who'd held back. But I didn't see how I'd have time to drive up the keys again until the middle of next week. Besides, he was professionally trained and cagey about sharing information—what more would he tell me? Hopefully, by then, the authorities would have wrapped up the whole situation and arrested whoever needed to be arrested and put the fears of the locals on Big Pine Key to rest as well.

I typed Catherine's full name into the search bar, thinking it might help if I knew more about what she'd been writing over the past ten years, or even longer. As she'd told me on the first day I met her, she had dozens of publications on various shades of toxic love. In my search, I found several of her articles, including "Healing the Wounds of Toxic Love," "How to Say No to an Abusive Relationship," "Poisonous Love: How to Recognize and Confront Toxicity." And then this one: "How a Toxic Family Can Poison Future Relationships." This surely had to do with Hemingway, and maybe Veronica, but I wondered if it applied to Catherine as well? The next link really grabbed my attention: "The Mother Wound: How to Identify and Escape from Toxic Love in Your Family."

I clicked on that title. Catherine had begun the article with a quote from Hemingway's third wife, Martha Gellhorn, about how a woman should know better than to marry a man who hates his mother. That was followed by another quote from Gellhorn's letters: "Deep in Ernest, due to his mother, going back to the indestructible first memories of childhood, was mistrust and fear of women."

Somehow this was related to the 1978 campground and the recent murder and the disappearances—now two—that had ensued. Feeling a wave of exhaustion, I glanced at my watch. It was getting late and tomorrow night's wedding party would be even later. Before shutting down the computer and heading off to bed, I texted the private investigator, Simon Landry.

I'm wondering what you might know about Catherine's family? Their psychology, I mean.

Chapter
Twenty-Four

"This was such honest, warming food, served by such a dif-fident man. I couldn't work him out at all."
—Jenny Colgan, *The Summer Skies*

Simon Landry called me the next morning as I was having coffee on the deck. "I phoned Catherine's family home after you messaged me. Her parents have passed away, leaving only the younger sister. There was no love lost between the two of them. She has not heard from her, though she said this isn't unusual. They could go months without speaking."

"But did she seem worried?" I asked.

"Not much," he said. "There was a lot of dramatic sighing. I asked if she cared to spell out what the trouble was between them. She said not really, but Catherine was always jealous of her. Was it her fault that she got the looks *and* the brains in the family? Then she got on a roll, saying they'd really fallen out when Catherine wrote an article about the family."

"An article about the family?"

"I think she called it—"

"'The Mother Wound?'" I asked.

He laughed. "I should have figured you found it already. You'd make a fine PI. According to the sister, Catherine didn't use their names, but she described them in such detail that it wouldn't have been difficult to identify members of the family."

"Did she describe the family dynamics any further?"

"She said that their father was distant and uninvolved, but their mother encouraged competition. She admitted that it may have gone too far and that she herself definitely felt like the favorite."

"Does she remember Catherine leaving home in 1978? Did she ever meet Veronica?" The questions tumbled out of my mind, faster and faster.

"She said their mother didn't like any of the plans Catherine made for after graduation—she was very critical, saying things like 'This is what we get for paying for your education?' and 'I knew you'd never amount to much,' and so on. The sister doesn't remember meeting Veronica, but she does remember the girl's father coming to the house after she disappeared from the commune. He was furious and blamed Catherine for everything."

I thanked him for this help, and we made promises to stay in touch. Considering what Simon Landry had learned from Catherine's sister, it didn't seem a stretch to me that her interest in toxic love began with her own family. As Sam said during his birthday dinner, when given free rein, many writers seemed to write the same story over and over in different forms, working out a knotty personal issue as they wrote. Even if you didn't think you were revealing your personal psychology and opinions, most writers were painting a picture of themselves through the subjects and words they chose.

My themes seemed to be centered around food as a language of love and family. Readers had pointed out in my reviews that I tended to prefer homier, simpler meals and rarely visited and reviewed the fanciest and most expensive places on our island. I wanted the food I described to be accessible to most people, and I wanted families to come together over their meals. I hadn't quite figured out why I chose what I did, but I was sure the meaning was in there. For sure, I was a product of a broken family, and that had always left me sad, yearning to piece things back together.

I turned my thoughts back to the cast of characters at the mangrove camp. Were they all running from problems in their family life? Clearly Veronica and Catherine had them in spades. I hadn't learned enough about either Susanne or Arthur Combs to understand what drove them.

And what drove one of these people to one murder, possibly two? Love, lust, loathing, lucre. Those were the motives that PD James insisted encompassed all the possibilities for a murderer. Minus, of course, mental illness, which should not be discounted, although none of the people we'd interviewed obviously fit into this category. There had been other people camped out in the mangroves too, but they were apparently not still in the area and didn't seem to be major players.

I pushed myself to bring up the details of our first interview with Ginny at the No Name Pub. I was pretty sure she'd described Arthur as pathetic and Susanne as a nag. Was Ginny telling a story that didn't exactly match up with the others? I'd have to go back through my notes. It would have been even better if I had Catherine in front of me to compare notes, but I didn't.

A Poisonous Palate

After coming to zero conclusions, I began to scroll through Facebook. Sometimes the local groups shared information that even the authorities weren't privy to. Forget Twitter and Threads and Instagram or any of the other current social media apps—the Key West locals ran on Facebook gossip. I checked in with several groups but found nothing new.

Then I noticed that today was open house day at the Monroe County Sheriff's Animal Farm. Farmer Jeanne (a deputy who cared for the animals) and Dr. Arthur Combs would be on duty talking about how the animals ate, where they came from, why they landed in the Florida Keys, and necessary veterinary care. Arthur would help introduce the newest animal, a capybara named Simon. Simon was a large barrel-shaped rodent with shaggy hair. He'd drawn a lot of attention when he moved into the animal farm. The open house was a stroke of luck. I'd always meant to visit the little sanctuary underneath the Stock Island detention center and if I went early, maybe Arthur would answer a few more questions.

I drove north to Stock Island at 11:45 so I could be first in line and hopefully get a few minutes with the veterinarian before he was mobbed with kids. The farm was located beneath the jail, which was raised up eleven feet to meet hurricane standards, leaving parking and other space below. Animals in need of fostering had been arriving since 1994. I was greeted at the entrance by a uniformed deputy. Inside, I saw Farmer Jeanne, the main caretaker of the animals, showing some children one of the newer additions, a skunk named Squirt.

"He has been de-scented," she explained, "so no one will get sprayed and go home stinking of skunk."

The kids roared with laughter and pushed forward to stroke the little animal. I moved past them, quickly admiring the small ponies, a tortoise worthy of a position in the Galapagos, a hybrid crocodile with a gorgeous checkerboard pattern, and Juju the hedgehog, bristling with whiskers all over. At the back of the farm underneath an awning, Dr. Arthur Combs was examining a large sloth with the help of a jail trustee in an orange uniform. I remembered Nathan telling me that the most reliable inmates were promoted to do outside work, including animal care at this farm. I could imagine that this was a very popular position since it was an opportunity to get out of the concrete prison and into the real world.

The trustee carried off the sloth, and I hurried forward to catch a word with Dr. Combs. His face fell when he saw me, but he quickly changed his expression with a smile.

"Welcome to the zoo," he said, gesturing toward the array of cages. "Have the authorities located Catherine or found Ned's murderer?"

"Neither," I said, thinking that he probably knew the answers to those questions. Since he was working at a Sheriff's Office facility, wouldn't he have asked someone these very things right away? "That's why I'm here. I talked with Ned's most recent ex-wife, Arden, yesterday."

He looked genuinely sad. "She's a nice person, and their son is adorable. I told Ned he ought to try to work things out rather than run away from problems, but I don't suppose it was in his nature. He was a good friend, but not a good husband." He paused, one hip leaning against the table where he'd been examining the sloth. "Why were you visiting Arden?"

"I hoped that she might have some insight into Ned and why he was killed, and I thought maybe she'd heard things about Veronica's disappearance that others had not."

"Did she?" He quirked one eyebrow as though he thought it doubtful. "That was a long, long time ago, and she probably wasn't even born."

"No, but spouses talk." I narrowed my eyes. "She said she thought all the men in the camp, including Ned, were in love with one girl. That would probably mean you too, right?"

He cleared his throat and tucked a flyaway strand of gray-blond hair behind his ear. "She was a very attractive girl and knew how to make the most of what she had. More than that, she was flirtatious and knew how to play one person off against another. To be honest, I was infatuated for a time, even though the wiser part of me saw through her."

"Were you involved with her?"

He shook his head, staring me down.

Whether I believed him or not, this was as much as he was going to say on the subject. "We also talked with Susanne again," I told him.

"For what reason?" Now he looked genuinely appalled.

"I'm trying to get a better sense of exactly what happened the night before Veronica disappeared because I believe it might be connected with both Ned's murder and Catherine's disappearance."

I waited him out until he finally spoke.

"That night, we all drank too much and, against my better judgment, smoked some of the marijuana that Billy and Peter brought in on their boat that day. If the details are fuzzy, that explains it. The next day, Veronica was missing. Susanne agreed with Catherine that we should report it to the authorities. I did not."

"Why not?

"Because Veronica had worked everyone in the camp into a frenzy, turning friends against each other. She had ruined the sense of community that we'd built. It made total sense that she'd split—there was no one left to conquer. This mirrored what had happened with her family of origin, she left them in ashes too. We'd talked enough over the weeks leading up to this that I could see the parallels." His voice sounded bitter but also sad. "Besides that, I knew what the outcome would be. Unfortunately, I was right. Catherine went to the Cudjoe Sheriff's Office substation and reported her tentmate's absence. I'm fairly certain she also told them about the drugs, although to be fair, they weren't a big secret since Ginny's father was a customer. That night, the authorities cleared out the whole camp, which was probably for the best."

I felt my frustration building. Why was it that all these people were only willing to tell the smallest bones of the story? "Before she vanished, Catherine told me that you should've been the one to take the fall. Do you know anything about that? Do you know what she meant?" I waited to see how he would react, sort of expecting that he would calmly explain it all away. All along, he'd presented himself as the wise man, not getting sucked into other people's drama.

But instead, he got angry. "That's not fair," he said through gritted teeth. "It's not fair at all. I did my best to act like an adult when no one else would even try, and yet I still got blamed for the problems. At least Ned took me as I was, same as I did him. Neither of us were perfect, but we tried to be good enough. Now if you'll excuse me, we have a lot of children who've come today to meet our new resident capybara."

A line of kids had begun to form behind me, jostling for a chance to talk to the vet and see the new guy. I wasn't sure how much time I had left with him. I was guessing only a little. Actually, none. I lowered my voice so the children wouldn't overhear.

"Did you have a relationship with Susanne during those months in the camp?"

"We certainly had a relationship. We were friends," he said through gritted teeth.

"I hate to be intrusive, but I feel like I must ask, not lovers?"

"You *are* intrusive, and I can't see why that's any of your business."

Color flushed his stony face, and then he turned to help the trustee who'd returned with what looked like a giant though bristly guinea pig. Dr. Combs smiled at the first kid in line.

"This is Simon. Two things you might not know about capybaras: First, their closest animal relation is a guinea pig. Second, they are semiaquatic, meaning he loves the water. Look at his webbed feet . . ."

He appeared completely engaged, professional, and interested in both the kids and his animals. But for some reason I thought of the words to a song by Mary Hopkin, "Those Were the Days" . . .

1978

Catherine

After talking with Deputy Lopez, I went to work for a couple of hours, dragging my tired bones through the shift until I could get back to camp and go to bed. By the time I hitched a ride home from work, showered, and changed, most of the others were gathered around the campfire, except for Veronica, which surprised me. She was usually first in line for beer and chow. It was a relief too, if I was honest. She had a big personality, and everyone loved her, reminding me of my younger sister. I was feeling a little sheepish about making such a stink that she was missing. Part of me didn't really believe she was gone for good. She loved to make an entrance.

Arthur and Susanne were making dinner, and that meant vegetables. Yesterday we had roasted hot dogs on sticks, so today they insisted on something healthy. Susanne was telling everyone about their adventure rummaging through a dumpster just off Route 1. "Susanne found vegetables and declared them perfect for peppers and potatoes with eggs," Arthur said. "An Oklahoma omelet, she called it, just like her mama used to make."

Susanne blushed, and everyone could see how pleased she was to get his attention and approval. She'd been wound up so tightly the past couple days, but tonight she seemed relaxed and happy.

"Where's your roommate?" Arthur asked me.

I was pretty sure they'd had a fling a couple weeks ago, though after that Veronica had declared him a stick in the mud with a Jesus complex. That wasn't quite fair, in my opinion. I felt better with someone acting like they were the only grown-up in charge. I hadn't felt like this at first, but a lot could go wrong with a bunch of kids partying in the woods without any rules or any authority to enforce them.

I glanced around the circle, looking for who else might be missing. I'd been wasted when I crawled into our tent last night, so I honestly couldn't say whether she'd come home or not. By "home" I mean snoring alongside me in her sleeping bag. Ha! That reminded me of my father, which was not a happy memory.

"I don't know where she is," I said, leaving out the part where I'd spilled everything to the deputy. Maybe if I pretended nothing had happened, it would all be true. "Haven't seen her since yesterday. She was here for supper, right?"

"Have you ever seen her turn down a hot dog?" Ginny asked, pushing out her stomach as though she'd gorged. "I'm pretty sure she went into town after. She probably went home with some dude at the bar and now she's sleeping it off."

Chapter
Twenty-Five

"Armed with the strength of renewed commitment to each other, and a pair of forks, we reach out and choose the abundant sweetness that lies before us to erase the bitterness in the past."

—Stacey Ballis, *How to Change a Life*

E very detail of Danielle's wedding went like clockwork. Her figure-skimming gown was stunning, not too fluffy, and just the right amount of sexy. The hairdresser had shaped her blond mane into a mass of curls studded with a few white flowers and topped all that with Danielle's grandmother's veil. She beamed all the way through the service, her husband's eyes shone with adoration, and the sun dipped below the horizon at the exact moment that Reverend Torrence declared them husband and wife and invited them to kiss. The guests applauded, and I could feel the hope and the love circling around the new couple like heart-shaped glitter on an Instagram graphic. Maybe some couple among their friends and relations whose marriage was struggling would find hope in this moment. Or maybe someone lonely and alone would find the strength to keep looking for a partner who'd share their life. Feeling a rush of gratitude for Nathan's strong presence in mine, I reached for his hand, squeezed his fingers, and blew him a kiss. He squeezed back, grinning, and then I heard his phone buzz.

He glanced down at the screen and then leaned over to whisper, "Gotta go. It shouldn't take long. I'll meet you at the reception." He leaned over again to kiss me and tweak the peach-colored strap on my right shoulder. "You look adorable in that dress."

"Better than Saran Wrap?" I teased. Yet one more time, I thanked my lucky stars that Danielle had had the good grace to choose bridesmaids' dresses that didn't look like ruffled pink pup tents. After gathering up Miss Gloria and my mother and Sam, we drove from the beach to the Hemingway Home, with Miss Gloria chattering happily in the back seat about her wedding, and mine, and my mother's.

"Young people don't understand these days that it's not the production value of a wedding that matters, but rather it's the person you choose to spend your life with," she said. "You could get married in a closet, and all would be well if it was the right guy." We laughed because this had happened to my mother and Sam, and they couldn't be happier.

"It was an unusual setting," Sam admitted. "But it didn't cost a lot either. Our guest list was constrained by necessity."

I could picture the scene—the four of us, plus Steve Torrence and Nathan, all crammed into a walk-in closet the size of an elevator, clammy with sweat and fear, a hurricane raging and banging outside the apartment where we were hunkered. I barely knew Nathan back then, but even in that moment, I appreciated his calm presence. Even in those terrifying circumstances, I couldn't help noticing he was easy to look at.

Once we arrived at the Hemingway Home, Miss Gloria hurried off to find the ladies' room. I snagged a glass of champagne and followed a small group of guests into the building. Part of the joy of a reception at the Hemingway Home was the access to a private tour for any interested guests. While the tour guide launched into the opening description of the building's history, I wandered into the room across the hall from the living room. I'd first seen Catherine here, studying the photos on the wall. She was searching for something in Hemingway's family photographs that might unlock a mystery in her own past. I was sure of that. I just didn't know exactly what it could be.

I moved from photo to photo, looking for a new clue that might explain Catherine's preoccupation with the man and his wives. On one wall, a portrait of Hemingway dominated the middle, with photos of all four wives fanning out around him—Hadley, Pauline, Martha, Mary. Only Mary's photo— the wife who'd seen him through to his tragic end—included Hemingway himself. Another wall boasted pictures of his children, his fishing exploits, his travels, and multiple other social events. I thought again about the faded photos that had been posted years ago on the wall of the No Name Pub. Like Hemingway in his world, the missing Veronica appeared to be the center of that universe. I pulled out my phone and looked at the image I'd taken the other day when Miss Gloria visited the pub with me.

Ginny had identified each of the gang: Arthur, the dashing but serious leader; Susanne, the earth mother; Veronica, the siren and the beloved; Catherine, the gawky wannabe; Ned. Who was Ned to that group, anyway? Even Deputy Ryan Lopez hovered in the background, his expression both worried and fierce. Ginny herself stood a little distance away from the others, grinning widely—the sprite who was a little too young for this crowd in their early twenties. Now two of these people were missing, and at least one of them had been murdered.

I heard the loudspeaker out in the garden. The wedding planner was calling for guests to be seated. We found our places at the round tables set up under the tent on the lawn. Lorenzo was sandwiched in between my mother and Miss Gloria, looking dashing in a fawn-colored linen shirt and russet bow tie. Eric and Bill sat to my right and my mother's left, and Sam was on the other side of Nathan. I felt so grateful to be surrounded by my dearest and most beloved family and friends.

"Have you heard anything new about Catherine's case?" Eric asked as soon as everyone was settled.

"I've gotten lots of opinions, but nothing's been resolved. I'm certain the Sheriff's Office and the police department have the case firmly in hand." I smirked in Nathan's direction and then described my conversations with Susanne, Arden, and Arthur Combs. "Dr. Combs was quite annoyed with me for hounding him at the animal farm."

"Annoyed like he was guilty?" Bill asked.

I thought this over. "Hmm, it's possible. Oh, and the private investigator from Michigan who was involved in the case right after Veronica first went missing called me back today as well." I nodded at Eric and then Lorenzo in turn, as I'd discussed the PI with each of them. "I had noticed that much of Catherine's work is devoted to examining toxic love in families, including Hemingway's family. The PI was able to make a connection directly to her family. Apparently, her mother fostered an ugly competition between the sisters. That may have been partly why

Catherine decided to take off and head south with a girl whom she barely knew."

Miss Gloria said, "I bet you anything there's a parallel to those girls who were living in the commune. The centerpiece of the action seems to have been Veronica. She must've been a hot number. Everyone got their hormones stirred up and their knickers in a knot, and one of them apparently got them twisted tight enough to commit murder."

"Now that's a big leap, my dear," said Nathan, grinning.

But Lorenzo leaned forward, nodding vigorously. "All of your cards spoke of betrayal yesterday," he said to me, his expression grave. "I will not be at all surprised if Miss Gloria is right."

"But I adored that veterinarian," said Miss Gloria in a mournful voice. "I would be so sad if he turned out to be a murderer, especially since my T-bone liked him so well. That would mean we'd have to find another vet. Maybe it was Catherine herself—she wasn't going to win Miss Congeniality among that group. She killed Ned because he finally figured out that she'd offed Veronica back in the day, and now she's run away to avoid facing the consequences. Or maybe she killed him once she realized he'd killed her tentmate."

"Really?" I asked, looking at her. "Why in the world would she take that into her own hands? Unless he taunted her to the point where she lost her cool. But anyway, I don't think Ned killed Veronica," I said. "You heard it too—Arden, his fourth wife, said he wasn't a violent person. She seemed to understand him well, and she'd have no reason to lie to us, would she? She did say he was a serial cheater, for sure. Even though she was his fourth wife, he even cheated on her. Apparently, he wasn't capable of learning anything from past mistakes."

Nathan was shaking his head. "Four wives. That's excessive. One very lively, nosy wife is quite enough for me."

I snickered. "Actually, to be accurate, I am your number two wife."

He dropped his face to his hands. "You did have to call me on that, didn't you?" He lifted his head back up. "This old commune is not the only angle the authorities are considering. We're learning that Ned had a drug business on the side, and seedy, unsavory types are always drawn to that. Someone may have come to the motel figuring he had guns or drugs or money, or all of the above. We're pretty sure his business got started as early as the late seventies, when bales of marijuana frequently washed ashore. He wasn't the kind of man to leave an opportunity on the table."

"That confirms what Arden told us," I said.

"I can see it now," said Miss Gloria. "Someone comes into that dreadful motel to get paid, and Ned says he doesn't have the dough. He probably doesn't have any money because he has to pay alimony and child support to four different women. Then the dealer guy gets enraged and stabs him in the back with the scissors. It is possible. That scenario would be much more straightforward."

"Yes, it is possible, I suppose," I said. "That would make it simpler, wouldn't it? We could leave the rest to the authorities since they are proficient at tracking down career criminals, and we are not. It still doesn't answer the question of what happened to Catherine, and Veronica before her. It's like there's a black sinkhole on Big Pine Key." I tore off a small piece of buttered roll and chewed for a moment. "I still wonder why Catherine would decide to travel with a girl who reminded her of her sister, the very person she was trying to get away from."

Eric held up a finger. "Might I answer that? I've mentioned before that people repeat the trauma that they know because it's familiar. It can happen over and over and over as their subconscious attempts to master the experience. Sorry if I'm a broken record. It's difficult to break out of this cycle, unless the individual finds a good therapist who can help them recognize the pattern."

I knew that because he'd said the same thing in different words the other day. "Catherine didn't strike me as the therapy type," I said. "In fact, she's still repeating trauma through her writing, or she was up until three days ago."

Waiters dressed in crisp white shirts and black pants came to our table to deliver the food, and we moved on to lighter subjects. The dinner was delicious—I slid most of my steak over to Nathan and focused on the lobster tail—and the wine flowed generously. Toasts were made—sweet sorority girl stories for Danielle, dangerous rookie police officer stories for Jeremy. Danielle's father barely made it through a toast to his darling daughter and her new husband without breaking into tears. The wedding planner hurried up to pat his back and relieve him of the microphone.

"We will take a break for mingling and dancing," she announced, "and then return to our places for coffee and dessert. The bride has chosen profiteroles, in addition to the more traditional wedding cake. Profiteroles are puffed choux pastry stuffed with homemade ice cream and drizzled with homemade hot fudge sauce. You can choose coffee, vanilla, or chocolate ice cream. Meanwhile, enjoy the music!"

"Profiteroles!" my mother exclaimed. "How fancy and unusual. I'm glad she didn't ask me to bake all that choux pastry. I cannot wait to try one."

"Come, my princess, let's cha-cha some calories away," said Sam, holding his hand out to her and sweeping her off into a sprightly swing dance.

I stood up to stretch my legs and admire the cake, a glorious pale-pink, three-layer confection decorated with edible pearls, along with a collection of sand dollars, shells, and starfish. Two miniature white Adirondack chairs were perched on the very top of the cake, with *Mr.* and *Mrs.* written on the backs. Danielle had every intention of living out a traditional marriage to match the wedding, including hopes for a flock of children. Ready or not, Palamina was going to have to think about replacing her unless the journalism bug bit her hard and she decided to delay having a family.

I stood away from the tipsy crowd for a few moments, taking a breather from the breakneck pace of the past week. It was fun to watch Nathan joke and talk with the other officers, representatives from both the Key West Police Department and the Sheriff's Office—these were his people. As he sometimes reminded me, if I grumbled about his long hours or devotion to his colleagues, part of their bond came from their shared worldview. Something would always go wrong in the world, and it was their job and their duty to anticipate that and react to it before anyone was hurt. He tried to help new recruits understand how important their team of fellow officers would become. "To protect and to serve," he reminded them over and over. He was absolutely passionate about what he taught these young men and women. By now, I could have given the speech for him.

"Remember the most important rule: Keep your focus on doing things correctly, by the book, so that you go home safely at night along with the civilians. Remember that you will have more power than most people by virtue of your uniform and the privileges it conveys. Don't abuse that. Use it for the good of the people you serve. Don't even imagine you can get away with anything less than that. People are always watching."

Across the room, I spotted Darcy Rogers, who was wearing a glittery black dress that emphasized her square, solid shape. She saw me too and came bearing down on me, sparkling like a steamship at night.

"What a wonderful evening for a wedding," I said, hoping to keep things light.

She ignored the invitation for pleasant small talk. "Listen, I have gotten word that you are continuing to interview people connected with Ned Newman's murder. You need to back off the sleuthing and let the professionals do their job. Somebody's going to get hurt by your meddling, and it's likely to be one of us." She was jabbing a finger at me now, caught up in a lecturing loop about the dedication of the sheriff's deputies and how my interference with their work would only cause problems.

I waited for her to take a breath. "Thanks for the advice," I said, my jaw tightening. I had a million other comebacks in mind from reasonable to flat-out rude. But none of them would change her mind. She barreled off to join a cluster of deputies.

Had she not been such a pain, I might have passed along my new insight about the Hemingway/Veronica connection. As Hemingway was the center of his world, Veronica had been the center of hers. There were casualties along the way as Hemingway shucked off the skin of each of his marriages and moved on to a new life. I had to think that all the drama and disappointment damaged him as well as those around him. Was this also true of Veronica's circle? Whom had she left behind, seething quietly until the feelings led to murder, maybe both years ago and now? Or was it as simple as a drug deal gone wrong?

I shrugged away those gloomy thoughts. The band struck up "Try a Little Tenderness," and I went to find Nathan. He'd been romantic enough to propose to me while Key West blues legend Robert Albury was crooning that song on a pier overlooking the Gulf. Astonishingly enough, I learned later that he'd arranged the whole thing. He wasn't the kind of guy who'd want his wife displayed semipublicly in Saran Wrap, or even a guy who'd cut a rug in public.

But I knew he'd remember the song and agree to a slow dance tonight.

Chapter
Twenty-Six

"She laughed, an icy, uncanny sound. 'But it ruined all our lives, anyway, like drinking poison, every bloody day.'"
—Ragnar Jonassen and Katrín Jakobsdóttir, *Reykjavík*

The next morning, I was up early, but Nathan had already left for work. My head felt a little fuzzy from the late-night dancing and the more-than-usual number of flutes of champagne I'd enjoyed. I had drifted off to sleep, thinking of the lost loves in Big Pine Key. This morning, all the bits and pieces of what we'd learned circled through my mind. Much as I hated thinking of Chef Susanne this way, I could not get her yearning look in the photograph on Arden's wall out of my mind.

Ned too, seemed to be a searcher for love, never satisfied with what he had. And he'd had plenty. Why couldn't he have been happy with one of those women? Instead, he was obsessively aspirational with his marriages. Could he possibly have murdered Veronica because she spurned his advances? Might someone have realized this last week and murdered him in turn? Was Catherine the murderer? It seemed so extreme, and it seemed impossible that no one would have noticed the intensity of the feelings that he held for Veronica. I was beginning to think that the killer had to be Catherine, because of the way Simon Landry described her relationship with her younger sister. Veronica was too much like the sister Catherine had fled from. At some point, perhaps she could no longer tolerate the competition, and especially Veronica's taunting, and had to act.

Once again, I reviewed the photograph from the No Name Pub in my mind, thinking of the two people who orbited on the outside of this inner circle: Deputy Lopez and Ginny. Both were worth another visit. It puzzled me that the deputy hadn't looked harder for the missing woman over the years. I almost phoned him to ask about the revelation I'd had last night but remembered that he started most days with his old pals. He had told us they spent most Monday mornings drinking coffee and shooting the bull, followed by lunch and a couple beers. He wouldn't answer the phone, and even if he did, he wouldn't answer my questions in front of an audience. I decided to drop in on him instead. Never mind what Darcy Rogers thought of my nosiness. I was invested in finding the answers in a way that I couldn't quite explain but also couldn't ignore.

I drove up the Keys to Big Pine and retraced the route I'd taken several times this week. There were a few trucks and several Jeeps, like the one I'd seen at Deputy Lopez's house, parked among several Monroe County Sheriff's Office vehicles. I paused inside the door to let my eyes adjust to the change in light. I spotted him across the room sitting with a knot of men, some in uniform, some in the casual clothes of the retired. Ginny was bustling around their table, joking with the guys, picking up empty glasses and plates, and delivering coffee refills. She waved hello when she saw me in the doorway. She held up a white mug as if to ask if I wanted coffee. I smiled and shook my head.

I wanted to talk to her again about what she remembered about those last days in the camp, but she wouldn't welcome my intrusion in the middle of another busy shift. Ginny was a watcher, someone who sat on the sidelines, drinking and probably smoking dope, but she was not necessarily in the thick of the drama among the campers. Maybe I'd come back when she got off work to interview her another time, although she hadn't been that forthcoming up to this point. She would not want any fingers pointed at her about Catherine's disappearance.

Instead, I waved at Deputy Lopez. He did not look happy to see me, but he stood up and stumped over to greet me.

"I'm so sorry to interrupt your morning, but I had a thought about those campers, specifically about the connection between Catherine and Veronica. I had to ask because you might be the only one to remember."

"You're like a dog with a fresh bone," he said, grimacing.

I grinned in response. "Yes, my husband says the same thing. I have to tell you, that girl's disappearance bothers me a lot. Why did no one really care what happened to her after she'd vanished?" I beckoned him to follow me to the wall of photos. He trailed along reluctantly.

"I thought of this because Catherine is studying Hemingway and his marriages, and there are a ton of photos at the Hemingway Home, sometimes with future wives and current wives in the same shot."

Deputy Lopez looked confused and annoyed. "Your point?"

"My point is that the relationships overlapped, exactly as it sounds like they did back in the day on Big Pine Key.

Veronica seemed to be the epicenter of most of the drama, and I can't believe there weren't strong feelings in the people she left behind once she moved on to a new love. Does this sound familiar?"

He didn't say no but crossed his thick forearms over his stomach, then sat on the bench facing the photos.

I took that as a sign to continue, so I explained how the pictures we were now looking at reminded me of those photographs posted on the walls at the Hemingway Home. "What troubles me is that, on the one hand, the campers seemed so close for a time. But on the other hand, no one really pushed to get help from the authorities when Veronica went missing." I paused to give him a chance to jump in, but he said nothing. "Now Ned turns up murdered, and Catherine is gone. I haven't heard a peep from her after she begged me to help. You haven't heard from her, have you?" Why would she contact him, really? But I asked anyway to see what he'd say.

"Nope, nothing on my end. The story is puzzling, all right. I told you I always wondered about Ned and Veronica. Whether they ever connected. But I don't think that's true. You knew if she'd chosen you."

He had that wistfulness in his voice again. I decided to wait to see what else he would tell me before asking anything more. He seemed softer, with a small smile on his lips, as though he'd made a connection in his mind with the good parts of those old days. He might be willing to tell me more about them if I was careful in how I asked.

"Were you there the night the sheriff's deputies came to throw out the group? I'd love to figure out what exactly happened. You didn't make the decision on your own, right?"

He frowned and stood up from the bench. I'd made a gaffe already, but I had to keep going. This could be my only chance.

"Maybe some neighbors complained about the cars coming in and out, and all the noise?" I asked. "I can believe that folks living nearby wouldn't be so thrilled about the so-called hippie commune."

He stood over me, squinting. "Nobody lived too close to the campsite. You've seen Big Pine. It's no Key West."

I nodded my agreement but pushed forward, babbling a little, hoping to get a better picture of exactly what happened on the night Veronica disappeared. "Were Ned and Arthur playing ukulele? Maybe it was a sing-along? I got the sense at the Green Parrot that they'd been playing together for years. They seem to have kept their musical connection right up until Ned was murdered."

"Nope." The deputy gestured for me to follow him outside the bar, and we both blinked in the sunlight like a couple of bears emerging from their shadowy dens into spring.

"I stopped to talk with Catherine on the side of the road earlier that day. Turns out she was headed to the station to report her roommate was missing. She couldn't get her car to start, and she was so hysterical that I picked her up and took her to the station to calm her down. I informed her that an adult couldn't be declared officially missing until they'd been gone for forty-eight hours. I asked her what it was exactly that made her worry that something nefarious had happened. She said that the night before, those kids were stoned and drunk out of their minds and half stripped naked, playing some kind of game. Veronica was the instigator as usual, and she was baiting all the guys and flaunting her success to the women."

He paused, studying the line of yellow cabins across the street from the restaurant. "Catherine said she didn't remember much else until she woke up the next morning, hungover. Veronica had not slept in their tent. Catherine thought she'd overheard people fighting, a man and a woman. The woman argued about something being wrong with someone, a major screw loose. She assumed she meant Veronica. Who else could it be?"

He heaved a big sigh and glanced at his watch. "I suspected Veronica was pitching another snit, maybe hiding out to scare people. But to be thorough, I agreed to investigate. I gave Catherine a ride to work and later interviewed some of the campers, but no one seemed to know anything. Several of them believed Veronica was getting antsy and was on the verge of leaving anyway."

Something wasn't holding together in his story. From what he'd told Miss Gloria and me, he'd spent a lot of time cruising the area around the camp and watching these people. Wouldn't he have known them better? "Are you sure this was only hearsay? You didn't see any of it happen the night before?"

His teeth were gritted, and he looked about to explode, so it surprised me a little when he continued to explain. "No! I didn't see it happen, but I knew the whole situation was headed downhill. I knew this could only have one ending, and it was going to be a bad one. Someone had to clean things up and make things safer for all of them and the Big Pine residents, and that was our job. Exactly as I said, when I got back from those interviews, I told my captain about the camp spiraling out of control, and he agreed it had to stop. He spoke with the sheriff, and later that evening, he sent a few of us in squad cars to drive over—no sirens, just lights."

I nodded, keeping my voice low and thoughtful. "So, what, you guys got out of your cars and announced you were with the Sheriff's Office, and then what?"

"We told them the sheriff wanted us to close the camp down," said Deputy Lopez. "And he did. He didn't mind turning a blind eye sometimes, but in this case, they'd overstayed their welcome by a lot."

"Did you and the others from the Sheriff's Office insist on taking Ginny and the other locals home? Is this part of what happened, parents had begun to complain about kids congregating here?"

"No," he said. "Most of those kids had their own cars, though they shouldn't have been driving around loaded and high. From time to time, one of us would stop them so they understood who was in charge." He fell silent for a minute. "I remembered something else after we talked last time. It's probably not related, but it was an oddity. Those kids were dedicated to the Gods of Love. I should have thought of this sooner, but for some reason I blocked it out. They kept a place that was something like an altar. It was back in the brush, a short way from the camp." Deputy Lopez swiped a hand over his forehead, pushing a few sprigs of gray hair out of the way.

"An altar?" I nudged, feeling a surge of excitement that came from finally getting close to an answer.

"Candles and beads and such. Someone had carved 'love me tender' into the stone top. Kids would put items from their love interests on the altar and say a prayer or something. This was supposed to attract the loved one, with the assistance of the universe. That's what one of them told me." He rolled his eyes, but he had described it so well that I had to wonder whether even he had snuck over one night and placed his own offering to the Gods of Love. "I remember that Veronica's hairbrush had been left on the surface right before she disappeared."

"A hairbrush?" I asked. "Any idea who left it there? Wouldn't she have taken it back? To brush her hair, I mean."

"No idea. You didn't take things back," he said, pinching his bottom lip between his fingers. "It was a sacred place to those kids, and nobody messed with it. I doubt they ever talked about what it really meant either. They were what you might call woo-woo." He made air quotes with his fingers. "I don't know who exactly they were praying to, maybe hoping the God of Good Sense would show up?"

He snickered, and I had to laugh along with him. I could totally picture this crowd—at least the girls—setting up a place to call in the unconscious to speak to their crushes.

"What did it mean if they placed something on this altar?" I asked, not wanting to assume I understood anything about those times.

He paused, squinting his eyes in a shaft of late morning sun that filtered through an umbrella on the nearby picnic table, making his face an unearthly blue color. "Like I said already, and mind you, no one put this in exactly these words, but I think that if they loved someone and wanted their love in return, they'd place something belonging to that person, or something representing that person, on the altar. The hairbrush was not subtle. That girl was hair proud. She tossed about all those golden curls when she was flirting." He chortled again, a laugh dry enough to start a brush fire.

"When the camp was cleared out not long after Veronica disappeared, you can imagine the trash that had been left behind. Everything those kids no longer needed they discarded as if the backcountry was a giant dump. Monroe County sent a front loader to scrape some of it into the ravine behind the camp and take the rest of it to the real dump on Stock Island. But that altar, it was back in the trees. I hadn't remembered it until now."

"You think it could actually still be there?"

"Could be," he said, squinting his eyes at me.

My excitement was mounting. "Could you point me in the right direction so I can see if anything's left?"

"You'd never find it on your own. In fact, there's probably not much left of it after forty years. But if you could persuade one of those experts to come down from Miami, maybe there'd be some DNA. Maybe your husband would have some pull. The authorities won't listen to me. They didn't listen to me back then, and there's no reason for that to change. They would have fired me if they could have. Somebody, I don't know who, complained that I was spending way too much time with those kids. Believe me, they were waiting for the smallest screw-up on my part. I was glad to see that mess cleaned up and those kids gone. They were a big cramp in my side."

I felt sorry for him, the way he felt like he'd dedicated his life to something that wasn't appreciated. He'd wasted his youth in that job. "I had a boss like that," I said, "only she wasn't quietly waiting for me to make a mistake. She vigorously pursued getting rid of me. It was only dumb luck that she was poisoned." That sounded terrible, especially told to a former law enforcement professional. I scrambled to straighten that impression out. "I didn't do it, of course, and it wasn't lucky for her, but it saved my neck."

He glanced over at me with a little grin. "We have something in common, then. But no one ever promised that life would be fair, at least not to me." He got up from the bench where we'd been sitting. "I have a few things to take care of at home, but I'm happy to meet you at the Blue Hole in forty-five minutes or so. Then I'll drive you over to the place where they camped, and we can take a walk back in the brush to the location where the altar used to be. I doubt much, if anything, is left to see there now, but we can try."

I squirmed, not wanting to insult him but not wanting to get into a car with him either. I wanted to trust him, but I didn't. "I'd feel better if you told me where to meet you."

He squinted again and shrugged. "Suit yourself."

1978

Catherine

Before dinner, two of the guys lit a bonfire, and Ginny brought out the bottle of Kentucky Gentlemen's bourbon that she'd probably lifted from her father's liquor cabinet. Did he not ever notice how much booze was missing? No one really felt like eating yet because it was too hot. The fire didn't help, but we loved it anyway.

Arthur stood up and pointed to the bottle. "Where'd you get that? We need a family meeting to talk about some issues and lay down rules."

I figured he also meant the square groupers two of the guys had dragged in from the canal last night. Square groupers were bales of marijuana that had been unloaded by drug runners worried they were in danger of getting caught by the authorities. It wasn't unusual to find them washed up on the island beaches or bobbing in a shallow current. Some of our gang wanted to dry the stuff out and sell it. Arthur wanted to turn it over to the Sheriff's Office. They'd been arguing all day.

"Ix-nay to family meetings. Rules are boring!" Veronica said. "Let's play Truth or Dare."

I was terrible at guessing liars, and she was worse. She wouldn't care about that, though, since the point was to get drunk. "Losers do shots until the bottle's gone."

Arthur protested again, but she got her way; she always did. The more I drank, the sicker I felt, and the harder Veronica flirted. I staggered off to pee, and by the time I got back, she'd changed the rules of the game.

"Strip poker, Kit Kat," Veronica yelled, patting the empty camp chair next to hers. Her curls were wild, and she was no longer wearing a T-shirt, just a lacy bra that showed off her assets. She was gorgeous. I could smell her from feet away, a combination of sweat, alcohol, and the lily of the valley perfume she'd brought from home. "Mue gue ay des boys," she called it, thinking she was so fancy when anyone who'd taken basic French would know she butchered the words.

"I've already lost my shirt. Ginny's lost more than that!" Laughing, Veronica pointed across the circle at the girl, who waved and giggled, not seeming to care one bit that she was in her underwear.

The next morning, I felt like I'd had a terrible case of food poisoning, but it was more likely a vicious hangover. I *couldn't remember if I'd eaten or not. The rest of the night was a gray haze in my memory. No way I was going to work. Besides, I was sick to death of twenty-four hours a day spent with Ronnie. Sick of her flirting, sick of her luring all the men to her honey, sick of her bigger tips at the end of the night if we worked the same shifts, sick of having to leave our tent because she wanted some alone time. Ha! As if she had ever spent any time alone.*

So I didn't get up. "Wake up, Kit Kat," said someone who sounded like Arthur. He was shaking my tent poles. "Where's your roommate?"

I just rolled over. "Too sick," I remember mumbling. They finally left, and I fell back asleep, sleeping hard until the heat building up in our canvas cave woke me.

Or maybe it was voices in the camp. People fighting again, one deeper voice rumbling and the high reedy sound of a woman, maybe Susanne. "You're part of the problem," said the woman, "only you don't want to see it. Did you sleep with her last night?"

"Of course not. I have no idea where she went."

I had to get help. I had to say something to someone.

Chapter
Twenty-Seven

"At home I peeled the apples, listening to the seductive way they came whispering out of their skins."
—Ruth Reichl, *La Briffe*, September 8, 2023

Rather than sit around battling insects at one of the picnic tables outside the pub, I decided to return to town and visit the Big Pine Library. With any luck, I could do a quick search of the history of the island around the time that Veronica disappeared.

In contrast to the charming pink stucco of the downtown Key West Library, the Big Pine Library was located in a small strip mall attached to the Winn-Dixie grocery store. Inside, I found the refrigerated air very welcome. An older man in a blue plaid shirt, with deep set blue eyes and a shock of white hair, was manning a desk behind a sign that read, "My name is Bruce. Ask me anything."

I gestured at the sign and grinned. "I hardly know where to begin."

He flashed a smile in return. "At the beginning, of course," he said. "I'm Bruce, and I am very interested in the history of Big Pine Key. I also have some horticulture background, and

I've lived here for fifty years, so I've absorbed a lot of useless facts by osmosis. I own and run a website called BigPineKey.com."

"Very good," I said, thinking this guy might be able to fill in some missing pieces. "I'm Hayley Snow, food critic for *Key Zest* magazine. I'm doing some research into the disappearance of a young woman back in 1978. Rumor has it that it might have been related to drugs."

"Perhaps also to the murder of Ned Newman?" he asked, surprising the heck out of me. My astonishment must have shown on my face. "There's a very efficient coconut telegraph in this town. Secrets aren't kept for very long. The drug smuggling theory is quite possible. Have you read about the big bust that occurred in 1980?"

I shook my head. "Tell me about it."

"Thirty people were arrested, ranging from local merchants to plumbers to sailors. Three agencies were involved in the bust, and they seized 25,000 pounds of marijuana right here in town. They also seized three boats, three trucks, and a gold Cadillac." He snickered. "The sheriff was proud of the fact that no shots were fired, and he was pleased to take custody of the boats but not so pleased about storing the marijuana."

This was interesting, but was it related to Catherine's case? If smuggling was big business in 1980, it was probably starting to pick up in 1978. It made sense that the kids who were camped near the mangroves might well have been involved.

"Did you know any of the kids from the mangrove camp?" I asked. "I gather some of them were locals. Did you spend any time there?"

He was quick to respond. "Nope. I heard about them, but I was peripheral to the action at best," he said. "I was married with a brand-new baby and pretty much tied to home when I wasn't working. Everyone assumed that they were a bunch of hippies that came and went as they pleased. One of them disappearing was not a big cause for concern."

This confirmed what I'd heard already, including from Deputy Lopez.

"I do remember the excitement when the Sheriff's Office cleared out that camp," Bruce added. "There was a parade of patrol cars across Key Deer Boulevard like has never been seen since. Except for that 1980 drug bust, of course. My wife and I drove down to look at the campsite after all this happened. It was scraped off clear to the ground."

"Do you remember seeing or hearing about an altar dedicated to unrequited love?" That's what I'd figured out Deputy Lopez was telling me. Those campers were praying for a long shot in the romance department.

Bruce shook his head. "Nope. The camp and the missing girl were news for a while, but the lady who disappeared a few years later made a bigger splash. Apparently, she had moved down with her kids to be with her boyfriend. She sent them north for the summer, and that's the last anyone ever saw of her. Again, involvement with a drug operation was assumed. Her daughter tried to resuscitate the case in the 1990s, but by then, the investigating officers were gone, as were the witnesses. Cold cases are tough," he said, wagging his head in sympathy. "And the cops down here are spread thin."

"Tell me about it," I said. "Do you remember a sheriff's deputy named Ryan Lopez?"

"Yeah, I knew the guy. He was all right. Strict and a little green, but he did his job. He got better as the years went on. We always felt safe when he was patrolling the island."

"Do you think he could have been involved with the girl who vanished?"

"Nope. I doubt it. I think he loved his job and wouldn't have done something to sacrifice his career, though we all make stupid choices when we're young." He grinned and winked. "A wife and baby helped keep me from mistakes I might have tended toward."

"Hear, hear on dumb choices. Can you think of anyone else in town who might have been around in the late seventies that I could talk to?"

He rubbed his chin, thinking. "You know who spent a lot of time there? Ginny. She works over at the No Name Pub."

"I've met her," I said.

"Her father was one of the biggest perps in that 1980s drug bust," he added. He tapped the keys on his computer and turned it around to show me a photo of Ginny's father in handcuffs, a grim officer guiding him into a Sheriff's Office vehicle. "I couldn't blame her for wanting to get out of the house. He was a big drinker and mean as a diamondback rattler when he got drunk. He was too wrapped up in his own shenanigans to take good care of his family, but when he caught his girl doing something wrong, he went wild. I never thought she'd come back to the island and settle in."

I glanced at the wall clock above his head. I had ten minutes to meet the deputy. Pushing one of my *Key Zest* business cards across the desk, I said, "Please call me if you think of anything else related to the case."

Chapter Twenty-Eight

"The palette of flavors is unapologetically loud—'noisy,'
Mr. Ottolenghi would say. Garlic and lemon dominate. 'I
want drama in the mouth,' he said."
—Ligaya Mishan, "A Chef Who Is Vegetarian in Fame
if Not in Fact," *New York Times,* April 26, 2011

I arrived at the far end of Key Deer Boulevard a minute before
the deputy did, feeling better about the meeting than I had
before chatting with Bruce. Deputy Lopez parked his vehicle
behind mine and got out. It was a military-style Jeep with the
words *Downrange Concepts* written along the side. Then I noticed
a sticker in the window: AmericanSnipers.org.

I tried to suppress the shot of fear I felt, not wanting it to
show on my face. A smile spread over Deputy Lopez's face. "It's
an organization in which snipers support other snipers, usually
guys who are deployed as marksmen but don't have the equipment they need. Nothing shady about it.

"As you would expect, I know my way around a gun. It's
perfectly normal for an officer of the law. Didn't your husband
ever tell you that choosing a gun for a cop is like buying a purse

for a woman?" He paused, studying my face. "I can see you're nervous. We don't have to do this."

"No," I said, straightening my shoulders. While still in the car, I'd pocketed my phone with 911 punched in and my finger poised to dial if needed. "I want to see the altar. Or what's left of it."

He motioned for me to follow him down a narrow path into the mangroves. I pulled on the light sweatshirt I'd brought as protection from the sun and bugs, shouldered my backpack, and started after him. I felt better staying behind him so I could run like hell if I changed my mind. As curious as I was about what we might find, I was beginning to feel just as scared.

"I've done a lot of thinking about the old days since you showed up," he called back over his shoulder. "I can't help believing that Catherine killed Veronica, not Arthur, not Ned, not Susanne, and not anyone else either. She couldn't stand one more minute with that girl. That's the impression she gave me that day when I picked her up and drove her to the substation. On the other hand, she was genuinely worried about something. Maybe they had a big fight at the end. Maybe she didn't mean to do it, but she lashed out, and she had to hide the body. Then she came to the station to report her missing so she wouldn't look guilty. Maybe last week she had to kill Ned because he started stirring things up all over again and asking questions about what really happened back then. Who knows? Maybe he'd gotten in touch with her, and that's why she returned to the Keys."

"Hmm. It sounds like it would've been difficult, if not impossible, for her to murder Ned," I said. "Especially since she was the one who drew my attention to this mystery, and now she's also gone missing. Why bring it up if she was the killer, unless Ned was threatening to reveal that? But how could she have made it up to Big Pine from Key West, killed the man, then returned so I could bring her up a second time? How could she be sure that no one would find him in the interim? Disappearing would make total sense if she believed the current Sheriff's Office was going to come to the same conclusion that you have." I wasn't sure why I was fighting against his theory when it was a contender in my own mind too.

He paused for a moment to look back at me, his face red and beaded with sweat. "Maybe she wanted someone else to find him first, but when that didn't happen, she talked you into driving around with her. When you two ladies arrived at the motel office, did she seem surprised, or did it seem like she might be faking it?"

I clearly remembered her reaction to the discovery—horror and shock followed by getting sick to her stomach. "It seemed real to me," I said, following him as he started forward again. "Unless she is a top-tier actress, she wasn't pretending."

I felt my feet squishing into the tidal wash, soaking my favorite red high-tops whenever I lost my footing. He stumped on steadily without a missed step, lighter on his feet than I would have imagined for a heavyset man.

"It didn't used to be this wet," he grumbled. "Climate change is killing us. We're slowly sinking underwater, and we've only seen the beginning. Half the morons I drink coffee with every morning still don't believe in it."

The farther in we walked, the more nervous I felt. It dawned on me that I could have the truth completely turned around. Deputy Lopez could be the killer—not Arthur, not Catherine, and not Ned. I took a quick peek at my phone. Two bars of service. The 911 call was still ready.

"Everyone in the camp had fallen in love with Veronica, hadn't they?" I asked once we'd reached a more open area where he could hear me. "Including Arthur and Ned. Maybe even Catherine was bewitched by her friend. Maybe she loved her too."

He grunted in agreement. "Maybe. For a lot of them, it was love and hate. Veronica was a tease. She teased them all one by one, and the men started to turn against each other. I watched the group spoil from the inside out, like a rotten potato that looks fine from the outside, but cut into it, and you turn up a black heart and an awful smell. Gradually the women caught the same rot."

Suddenly my little burst of nervousness blossomed into a wave of fear. I had to get out of here—after I convinced him to tell the truth. Now or never. "I can understand why you had to do what you did," I said, scrambling for the words that might nudge him off guard enough that I could run back the way I came and get help. "You didn't have a choice. You had to get rid of Veronica and then call in the Sheriff's Office because everyone was turning on each other. Instead of controlling those kids, you'd gotten involved with her too. That would have come out quickly."

"It was back here somewhere," he said, ignoring my words while striding ahead. "I left a stick to mark the spot. Oh, here." He jogged toward a big branch jammed into the side of the marshy path.

Oh Lord, had he trekked in here earlier to set that up as a weapon? Backing up quickly, I tripped over a protruding root, lost my balance, and dove into the dirt to avoid the blow to my head that I was sure was coming. I'd been an idiot to trust him and follow him into the wilderness, especially without anyone knowing exactly where I was. I'd been like every dumb girl who goes down to a dark basement alone in every pulp murder mystery. I groped for my phone—no service bars this time. But I punched the call button anyway. Then I cowered, arms wrapped around my head to protect it. But instead of him swinging that big stick so that it connected with my temple, he collapsed to the ground clutching his chest. I watched in horror as blood seeped out of a hole in his shirt below his heart.

It took me a few precious moments to comprehend that if he was down and he was bleeding, it wasn't him who was out to get me. There was another shooter. I'd had my serious doubts about Catherine, but I hadn't pegged her as a killer. He had, though, and he had a lot more experience with identifying bad people than I did. A bullet whizzed by my left ear, causing me to lurch and yelp. I belly crawled toward Deputy Lopez and whispered, "Are you okay? What can I do?"

He groaned. "I'm shot in the gut. Unless you're a trauma surgeon, there's not a thing you can do for me. Do you have any cell service?"

I pulled the phone out of my pocket again. "Nothing." I felt rigid with fear.

"Then you need to take my gun."

Feeling cold and sick with a rush of adrenaline, I pulled off my sweatshirt, grateful that I had grabbed it from the car to try to beat out the no-see-ums. They were seething the way Catherine had described, like when she decided she had to abandon her tent and move north so many years ago. Now they were seething around his open wound. I pressed the sweatshirt to the deputy's torso, trying to staunch the flow of deep red blood.

"Take the gun."

"I don't use guns," I said. I started to sit up, but he grabbed my hand.

"Stay low," he said, his jaw clenched—with what, pain? Fear? "Listen to me. You are going to need to either shoot her or be shot. She's pegged a former law enforcement officer. She has absolutely nothing to lose."

The last words that my nemesis Deputy Darcy Rogers had hurled my way at Danielle's wedding reception spun through my brain. At that moment, it felt more like the culmination of a lecture than anything else. "Sometimes the choice is between you going home to your family that night, or the bad guy who's done terrible things, and they will do more if you allow it. I am always going to choose me. That way, I will be out there the next day. By choosing me, I'm choosing you too."

"I don't know how to shoot," I told the deputy. Nathan had tried to show me the basics when we'd first gotten engaged several years ago. He'd wanted to buy me a gun, but I refused. In the end, he gave up trying because neither one of us believed I'd actually pull the trigger.

Deputy Ryan groaned, and I could hear a gurgling noise in his throat. He spoke distinctly and patiently. "Take the gun. Line up your forefingers on either side of the barrel, aim directly at her, and then pull the trigger. Don't bother to shoot at anything but the middle mass of her body. It's a bigger target. Winging her won't do you a bit of good."

"I can't kill someone."

His breathing was growing raspy and labored. "It's us or them," he said quietly. Another bullet whizzed by and buried itself in the brush to his right.

For the first time, I completely believed him. I did not want him to be killed, and I didn't want to die either.

"Hold on to this," I said, pressing his hand to the sweatshirt. "I'll take care of the rest of it." I reached across his body and pulled the gun from the holster on his belt.

"For God's sake, don't put your finger on the trigger until you're ready to shoot. And please don't shoot me because I'm already riddled with holes." He tried to smile at his own joke, but I could see the pain ripple over his face. "I'll draw the fire this way while you flank her. Once you get close, you shout at her: 'I'm with the Sheriff's Office. Drop the gun and put your hands on your head.'"

I muttered those lines under my breath.

"If she moves toward you," he added in a hoarse whisper, "then yell 'Stay right where you are. If you even twitch, I will light you up.'"

I felt a bubble of hysterical laughter rise up my throat. What were the chances I would say all that or even remember it? I pushed the hysteria back and arranged my fingers on the barrel as he'd instructed me. As I crept into the brush, he called out to Catherine.

"Come and get me. Don't be a coward. Finish the job."

Chapter
Twenty-Nine

"Julia Child had a mayonnaise problem."
—Colleen Cambridge,
Mastering the Art of French Murder

I edged carefully through the thicket of vegetation, hoping I wasn't brushing up against the poisonous trees that Ginny had warned Catherine about all those years ago. But with a desperate shooter on the loose, a case of pruritis was the least of my possible problems. A branch cracked under my foot, and I froze, listening for Deputy Lopez to shout again and distract the killer. Instead, I heard the thwack of another bullet and felt a sharp pain in my thigh. I dropped to my knees, smacking my head on the tree in front of me, still clutching the gun. I stayed there stunned for a moment and then took a deep breath to assess the damage. My leg was bleeding, but not badly. It hurt, and so did my head, but not enough to quit trying and die out here in the woods.

Scrambling back to my feet, I crept closer, pushing off the pain, taking cover behind the bigger trees, and listening. Once I could hear the rustling of the shooter nearby, I jumped out from behind a big poisonwood tree and shouted, "Freeze! Sheriff's department! Drop your weapon and put your hands on your head."

She fired off two more shots. Without thinking further, I pulled the trigger. She screamed.

After taking one more look at my useless phone—it was me or no one, I staggered over to her and kicked the gun she'd dropped as she fell out of reach. The adrenaline that had been pumping so hard just minutes ago whooshed out of my system, and I collapsed to the ground. Gripping the deputy's gun with both trembling hands, I pointed it at her chest, and finally her features came into focus. "You?!"

It was Ginny, the waitress. We were both dripping with sweat and blood. Everything hurt, and on top of that, I was so angry. "Why were you trying to kill us?"

"You shot me," she said, pressing her hand to her ribs below her breast and then looking in astonishment at the blood.

"You shot us first. Did you kill Veronica and Ned? Where's Catherine?"

Her face looked pasty and sweaty, and I was afraid she'd pass out or even die.

Finally, she whispered, "Didn't you ever have a moment when you were fiercely, desperately in love, and you had no way of letting them know, and no chance of them loving you back? I watched while the men used her just because she offered. It made me crazy that she would give herself away like that. I loved her so much."

"Catherine?" I asked.

She spat. "Not that loser. Veronica. I knew Ronnie wouldn't run away with me because she thought Arthur really loved her, and she couldn't resist that. She wasn't finished playing with him, teasing him. Ned figured it out."

"You're the one who left the hairbrush." She just stared at me. "What did you do to Veronica?" I asked.

She told me.

I felt a wave of wooziness, sank flat to the ground, and passed out.

Chapter Thirty

"I sought refuge in the kitchen, where I've always found grief to be at its most reasonable. Grief occupies all of the senses, but in the kitchen, it neither aids in my cooking nor meddles with it."
—Yewande Komolafe, "The Many Lessons of Kouign-Amann," *New York Times,* January 24, 2023

When I came floating up to consciousness, everything looked blurry and white, and I could hear an annoying beeping. I recognized finally that I was lying in a hospital bed and both my thigh and my head hurt like heck. Faces came into focus on both sides: my mother, Nathan, Steve Torrence, Miss Gloria, and then several uniformed figures hovering near the door.

Mom reached over to brush the hair off my forehead. "You're back! We were so worried."

"What happened?" I asked.

"One of her bullets grazed your thigh," Steve said. "You lost some blood and got a few stitches. Other than that, you're right as rain."

"Other than that giant purple egg on her forehead," my mother added, glaring at him. "I hardly call that right as rain."

He reached over to wrap her in a big hug and chuckled. "Point taken. I was trying not to scare her. Or you."

"We want to hear everything that happened, blow by blow," said Miss Gloria. "And I'll go ahead and say this so Nathan doesn't have to. What the heck were you thinking, traipsing off by yourself in the wilderness? Plus, how in the heck did you get yourself shot?" She patted my leg, and I winced.

A chorus of weak laughter came from the people around me. My throat felt parched and my mind fuzzy. "Can I get a milkshake or a Coke or something? And maybe tell you the whole story in a few hours? I feel kind of loopy." Then my eyes flew wide open. "What about Deputy Lopez? Is he okay?"

"Ice chips for now, my darling." Nathan fed me a chip, then stroked the back of my hand, his face lined with worry. He exchanged a glance with Chief Brandenburg, who stood behind him, also looking concerned. A tear trickled down my cheek as I remembered Deputy Lopez teaching me to shoot. He'd saved me, but had it been too late to save him? To push my mind off the worst possible outcome, I focused on the tattoo on the chief's arm.

"I never noticed your tattoo before. What does it say?"

"My sister's protector."

"Nice. Does your sister have one too?" He nodded. "What does hers say?"

"My brother's keeper."

"That is so sweet. I wish I had a brother. I have a half-brother, but he's a lot younger than me, and we didn't really grow up together so that's not quite the same." My mother's concerned look made me realize I was babbling.

But the chief laughed. "You might not have wanted one growing up. But sisters are special, and the entire police force considers you to be an honorary one. That means you've got more brothers than you'll know what to do with. I'm pretty sure the Sheriff's Office feels the same way." He gestured to three green uniforms behind him who all waved. "You're kind of a hero."

A woman in green edged a little closer. "I'd rather be considered an honorary sister." That was Darcy Rogers's voice, only a lot gentler than she usually sounded.

"Whatever you want," I said, smiling, then turned back to the chief. My head was beginning to feel achy and fuzzy. "I'm worried about the tattoo now," I said, my eyes fluttering shut. "How will I fit all the officers in one design? Between the Sheriff's Office and the KWPD, that's a lot of names," I lapsed into silence when I realized I was making no sense. "How did you guys even know where I was?"

"I can answer that," Miss Gloria piped up. "It was my new Apple watch. Remember we were talking about how my sons gave it to me to keep track of me? It felt so clunky and then it got to bothering my wrist, and I took it off and dropped it in your pack. Actually, that's not the whole truth, nothing but the truth."

"Go on," Nathan said, shooting her a fierce glare.

"The boys are keeping track of me, making sure I get enough exercise and get to bed when I say I'm going and all that. I thought it would be a hoot to have you carry it for a while. You walk a lot more than I do so I'd get a big boost in steps and maybe they'd get off my back." She looked sheepish for a minute but then grinned. "Lucky thing I did because you two could have been rotting out there in the wilderness until you were nothing but bones."

I heard Darcy Rogers's instant protest, informing my friend they were hot on my trail and that the Sheriff's Office was all over it, very close to finding us. But then my consciousness faded away, along with their voices.

By the time I woke up a second time, I was feeling less groggy, and the room had cleared out. Only Nathan was sitting in the chair beside the bed.

He looked up from his phone and smiled. "You scared me this time, sweetheart. How are you feeling?"

"Like I've been shot at and dragged through the mangroves." I reached for his hand. "I need you to tell me the truth about something. Did I kill Ginny?" I felt tears well up in my eyes and tip over onto my cheeks.

He squeezed my hand back. "She's going to be fine. You only winged her. The bullet went right through her and didn't nick anything she needed to live." He had a grim look on his face. "For better or worse. She was the person responsible for Ned's death, not Catherine. She probably killed Veronica too."

I nodded slowly. "I'm not surprised, though part of me finds that so weird, if that makes sense," I said. "I never seriously suspected her. She didn't strike me as having a big enough personality to kill someone."

That made Nathan laugh. "Haven't you heard of those neighbors who are always astonished when a murderer is found living next door and all along they believed he was a bland milquetoast of a person?"

I chuckled too, but then the memory surfaced of my crawl through the brush with Deputy Ryan Lopez's gun gripped in my hand. I remembered confronting Ginny and listening to her tell me bits and pieces about what had happened back in the day. She'd come up with a plan to make Veronica super sick by adding relish to her hot dog made from the fruit of the manchineel tree. She made homemade relish for everyone, but only Veronica got the special ingredient. I described all of this to my husband.

"She told me that she never imagined that the hot dog would kill her. She figured she was too drunk to eat much and would take only a bite or two. But she hoped she'd get good and sick, leave town, and go back home where she'd come from. She insisted that Veronica's presence in the camp was poisoning everyone. She couldn't stand watching her flit from one dalliance to another, and finally land on Arthur. Ginny believed her love for Veronica was true and real, but Ronnie would never love her back." I took a deep breath, then continued the story. "But Veronica loved the sweet relish and ate the whole thing. Ginny could see she was beginning to feel nauseous. She staggered off into the woods. Everyone was so drunk, Ginny was the only one who noticed and followed her."

I started to shiver, imagining the scene. "How did she make that relish without harming herself? I'll tell you how, because she told me. She planned ahead. She intended to hurt Veronica. She used gloves. This was no spur of-the-moment decision." I practically spat the words out, as though they were poison too.

Nathan nodded. "Take your time," he said. "You don't have to talk about it now if you don't want to."

But I did want to. I needed someone else besides me to carry the awful story in their head. I pulled in a ragged breath. "Ginny watched Veronica curl up in the bushes, gasping for air, until the breathing noises stopped. I think she couldn't believe what she'd done, and even if she wanted to fix it, it was too late. Then she panicked and rolled Veronica's body into the ravine where the crocodiles sometimes crawled in from the Gulf. That was it. She drove herself home, and when she returned to camp the next evening, the sheriff's department was there telling everyone they had to leave. Then she got lucky because they scraped the camp detritus into that ravine and covered the body up." I looked at Nathan, thinking how strong he was to face this kind of evil every day. "After she told me all that, she started to sob, saying, 'I knew she'd never love me.'"

Nathan shook his head.

"What about Ned?" I asked. "Did she confess to his murder?"

He nodded slowly. "She told Darcy Rogers the rest. As you figured out, Catherine did come into town a few days early to hire someone to drive her up from Key West to talk to Ned about what really happened to Veronica. He got worried, wondering if his friend Arthur had killed Veronica, or even Susanne. He mentioned that old photo in Arden's home with Arthur and all the girls—Susanne, Catherine, Veronica, and Ginny. He thought it was time the truth come out, and he was certain that they would find it right there. The authorities hadn't tried very hard back then, but these were different times, and different people were in charge. After Catherine left Ned's motel, he texted Ginny and asked her to stop by after work. He wanted them to go to the Sheriff's Office together and request that they reopen the investigation. She couldn't risk that happening, they argued, and then she killed him."

I collapsed back into my pillow, trying to slow the pounding of my heart. "When I was crawling through those bushes, I thought I was a goner."

Nathan took my hand and held it gently. "You pulled the trigger," he said. "You surprised me."

I could feel the tears running down my cheeks. "When I saw how desperate Ginny was and realized she'd already tried to shoot us and probably killed Ned, I had no choice. It was exactly as Darcy Rogers had warned me, and Ryan Lopez too: it was her or me."

Now it occurred to me that no one had said a word about the retired deputy and that scared me a lot. "How is Deputy Lopez?"

The line of Nathan's jaw tightened. "He's out of surgery. They're not saying that he's out of the woods. He took a second bullet to the torso before you nailed the shooter."

I pushed the bed covers off so I could sit up. My bandaged leg hurt, and so did my head, but that man had put his life on the line for me. A little discomfort meant nothing in comparison. "I want to see him."

"The nurses aren't going to go for that. I don't much like it either."

"I want to see him," I repeated in a low voice. "We will all feel terrible if he dies, and I didn't have a chance to thank him."

Nathan gave a quick nod and went out into the hall to speak to the charge nurse. He returned with a wheelchair and the nurse, who unhooked my IV. Then he scooped me out of bed, settled me gently in the chair, draped my legs in a clean sheet, and tucked the edges behind me.

"Not gonna lie," I told him. "That was sweet, but it hurt like hell. Let's go."

He rolled me through the hallways to the surgery unit. We could tell which one was Deputy Lopez's room because a uniformed sheriff's deputy was posted outside of it. He and Nathan conferred briefly, and then he waved us through.

The deputy had tubes everywhere: oxygen, several IVs, a chest tube, and a catheter. His face looked ashen against the white pillow behind his head. The machines beside him beeped and whirred. He blinked his eyes open as Nathan rolled me up next to him.

"It's me, Hayley," I said, feeling suddenly so choked up I could barely get the words out. "I wanted to thank you for saving my life."

"And likewise," he said in a raspy voice. His hand reached for mine, and he gave me a weak squeeze.

"This is my husband, Detective Nathan Bransford."

They exchanged awkward greetings. "Thank you for being there and for showing her what to do," Nathan said. "She told me how you taught her everything she needed to know in under five minutes."

Deputy Lopez smiled. "Probably under two. She was a trooper. You should get this woman a gun and take her up to the Marathon Range so she can learn how to shoot properly. She's got the makings of a fine markswoman already."

Nathan laughed and shook his head. "I tried. She told me she wouldn't use a gun."

"Do you believe everything your wife says? I say try again." The two of them chuckled as a nurse bustled in.

"Time to go," she said briskly. "Dr. Canter's here to examine his patient."

"Thank you again," I said to Deputy Lopez, my heart so full I could get no more words out. I leaned over to peck his cheek.

"I'd like to take you to lunch or dinner when you're sprung loose from here."

Nathan saluted him. "I thank you too. You are a hero." His voice sounded as shaky as mine had.

When we'd returned to my room and I was settled back in bed, Nathan asked, "Ginny claimed she loved Veronica and yet she killed her?"

I nodded. "I know it sounds bizarre—it is bizarre. She asked me if I'd ever had that experience of loving someone who didn't love me back, because then I would understand what she did." Even though the question seemed absurd in this situation, I took a moment to think about it, and then explained. "You remember Wally, my ex-boss? He was a flash in the pan. A nice guy, but not the kind of guy I'd feel desperate over. Instead, it was a time in my life when I was generally feeling desperate about where I was headed, especially, if I'd ever find a mate. I kind of transferred that feeling to him, even if it didn't quite fit. Luckily for both of us, we didn't push through the doubts.

"You, on the other hand, are a soulmate. It took us a while to wipe the cobwebs from our brains to be able to see it." I reached for his hand and laced my fingers through his.

He grinned and the adorable dimple in his chin deepened.

"Honestly, when I think of you, I don't know what I might do to someone who tried to get between us," I added. "Not sure I would have stabbed someone with a pair of scissors or fed them poisoned relish, but it could have been ugly."

Chapter
Thirty-One

"I think every woman should have a blowtorch."

—Julia Child

The next morning, I was released from the hospital, feeling much better except for the occasional twinge in my leg. My mind, however, was a different story. I kept replaying the shooting incident in my memory, over and over. Plus, the fact that Catherine had not surfaced yet bothered me a lot. I'd checked in with the PI, Simon Landry, but neither he nor her family in Michigan had heard from her, so I didn't believe she'd gone back home. I wished I'd thought to ask Ginny, but I was too shocked and too focused on staying alive and getting help. Catherine obviously wasn't the killer, so why did she flee? If she was hiding out and heard about Ginny's capture, wouldn't she have emerged again once she realized she was safe? The whole story had been plastered all over the local news, and it was even picked up by the Associated Press.

Nathan would hate the idea of me returning to Big Pine Key, but I hated the idea that I hadn't gotten to see what remained of the altar of love and, even more important, that Catherine was still missing.

"I'd like to talk with Ginny again," I told my husband as we were having a late breakfast on the deck. He'd stopped at the Cuban Coffee Queen on the way home to buy me a café con leche, and then he bought an enormous cinnamon roll, glistening with sticky sweetness, at Old Town Bakery. Evinrude was curled up on my lap, and Ziggy panted at my feet. Half the neighbors on the dock had come by with well wishes and food and flowers. I paused my inhalation of the sticky bun to lick the fingers that were carrying the heaviest load of caramelized sugar.

"Maybe she killed Catherine too, and maybe she'd confess that to me even if she refused to tell the authorities. We're sort of connected now, in a weird way. Maybe we could ride back over to the hospital for a few minutes, and I could ask her?"

"Not gonna happen," Nathan said, looking up from his phone with a firm shake of his head. "She's a suspect in attempted murder in the first degree, two counts, one of them involving an officer of the law. Plus, stabbing Ned is first-degree murder and hard to plead away. You can't claim self-defense if you've stabbed someone in the back. And that's not even counting what she did to Veronica. She's already in the Stock Island jail, probably in solitary confinement. She was transferred there early this morning from the hospital, and believe me, no one other than her lawyer will be engaging her in conversation. That will be a video conference only." He studied my face. "What is it that you want to know?"

"I want to know what happened to Catherine. I'd also like to see the remnants of the altar of love. That's where Deputy Lopez was taking me before we got ambushed."

"You heard the doctor as well as I did," he said. "She said rest, rest, rest."

We argued back and forth for a few minutes. In the end, Nathan agreed to drive me up to Big Pine the next day if I promised to lay low for twenty-four hours. He folded because he was afraid I'd go on my own if he didn't take me.

* * *

I dozed on the drive north along the Keys after checking that Nathan was okay without chatting. He was. He woke me as we pulled onto Big Pine Key and turned left on Key Deer Boulevard. As we approached the end of the long road, I caught myself shivering a little bit. Nathan glanced over and took my hand.

"We don't have to do this. This isn't your job."

"I would feel a lot better if we put this to rest. If we don't find her up here, I promise I'll leave it for the Sheriff's Office to figure out."

He pressed his lips together. He wasn't happy, I could tell, but he also knew that I was stubborn as an ox in deep mud. I directed him to the entrance to the path where I had walked with Deputy Ryan Lopez the day before yesterday. It had been only two days earlier, but it seemed like eons.

We trudged through the shrubbery, and I pointed out the poisonwood tree that he should avoid touching as we dodged the bigger pools of water on the path. "Is Ginny's poisonous manchineel tree still here too?" Nathan asked, looking nervous.

"Apparently it exists, but it's not that common and not found on nature trails," I said, not wanting him to get cold feet. I motioned for him to stop walking.

"Here's where the deputy was first shot." I paused beside the big branch that I'd thought Deputy Lopez had meant to hit me with. A dark patch in the dirt had to be his blood. I pointed to the left. "Then he sent me up through the woods, which is a path I'd prefer not to take again."

I kept plodding along the trail, even though my leg was beginning to ache, and I suspected that I was limping and that would make Nathan worry. We finally reached the point where the shoot-out had occurred. A hundred yards ahead through the limbs of several stunted pine trees, I thought I spotted the remains of the altar. I stopped to rest for a moment, then we trudged forward until we stood next to it.

"It's pretty anticlimactic," I said, glancing at Nathan and then back at the large, flat stone lying on the ground. If I looked closely, I could make out the words *Love Me Tender* carved in a spidery script. But as far as items that had been placed on the altar by the campers, as expected, nothing was left. "Ryan Lopez did say there was a dilapidated hippie shack not far from here where some of the campers went if they needed space or wanted privacy for romantic encounters."

"Sounded like there were a lot of those," Nathan said grimly. "More primal sex than romance I suspect. Why don't you stay here, and I'll go poke around and call you if I find anything?"

I wanted to refuse, but my leg hurt. "Okay, but don't leave me out of something important."

"Never," he said with a grin, then marched into the brush. A few minutes later, he whistled, and I hurried after him. In a small clearing encroached by bushes and scrub trees, he was standing by a rickety cabin. He helped me climb over the logs that had fallen in front of the door, and we began to search. I heard a muffled thump from inside what must have been the bathroom. I tried the handle. Locked.

"Nathan," I called. The thumping got louder.

He sprinted over and slammed his hip against the door until it finally crashed in.

Catherine had been hog-tied and left in the rusty old tub with a bandanna stuffed into her mouth, the same pattern that Ginny had worn when we visited the No Name Pub. Her eyes were wild, like she was afraid of us, and she looked pale and sweaty, soaked in her own fluids.

"I'm going to call for help," Nathan said. "You stay here and try to reassure her."

"Of course." I noticed that the hair on the back of her head was thick with blood. I hoped we weren't too late. As I knelt beside the tub, she mewled like a kitten.

"Catherine," I said as I gently untied the bandanna and worked it out of her mouth. "We're here to take you home." I poured a bit of water from my bottle onto the bandanna and dabbed her forehead and squeezed a few drops on her lips, remembering that I'd only been allowed ice chips after my trauma. I tried to untie her arms and legs but the knots had been pulled cruelly tight, and I was afraid to hurt her. "Nathan's calling the sheriff and an ambulance. They should be here any minute." I had a million questions, but she looked too shell-shocked and exhausted to answer anything.

Once the EMTs arrived, we moved out of the shack to let them work. Ten minutes later, as they trundled her out on a gurney, I asked if I could accompany her to the hospital.

"That's a hard no," said the guy in charge. "You can check on her tomorrow in the hospital."

Lucy Burdette

1978

Catherine

At first, Veronica's absence felt like a relief. It was the kind of relief you might feel when an abscess is pricked and all the pus drains away. She took up so much air no matter whose space she was in. It felt suffocating. On the other hand, once she was gone half a day, I felt her absence in a different way, as though something lively and funny and buoyant had gone missing and my life was reduced to black and white.

None of the others knew where she'd gone, or so they said. I watched their faces to see what they weren't saying, like the negative space I couldn't help noticing after I'd broken my mother's favorite glass pitcher. "It was an accident!" I'd insisted. She hadn't said a word as she'd swept up the shards, leaving the dust that marked exactly the place where the pitcher had been. She left that empty space unfilled so everyone would remember it was gone, how much she'd loved it, who was responsible, and how very angry she was.

Finally, I couldn't stand it. Something terrible had happened to her. I could feel it. My car wouldn't start, so I began the long walk to the Sheriff's Office across the road from downtown. When I was still a mile away, Deputy Lopez drove by and rolled down his window.

"What's up?" he asked.

I began to cry.

"Veronica. Veronica's missing."

Chapter
Thirty-Two

"Besides, I hate seeing someone unsatisfied with their food. It means they're going unnurtured. Unfed."
—Mia P. Manansala, *Arsenic and Adobo*

Nathan pulled whatever strings he could to allow me to visit Catherine the next day. He'd agreed that she and I needed some solo time for closure, so he accompanied me only as far as the unit's front desk.

"You can't stay long," the charge nurse told me.

"Got it," I said, already limping down the hall. I knew the drill. I'd heard the same thing while visiting Deputy Lopez.

Catherine's eyes flew open as I entered the room, and she winced as though I was about to harm her. She had an IV in her arm and an oxygen tube in her nose, and she was wearing the same faded-green cotton johnny coat I'd worn only days before.

"It's okay," I said in a soothing voice. "I'm not here to hurt you. I just want to talk."

"Sorry," she whispered. "I'm still feeling anxious."

"No wonder, after what you've been through. Do you feel up to telling me what happened?"

"I already told the detectives," she said, smoothing the sheet over her chest. "But I owe you an explanation as well." She seemed to sink further down into her pillow, her face pasty white like the sheets. Like Deputy Lopez's face had been. There had been too many close calls this week.

She drew in a big breath and started to speak. "Ginny called me Thursday afternoon, the day after we'd seen her at the pub, supposedly so we could support each other in the wake of Ned's murder. She said she'd been thinking a lot about those old days, and she had some ideas about what happened in the camp and about Veronica. She was convinced that Veronica herself had returned to the Keys, fought with Ned, and killed him. She asked if I'd go with her to look at the site where the camp was, including that stupid altar."

"Why would Veronica come back after so many years and murder Ned?" I asked.

Catherine plucked at a string on her johnny coat. "I know. It doesn't really make sense. But I'd been so shocked by how you and I found Ned's body, and I desperately wanted answers. In a way, anything Veronica did wouldn't have surprised me. What if he'd taken something from her? Maybe he'd promised her a cut of drug money. It seemed possible that she'd come back to haunt him or make him pay."

She heaved a shuddery sigh, and I waited. "Ginny drove down to Key West to pick me up and take me to Big Pine. We started along the path to the old altar, stopping to look at that stone: *Love Me Tender*. We were remembering stories about who had left what on the altar, and laughing about how young and foolish we all were. She wanted to see the cabin too, and I agreed to go. Once we got there, she walloped me in the back of the head. Knocked me out cold. I woke up exactly where you found me. I'd about given up on getting out of there alive." She held up her wrists, looking at the bruises and cuts she'd sustained from Ginny's ropes.

I patted her shoulder, thinking she really might not have escaped if Nathan and I hadn't found her. Another day or two and she'd have been gone. In fact, I couldn't help wondering why Ginny hadn't killed her. Why bother to leave her tied up in the old cabin?

Catherine closed her eyes for a moment, then opened them.

"Since we've been talking about this, and I had all that time alone to think"—she snorted out a laugh—"I finally figured out how much Arthur was like Ernest Hemingway, at least in his charisma and his sequential relationships. Susanne was his first love, his Hadley."

"Do you think he really loved Susanne like Hemingway loved Hadley? Does he still?" I asked.

"She really wanted him to love her, as she adored him. That kind of adoration can feel like a drug while you are in the spotlight of that person's love." She looked hard at me until I nodded. "However, I think when Veronica and I arrived, he had already started to see that Susanne's love was never going to feel like enough." She tapped her chest. "He had a hole, right here. Just as Ernest Hemingway had."

I waited until she started speaking again. I knew there was more.

"I fell hard for Arthur the minute he showed up in the camp that first night, after we'd pitched our tent. He was trying to take charge of a group that was basically unmanageable, but in a quiet, calm way. I could tell he was a decent

253

man and so handsome besides. He seemed normal, you know? I spent as much time with him and Susanne as I could. She let me watch her cooking and taught me how to take care of people by feeding them. Then one day she went up to Miami for a medical appointment, and I had too much to drink and persuaded Arthur to sleep with me. I'm not proud of that—he was never going to love me the way I wanted him to. He felt terrible about what he did. To make things worse, he told Susanne and that broke her heart. She trusted me, and I shattered that trust."

"So you were his Pauline?"

"That's not very complimentary, is it? Nor did it last as long as their marriage by any stretch."

I shrugged. "Who was his Martha Gellhorn?"

"Veronica, of course. She was a party girl—so pretty and lively, and that was attractive to him in a powerful way. His dark side was drawn to her. Plus, she figured out what happened with me and Arthur. She couldn't stand it if I had something that she was missing out on. As I told you, usually it was the other way around—she had the guy first."

"I guess Ginny would have been the fourth woman in his life, if he'd allowed it?"

"Who knows?" Her eyes fluttered shut.

She was so quiet that I thought she was drifting to sleep. But she opened her eyes again.

"I'm sorry I lied to you about visiting Ned and Arthur before I contacted you," she said in a small voice. "But once I talked to them, I felt like I was over my head and needed help. I thought you would tell me to go to the police if I thought someone's life was in danger."

"I would have," I said, frowning. She'd talked to Arthur too? I'd let her tell it instead of butting in with a rush of questions.

"Arthur, it turned out, was like catnip to at least three of the women campers: Susanne, Veronica, and me. But he wasn't a toxic man, just a man yearning to fill a chasm inside himself—and we women felt that. Honestly, it was irresistible. He was so torn; he wanted the camp to follow the rules of a healthy life, but he wasn't quite healthy himself." More silence. "I never figured Arthur out, what made him the way he was. He's never been married. I suppose he fills his empty nooks and crannies with his work, the animals."

Her eyes filled with tears, which made me think that she had really loved Arthur. Maybe studying Hemingway stirred up all those ancient feelings, and she'd come back to the Keys hoping to reconnect. I reminded myself again to be patient and let her tell her story.

"I've met him twice," I said. "He seems like a deeply caring man with, from what you've said, some big regrets."

She nodded. "I told Arthur that I remembered having overheard Ronnie making fun of Susanne, and I wondered if it could have been Susanne who murdered Ronnie. He told me absolutely not, and besides, no one cared anymore, and then he said I should let it go.

"Ned was a little more open to talking about the possibility that someone had killed Veronica, and he believed she hadn't simply disappeared. He seemed to understand that people always suspected he played a part in all that. He texted Ginny to talk it over because he felt confident the Sheriff's Office could figure it out now. When you agreed to take me up to Big Pine to see Ned again, Ginny had already killed him. I was never so shocked and horrified in my life as when I saw him with those scissors plunged into his back. The rest you already know—she had no intention of letting her past crime come to life, even if it meant killing more people, including me."

"How would she have been exposed?" I asked.

"Ned told her the clues were in Arden's photos. But I think she felt that the real danger to her was that if he went back to the cops and stirred up renewed interest in finding the killer, this time the Sheriff's Office would get to the bottom of it."

I let her collect her emotions for a moment, then explained that I had talked to the private investigator that she'd hired and hoped she wouldn't take offense.

Catherine smiled and said, "I chose you because you're nosy, and so I suppose I got what's coming. Besides, you did save my life. Thank you."

Now that she was feeling grateful, I thought this would be a good time to ask her about the article I was planning to write about Hemingway and his wives. I described my idea, ending with, "I could interview you and give you credit. But maybe it's different enough from what you'd planned that you wouldn't mind. I certainly won't be focusing on how to recognize toxic love."

She plucked at the sheet, looked up at me. "I've been thinking about this. I had a lot of time to think when I was tied up in that shed. I'm not sure I should be considered an expert on toxic love even though I've written about it for years. But I realized I don't want to study it any longer. I'm going to turn back my advance and retire. Maybe I'll list my name on Match or Tinder." She grinned. "I'll find a soulmate who isn't toxic and ride off into the sunset."

"That sounds so smart, except I don't know how many of those you'll find on Tinder," I said. We chuckled together. "I keep wondering what exactly happened in the seventies to bring you to the Keys and set up camp in the commune."

"I was so lost," Catherine said, "so exhausted by my family dynamics. My sister was always the star—she was bright and dramatic and beautiful, and it was obvious that my parents preferred her. I wanted her to love me as much as I admired and loved her, but I guess she couldn't. I wanted to get away from all that and find people who loved me despite my weaknesses and flaws. I thought I'd found it in that camp." She paused, her eyes shiny with tears again. "Don't you think I would have recognized how similar Veronica was to my sister? I suppose you can't help but carry your problems with you when you run away.

"I suppose this is another reason I felt drawn to studying Hemingway," she said. "My travel mate was so much like him. Veronica's attractiveness was powerful, but she, as Hemingway had with his wives, became dissatisfied once she'd landed her fish. Also, like Hemingway, she yearned to be taken care of but scorned and despised anyone who tried."

"She must have been something special."

Catherine nodded slowly. "You know, it wasn't only the men who loved Veronica. Ginny loved her too. She may have told you that she killed Veronica to keep her from stealing Arthur. But I don't believe that. She couldn't bear to share Veronica. She was obsessed with her."

I thought but didn't say, *What about you?*

"She was toxic, though, start to finish."

"Veronica or Ginny?"

"Probably both," she said. "All of us were running away from something. Healthy relationships didn't stand a chance because no one was looking under the surface. We were acting on urges rooted in our past problems. That's all."

I reached for her hand and gently stroked it. "I hope you find exactly what you really need."

Chapter
Thirty-Three

"In those moments when we are in the kitchen, when we're focused on a recipe, transforming basic ingredients into something that we can share, the noise from the outside world subsides and it's a respite."

—Dorie Greenspan, xoxoDorie newsletter,
March 4, 2022

Nathan was waiting for me outside the hospital. "How was it?" he asked.

"Sad, actually," I said, feeling myself tear up. "She had a sad home life, and she was looking to connect and feel loved. It was impossible to find that in Big Pine Key camp because the campers had brought their drama and trauma with them. We all carry old wounds, but most of us figure out how to move on in a healthy way. Those campers were struggling more than most. The drinking and drugs didn't help."

"You're a good friend," Nathan said as we got into his cruiser. "A kind person."

I felt wilted and tired. "It also made me think about things from my own past that I regret. Things that I hoped were so far buried that they would never be uncovered. I certainly haven't killed anyone, but I've made mistakes.

"I still feel awful about wrecking Eric's car right after moving here. Plus, moving here lock, stock, and barrel when I didn't even know Chad. What dope makes a mistake like that?"

He turned to look at me, his green eyes filled with worry. "It takes a long time for most of us to really grow up. Everybody has these moments. Yours truly included."

I thought he was probably remembering his ex-wife and how crazy he went when she was stalked.

I rested my hand on his strong forearm. "I probably don't give you enough credit for how hard it is to let me do what feels right, even if sometimes it's dangerous."

"Sometimes stupid dangerous," he said, with a grin spreading across his face. "It would break my heart if I lost you. You know that, right?"

I took his hand and brought it to my heart. "You won't, I promise. Not for the longest time, anyway."

Nathan took a right on Palm Avenue and pulled into the lot at Houseboat Row. As he parked his cruiser, I could see my mother and Miss Gloria and Sam waiting on the deck of our houseboat. I knew there would be food, lots of food, and something cold to drink, and hugs, and animals to stroke. I took Nathan's arm for warmth and steadiness, and we headed to our home.

My mother leaped up from a chair on the deck to make sure I made it aboard.

"I'm fine, really," I told her. "Just hungry."

"I have just the cure for that," she said. "I tried a new recipe for a chocolate layer cake. One of the commenters called it a 'cake in search of a celebration.' I couldn't resist."

"Unless you think it's too early, we also have champagne," said Sam, looking a little hesitant.

"When is it ever too early for champagne?" Miss Gloria said. "If you're that worried, we can add orange juice and call it brunch."

I laughed so hard that I started to cry. "I am so lucky. Every bit of love and community those kids were searching for, I have right here." I wiped the moisture off my cheek and leaned over to kiss Nathan. Then I got up to hug my mom and Sam. "Thank you all for being part of this life, and for helping to save me." Finally, I stopped in front of my dear friend Miss Gloria. "That watch in my bag"—I shook my head—"you are brilliant."

Recipes

Nathan's Favorite Italian Pot Roast

Hayley makes this recipe for her husband, Nathan. My version was adapted from one developed by Florence Fabricant for the *New York Times* Cooking app. She prepared hers in a heavy pan on the stove, while other cooks baked their version of the dish covered in an oven for several hours. I chose to make it in the slow cooker. It tastes even better if you cook it a day before you plan to serve it. Cool the meat in the sauce and refrigerate overnight. Before serving, skim off the fat, slice the meat, and reheat it in the oven along with the sauce. Serve with either cheesy polenta or mashed potatoes or macaroni and cheese and a green salad.

Ingredients
1 (3-pound) rump or boneless chuck roast
2–3 tablespoons olive oil
3 large cloves garlic, peeled and chopped
1 large onion, peeled and chopped
2 carrots, peeled and chopped
2 ribs celery, chopped

1 tablespoon tomato paste
½ cup red wine
1 14.5 oz can chopped plum tomatoes, drained
¼ cup finely chopped fresh basil
Salt and freshly ground black pepper to taste

Heat a tablespoon of the oil either in a heavy pan or in the slow cooker if you have a browning function. Add the meat and brown it well over medium heat. Remove it from the pan and set aside on a plate.

Chop the garlic, onions, carrots, and celery. Sauté them in the same pan until soft, adding oil if needed. Don't get too fussy about the size of the vegetables—whirling them in the food processor works fine and is easy. Add the tomato paste and sauté that a few minutes.

Stir in the wine, tomatoes, and basil, and cook for a few minutes. Add the meat back to the cooker and cook on low for 5 to 6 hours. Turn the meat a few times during cooking. Add salt and pepper to taste.

Refrigerate the meat in the sauce overnight. Several hours before serving, skim the fat off the top. Remove the meat from the sauce, slice it, and nestle the slices in the sauce. Reheat the roast in a 350°F oven for an hour.

Serve with mashed potatoes, polenta, or my personal favorite, macaroni and cheese.

Chicken Cacciatore

I have had this dish several times in one of my favorite Key West restaurants, Bel Mare. In this book, several family members order the same dish at a birthday celebration for Hayley's stepfather, Sam. Hayley's mother and Sam also make it for a crowd at their home in *A Clue in the Crumbs*. Since the visiting Scottish scone sisters were such excellent cooks and bakers, they think they'll be safer making something Italian rather than Scottish themed. This recipe is flexible, so you can add more or less of what you like or don't care for. I think the peppers and olives add a lot to the flavor, though I know they are probably not traditional.

Ingredients

1 red pepper
1 green pepper
1 red onion
1 pound cremini or other mushrooms
2 garlic cloves, minced
¼ cup red wine
14 oz diced tomatoes
2 tablespoon tomato paste
2 cups chicken stock
1 teaspoon dried oregano
Fresh basil and parsley

1 tablespoon honey
Half a large jar of pimentos
⅓ cup olives
3 pounds or so chicken thighs or tenders
1 Egg, beaten
½ cup or so flour
Salt and pepper, to taste
2–3 tablespoons olive oil

Slice the peppers, onions, and mushrooms. Sauté the peppers and onions until soft and beginning to brown, then add the sliced mushrooms, and the minced garlic. Once the vegetables are softened, add the red wine, bring to a boil, and scrape up the brown bits. Add the tomatoes, tomato paste, and chicken stock, then simmer until the sauce is thickened. Taste to see if it needs salt. Stir in the oregano, basil, parsley, pimentos, olives, and honey. Continue to simmer.

Meanwhile, dip the chicken pieces in egg and then flour seasoned with salt and pepper, and sauté until beginning to brown in a pan with olive oil. Add the browned chicken to the simmering sauce.

Once the sauce is thick and delicious and the chicken cooked through, serve it over spaghetti or polenta, with something green like peas. We liked it both ways, but the polenta was our favorite.

Crabcakes with Avocado and Mango Salsa

Hayley Snow's mother, Janet, in the Key West Food Critic Mysteries is a caterer whose reputation has blossomed in Key West. She caters the spread for Hayley's friend and coworker Danielle's rehearsal dinner, including these crab cakes. She makes mini cakes, topped with an avocado and mango salsa. I hope you find them to die for, but not literally!

Ingredients for the Crab Cakes

One pound crab meat, picked over to remove bits of shell
½ cup panko or fresh breadcrumbs
Two scallions, finely minced
1 stick celery, finely minced
¼ teaspoon celery seed or salt
½ teaspoon paprika
¼ tsp cayenne
1½ teaspoons Dijon mustard
1 teaspoon Worcestershire sauce
2½ tablespoons mayonnaise
Fresh black pepper
2 eggs
1 tablespoon olive oil
1 tablespoon butter

Mix the ingredients from the scallions to the eggs. Then fold in the crab meat and the breadcrumbs, sorting through the crab as you go to make sure no cartilage or shell remains.

Shape the crab mixture into ½ cup–size cakes. This should result in six cakes. If they are to be served as appetizers, make them smaller. Refrigerate for an hour or more to help the mixture set.

Heat a tablespoon of olive oil and a tablespoon of butter over medium heat. Add crab cakes. Sauté them until brown, then flip carefully and continue to sauté the other side.

Serve with avocado and mango salsa or cocktail sauce (one part horseradish to two parts ketchup).

Ingredients for the Avocado and Mango Salsa

One large ripe mango
Two ripe avocados
1 tablespoon minced red onion or 2 scallions
2 tablespoons chopped fresh cilantro
1 tablespoon minced jalapeno, or to taste
½ lime
1 to 2 teaspoons olive oil
Salt and pepper to taste

Cut the mango and avocado into small chunks. Mix this gently with the onion, cilantro, and jalapeno. Squeeze lime juice over the top and drizzle with the olive oil. Then add salt and pepper to taste.

You could also serve this with pan-fried yellowtail snapper or Key West pink shrimp. You could even serve it with tortilla chips as an appetizer.

Profiteroles with Hot Fudge Sauce

Danielle has this dessert served at her wedding reception, in addition to the traditional wedding cake. Guests were offered a choice of ice cream to stuff inside, then hot fudge sauce was poured over the top of each puff at the table. Everyone agreed that it was spectacular!

Ingredients for the Choux Puff Pastry

Note: Both the *Joy of Cooking* and Dorie Greenspan's *Baking Chez Moi* list these same ingredients, so it's hard to go wrong.

½ cup whole milk
½ cup water,
1 stick (8 tablespoons) unsalted butter, cut into four pieces.
1 tablespoon sugar
½ teaspoon fine sea salt.
Four large eggs at room temperature

Preheat the oven to 425°F with the baking racks positioned at the bottom and top thirds of the oven.

Add the milk, water, butter, sugar, and salt to a medium saucepan and bring to a low boil. Add the flour all at once and stir vigorously with a wooden spoon over medium low heat. Once the dough comes together, add the eggs one by one, beating thoroughly after each addition, so no signs of yolk and white remain in the dough. The dough will come together into a smooth ball by the end of the last egg.

Using a cookie scoop, place the puffs on parchment lined baking sheets, about 2 inches apart.

Put the baking sheets into the oven and turn the heat down to 375°F. Bake at this temperature for 20 minutes, then rotate the pans up and down and back to front, then bake for another 10 to 15 minutes. You will know they are done when they begin to brown and sound hollow when tapped. Transfer to a rack and let the puffs cool.

When it's time for dessert, slice the puffs in half and add a scoop or two of ice cream in between. Finally, douse in hot fudge sauce. Ooh la la!

Ingredients for the Hot Fudge Sauce

This recipe for hot fudge sauce makes a lot. You could make half the amount if you don't want it lingering in the fridge, or give it away in little mason jars to friends. The recipe was based on one in the *New York Times* Cooking app.

Ingredients

2 cups heavy cream
4 tablespoons unsalted butter
½ cup light brown sugar
¾ cup granulated sugar
¼ teaspoon fine sea salt
2 ounces bittersweet chocolate in small pieces
1¼ cups sifted good quality cocoa
½ teaspoon vanilla extract

In a medium pan, combine the cream, butter, sugars, and salt and bring to a simmer. Meanwhile, cut the chocolate into pieces and sift the cocoa. (I used King Arthur Baking's triple cocoa blend and Ghirardelli's chocolate.)

When the first ingredients are combined smoothly, add the chocolate pieces and stir until melted.

Add the cocoa and whisk everything well. Bring it back to a simmer and whisk until thick and shiny. Take the pan off the heat and whisk in the vanilla.

Serve over ice cream, waffles, profiteroles, or whatever suits your fancy! Store in the refrigerator and warm it over low heat on the stove or for 30 seconds or less in the microwave.

Cottage Cheese Oat Waffles

This past spring, we went to lunch with new friends at the Square Grouper on Cudjoe Key. I'm a sucker for fried chicken served over waffles, which was the special of the day, and that's exactly what I ordered. I had a feeling Miss Gloria would order it too. Here's my version of the dish, which started out as the one on the *New York Times* Cooking site. I made some tweaks inspired by Jane Brody's cottage cheese oat biscuits, which I've made and loved for years.

Ingredients

6 tablespoons unsalted butter
1 cup ground oats
1 cup all-purpose flour (next time, I'll try white whole wheat)
1 tablespoon brown sugar or maple syrup
1 teaspoon baking powder
½ teaspoon fine sea salt
½ teaspoon baking soda
1 cup cottage cheese
1 cup milk
4 large eggs
Chicken cutlets

Melt the butter and set it aside. Grind the oats until fairly fine in your food processor. You want a little bit of texture left.

Add the flour, sugar, baking powder, salt, and baking soda and pulse those into the oats.

In a separate bowl, whisk together the cottage cheese, milk, melted butter, and eggs. Pulse the wet ingredients into dry ingredients. The batter should look thick (and delicious!)

Preheat a waffle iron and lightly coat with butter, unless your brand of iron tells you this isn't necessary, as mine did. Cook waffles (using about ½ cup batter per waffle) until golden and crisp. Keep them warm in a 200°F oven until ready to serve.

For the chicken, I bought pre-fried chicken cutlets from Bishop's Orchards, a local grocery and farm near us. That way, I could simply heat them, slice, and serve over the waffles with syrup. You are welcome to make your own!

This made about eight waffles. You could cut the recipe in half, but why not make them all and freeze the ones you don't eat for an easy breakfast down the line? I can picture them next time with a big serving of fruit and plain yogurt drizzled with honey or syrup!

Acknowledgments

S ometimes a writer struggles for the nugget of a story, and sometimes the story comes to her. This time I got lucky! Huge thanks go to Kathryn Kraepel, a reader who emailed me out of the blue about her experiences camping on Big Pine Key in the 1970s. She said, "It was an unforgettable experience. We never discovered any dead bodies. It was a strange time where we were taking chances on strangers that seem reckless now, but we only encountered good people. We ended up going back to Michigan but wonder what if we had stayed there?" After we chatted on the phone, she gave me permission to use some of her experiences, and I was off. Her story is not this story, but it was the original inspiration—I'm so grateful that she got in touch.

While I was working on this book, the Monroe County Sheriff's Office offered a Citizens Police Academy. This was a wonderful hands-on experience, which brought the temptation to cram as many police procedural details as possible into this story. Hopefully I resisted that and used only the words that helped fire up the story in your imaginations. The deputies who taught us were fully engaged in sharing their work and their perspectives with civilians. Thanks especially go to Captain David E. Smith, Deputy Ryan Lopez (who also agreed to share his

Acknowledgments

name for a character in this book), Deputy Cecelia Hoversen, Lieutenant Lissette Quintero, and Sheriff Rick Ramsey, who sets the tone for his team. Thanks to my pal Pat Kennedy for attending the academy with me, thereby doubling the fun. Once the class was completed, I was asked to give the keynote speech at graduation. Here's how it ended: "These are challenging times for the relationship between police officers and civilians. We see the worst of the worst about law enforcement on television and in the news on a weekly basis. Thanks to every one of these Monroe County officers for showing us the good side, the dedicated side, the side that cares about each of us." Please know that any mistakes in police procedure are mine.

As always, I want to thank the actual Key West people who have become important characters over the course of the series. Thanks to Lorenzo, who is the real Ron Augustine—I channel his wisdom even when I'm not sitting with him; Rusty Hodgdon, a real guide at the Hemingway Home who kindly dished real details about his tours; chef Martha Hubbard, Police Chief Sean Brandenburg; and Steve Torrence, who has shared so much deep love with Key West across the years. I borrowed the chief's tattoo and his experience in the Blue Angel flight— I thank him for that. Thank you to the Big Pine Key Library book club, who invited me to join their discussion of *Death on the Menu* and cooked a fabulous Cuban feast to go along with it. Thanks especially to Kitty Somerville, who drove me around the island so I could get a sense of the geography, and Bruce, who sent ideas and notes about the history of Big Pine Key after our meeting at the library. Both of these kind people had ideas about the perfect murder method. Thanks to my friend Lyn for the catnip.

Acknowledgments

I am ever grateful to the usual suspects for their friendship and support: my stalwart writers group, Angelo Pompano and Christine Falcone; my Jungle Red Writers blog mates—Hallie Ephron, Hank Phillippi Ryan, Rhys Bowen, Deborah Crombie, Julia Spencer-Fleming, and Jenn McKinlay; my amazing agent, Paige Wheeler; the talented team at Crooked Lane Books, including Matt Martz, Rebecca Nelson, Madeline Rathle, Dulce Botello, plus many others; my astonishingly good cover artists, Griesbach and Martucci; and my equally talented independent editor, Sandy Harding. I was so pleased to add Ava Slocum to my team this year!

Thanks to each one of you readers for choosing to read this book, and to bookstore staff and librarians everywhere who make it possible by spreading the word and carrying the books. Last but never least, I couldn't do any of this without my biggest supporters, my sister, Susan Cerulean, and my husband, John Brady.

Lucy Burdette
October 14, 2023